THE ADULTERY DEPARTMENT

HOLLOW TARGET
THE CAT TRAPPER
HIRE ME A BASE FELLOW
COMING FIRST

THE ADULTERY DEPARTMENT

Paul Bryers

BLOOMSBURY

First published 1991
Copyright © 1991 by Paul Bryers

The moral right of the author has been asserted
Bloomsbury Publishing Ltd, 2 Soho Square, London W1V 5DE
A CIP catalogue record for this book
is available from the British Library

ISBN 0 7475 0841 0

10 9 8 7 6 5 4 3 2 1

Typeset by Hewer Text Composition Services, Edinburgh
Printed in Great Britain by Butler and Tanner Ltd, Frome and London

CONTENTS

1

The Saint, the Schoolboy and the Nun

He was, as a child, much obsessed with Holes.

Not common or garden holes, not those bodily orifices so absorbing to his contemporaries. Not holes in the ground.

It was the holes in the universe that troubled Preston, the kind of holes that St Augustine wrote about.

Preston was familiar with the works of St Augustine, or, at least, more familiar than the majority of seven-year-olds, from the teaching of Mother Bernard to whom he went for catechism once a week. There are holes in the essential goodness of the universe, St Augustine had written, through which Evil comes into the world.

This was an alarming concept to Preston. He used to look out for them on his way to school and on his way home in the evenings.

But what could you do if you saw one, he used to wonder, who would you report it to? And what form would the Evil take, as it came seeping through? Would you know it if you saw it?

And who caused the holes to appear?

And what if it was all his fault?

Sometimes Preston felt that St Augustine had raised more problems than he had solved with his theory about the holes in the universe.

Of course, Preston did not spend all his time looking out for the holes.

He also had to watch out for the bears that pounced on you if you stepped on the lines in the pavement, and the killer bats that hung upside down in the shadows under the roof of the railway arch, and the rats that came out of the cracks in the brickwork and infected you with their deadly diseases simply by breathing out into the same air that you breathed in.

Going to school and back was a hazardous operation for Preston. He couldn't relax for an instant. Sometimes he felt that it was only the power of his concentration that kept everything in order. If he ever stopped concentrating the whole thing could collapse in chaos.

He used to think it would get better when he grew up.

But it didn't.

It got worse.

2

Devil Dog Eats Man, 36

Here is Preston Moody walking across the Common. Shoulders hunched into the collar of his leather jacket, fists clenched inside the pockets, eyes little worry beads of suspicion. Thus might some fretful merchant have ventured through the medieval forest, nerves braced for the sudden twang of bow strings, the murderous rush from ditch or thicket.

It is Sunday morning in the suburbs.

'Mind the dog pooh,' shouts Preston to the two children running heedless before him, though dog pooh, even here, where it thrives like fungus after rain, is the least of his worries. Preston this dank October morn has encountered greater hazards and is prepared for more. Mad dogs, mad cyclists, mad kids hurling sticks at conker trees and forgetting that what must go up must come down, or, more likely, not caring either way. Mad model aeroplane enthusiasts practising ground attacks. And a mad old wino shouting Fuck the Pope at a party of church-goers, unaware that they are Jehovah's Witnesses.

'Mind the swings,' shrieks Preston as his charges finally reach their goal and narrowly escape decapitation by one, propelled through the air by a boy who is old enough to be banned, or, if he is not, should be.

Mind the swings, mind the shit, mind the psychopaths, sadists and prowling malignants, mind the drivers who should never be allowed out on the road, mind the child molesters, torturers and Satanists, mind the mass slayers and maimers of innocent victims, mind the drunk drivers, mind the aeroplanes that fall from the sky and the ones that are aimed at you, MIND THE HOLES IN THE UNIVERSE, PRESTON, MIND YOU DON'T DROP THROUGH.

And here is William, medieval scholar, sitting on a park bench, a plaque on the back of which informs the enquiring public that it is dedicated to the memory of a Mrs C. M. Elliott who so loved . . .

Quite what is obscured by William's lanky, sprawling, untidy frame.

William's young son, Edwin, plays on the Adventure Playground nearby. Edwin is named from the Anglo-Saxon 'Eadwine', meaning 'prosperous friend', but this is small comfort to him. His own friends call him Ed when they are feeling kind and when they are not, Winnie. His parents call him Pooh. When he is old enough to have a say in the matter he will change his name to Jack.

In the space next to William on the park bench there is a Sunday newspaper, as yet unfolded. William is reading a book entitled *Rats, Lice and History*. He has read it before but he dips into it from time to time as a priest might consult the Bible in preparation for a sermon, or a poisoner Feltman's *Toxicology* in preparation for a murder. There are probably other examples, but these are the two that most spring to mind while contemplating William on his park bench. It is hard to say why, just something about him.

William knows the book practically by heart. He is one of the country's leading authorities on medieval plague, in particular the Black Death of 1348, about which he has written numerous papers and articles in historical journals. He reads *Rats, Lice and History* as a kind of reassurance, a reminder of basic principles, and also, sometimes, to deter people from sitting next to him in pubs or restaurants, or on park benches.

After a while, there being no apparent threat of this, he closes it with a sigh and selects the review section from the thick fold of newspaper beside him. But he is in restless mood and his wandering eye, seeking distraction, is caught by the sight of an attractive woman walking beside the park lake. She has shoulder-length blonde hair and wears an expensive-looking leather coat. Even at this distance, and despite the coat, William can tell that she is quite slim. William likes thin women. Or, more precisely, and he likes people to be precise, and would be quite anxious not to be misunderstood, he is not overly fond of fat women. He does not like spare flesh. Big breasts hold no attraction for him.

His preferred mate would be a feminine version of himself, but William tries not to admit this, even to himself. Indeed, he resists it. His own wife is not thin.

He watches the woman by the lake. She is not alone. She is accompanied by a man and two children and two Labrador dogs. They all look quite thin, even the dogs. Fit. A very happy-looking, together, fit, thin family. See them laugh as they feed the ducks.

They are not actually a family, says the Demon inside William. The woman is married to the man's best friend who is away on a business trip. The man's wife is at home, preparing the Sunday lunch. The children are not related; the boy is the woman's child, the girl the man's. I'm not sure who owns the dogs, I'll come back to you later on that. The man and the woman are lovers. They have secretly wished to be lovers for years but the consummation of their affair is a recent event. They are still in the first flush of passion. And guilt. Soon they will return to the man's house and have lunch with his wife. The guilt will increase and the passion diminish. But the affair will continue. A few days before Christmas her husband will discover her adultery in a manner I will subsequently reveal to you, and in a fit of jealous rage he will push some sharp, thin instrument, a pen, perhaps, or a knitting needle, or a personalised automatic cocktail stirrer purchased from Global Inventions Inc. by mail order, up her left nostril, not to kill or maim, but merely to inflict some pain as a small, desperate expression of his own; pushing too far, however, he will accidentally pierce the brain.

She will become a vegetable in a wheelchair.

Her son, that small boy you see there, happily throwing his crusts at the waterfowl, will shortly afterwards contract some strange but deadly virus, possibly from the Labradors, and will lose the sight of both eyes. The man, her lover . . .

But William has had enough. He turns the voice off, a remedy still available to him, but for how long? And looking round, disturbed by a vague presence at his left shoulder, encounters his friend.

Preston.

'We used to meet in piano bars,' said Preston, sulkily, flopping down beside William on the park bench.

'Hi,' said William, smiling. 'Excuse me?'

Betraying, with both expressions, his American origins. But perhaps only to Preston.

'Piano bars,' Preston repeated. 'Don't pretend you don't remember.'

But was he pretending? It was, after all, so long ago, and had anything ever happened there worthy of remembrance?

'I mean, look at you,' said Preston. 'You don't even bother getting dressed any more.'

William, still smiling, shrugged. An amiable punchbag. He wore a baggy tracksuit with what looked like a jam stain down the front and egg yolk all down the sleeve. And on his head a woollen ski hat with a bobble on top.

Preston found the bobble particularly vexing.

'I mean, it's Sunday lunchtime,' he said. 'A few years ago we'd be down the piano bar listening to . . .'

He tried to remember what they used to listen to but the names that came were too embarrassingly ancient to be spoken in public, even to William.

Oh God, thought Preston, I'm only thirty-six and it's started already. This is it, Middle Age, and it will go on like this for the next thirty-six years until, without any big deal, without even noticing probably, it will be Old Age and we'll still be sitting here.

Old friends
Sat on their park bench
Like book ends.

That was one of the songs. Or perhaps that was earlier, surely, much earlier than piano bars, please.

Mrs C. M. Elliott who so loved. Once upon a time. Didn't we all.

'You know, meeting all the crowd, cracking open another bottle of sparkling Saumur. Now what do we do?'

He stared expressively in the direction of the climbing frames. It was a mistake. His small son, age five, was hanging from a steel bar eight or ten feet above the ground while William's, a year older, taunted him from a greater height and threatened to tread on his fingers to make him drop.

Don't scream, Preston disciplined himself, don't even shout. He'll be all right, you don't want him growing up a wimp.

But what if he was hurt and Polly found out? Would it be grounds for denying access?

The child dropped and Preston shot to his feet. But Daniel was already up and climbing again, yelling abuse.

William appeared not to have noticed.

'How are you?' he said.

'Fine,' said Preston. 'How are you?'

'Fine,' said William.

'Good,' said Preston.

One day, thought Preston, one glorious day when someone asks me how I am, I shall tell them. I shall detain them with my Mariner's ancient, emaciated claw and give them the full works. Thank you for your interest, comrade, sit down in the listening corner and I shall begin. And an hour or two later I shall leave them feeling considerably older and wiser than they were when I started.

'Newspaper?' said William.

'Pardon?'

'Do you want a bit?'

Preston sighed and picked up the news section.

The front page contained nothing to lighten his mood.

'Another jogger savaged to death by Rottweilers,' he commented with grim satisfaction. 'That makes five this month.'

William looked vaguely perturbed. Preston read on with mounting rage and dismay.

'If you think a Rottweiler is going to attack you, it's no good staring at it like you do with other dogs. Apparently staring doesn't work with Rottweilers. If you stare at a Rottweiler it thinks you are challenging it and goes for you immediately, knocking you down and tearing your throat out.

'The only chance you've got, it says here, is to run towards it waving your arms and shouting.'

His voice was hoarse with incredulity.

' "This may fool it into thinking you are not afraid and therefore more powerful than *it* is." '

He thought about this for a moment.

'Imagine running at one of those things, shouting and waving your arms. They can weigh up to eighteen stone, it says, of solid muscle.'

He read to himself for a few minutes while William perused the review section, but his agitation could not long be contained in silence.

'Good God,' he said. 'Apparently Rottweilers aren't the real problem. According to this, the real problem is cocker spaniels. There are more attacks on humans by cocker spaniels than any other species of canine.

'"Cocker spaniels,"' he quoted, '"become overwhelmed with an Avalanche of Rage. It only lasts seconds and then they are overwhelmed with a Wave of Remorse."

'Fat lot of good that is,' he observed, 'if they've chewed your balls off in the meantime.'

He turned the pages morosely in search of further confirmation of his own apocalyptic view of the world. You could usually trust journalists to come up with something.

'Listen to this,' he enthused, when he found it. 'There's a bloke here, junior minister of something or other, urging old people to cut fuel costs and keep warm by dressing up in newspapers.'

William was mildly sceptical.

'I'm not kidding,' Preston assured him. 'He says they should save old newspapers because, I quote, "folded up tight they make good logs for the fire and, *in extremis*" – that's what he says, the fucker, *in extremis* – "they make better insulation than wool."'

He shook his head in sheer admiration.

'I bet that's cheered a lot of old dears up,' he said. 'I bet that's given them a real sense of purpose. They're probably really looking forward to winter now they know that. They'll be pitching out their Agas all over the country. There'll be over-sixties' clubs planning wild parties on the money they're going to save.'

He folded the newspaper carefully, but not tight enough to make a log.

'They get it from my Auntie Ethel,' he said.

'Excuse me?'

'You must remember my Auntie Ethel.'

Even if he had forgotten piano bars.

'Remember her political theories? What she'd do to the unions, dole scroungers, the unemployed? How she'd eliminate Socialism, Inflation and the Wrong Element? We used to laugh at her then. Government policy now, most of it. You know all those government think-tanks? They're just cover for my Auntie Ethel.'

He indicated the headline.

'This is one of hers. She's got a thing about newspapers. Don't you remember, she used to make me wear them in my shoes to go to school when it was raining? It worked, too. I could hardly walk but it kept my feet dry. Once she showed me how to fold one to make a club. In case of attack by footpads.'

William shook his head.

'Your Auntie Ethel,' he said.

William was Preston's oldest friend. He was not the friend Preston might have picked for that distinction had there been any rivals in the field. If all Preston's childhood friends had lined up against a wall, as when they were waiting to be picked for football, Preston would most likely have left William to pretty near the end and then put him at left back, or somewhere he would do the least damage to his own side.

That little devil Billy Quirk, Preston's Auntie Ethel used to call him. Or, simply, Trouble.

Hello, Trouble, she'd say.

And it was a fact that William and Preston together led to more trouble than Preston alone, or Preston and any combination of other boys.

And now he was so respectable. And solid. And safe.

Just what Preston wanted, in his current state of vulnerability, with every nerve raw from the break-up of his marriage and all that had contributed to it. Preston needed an old friend, like he sometimes needed nursery food after a disappointment, or a hangover, and William was the only one left lined up against the wall.

Good old William.

So why this lingering unease? What childhood skeletons rattled so disturbingly in their cupboards?

Preston knew, if he cared to think about it. But he didn't. Let them rattle away, so long as no one opened the door.

9

William gave up trying to read the book reviews and stood up, revealing that Mrs C. M. Elliott so loved watching the children play.

And died of hypothermia, Preston surmised, because she didn't have enough newspapers shoved up her vest.

'Better be on our way,' said William. 'Lunch should be ready.'

3

The Freed Killer

Here is Kate in the kitchen chopping carrots.

Chop, chop, chop.

Chopping as if she really means it, the sharp knife hacking through the orange flesh, the bits flying, almost as if it is something personal.

It is.

Kate is William's wife.

And she is not happy.

She is in fact extremely irritated, and the carrots help, in some measure, to alleviate this, but not enough.

Kate feels put upon, a not uncommon sensation. She is trying to figure out why she is here in the kitchen preparing the Sunday lunch while William is on the Common with the Sunday papers and their child.

It is not, after all, *her* friend who is coming to lunch.

She knows that if she had pointed this out to William, and expressed her own wish to take child, and papers, to the Common, William would obligingly have offered to stay at home and chop carrots and peel potatoes and keep an eye on the lamb in the oven. But this does not make her feel less irritated. Because Kate also knows that if this had happened she would have returned from the Common an hour or so later to find the carrots unchopped, the potatoes unpeeled and the lamb burned.

And William standing in the middle of the kitchen looking pained and vaguely apologetic, and a reference book on *Deaths among Rural Clergy during the Black Death* lying recently discarded on an armchair.

Of course, Kate could have shrugged and let him stew in his own juice, or lack of it. She could have taken herself off to the local Italian with her child and a book of her own, for Kate also likes reading though her tastes are less morbific. But Kate is not made that way. Kate is a socialist. Kate cares. That is the advantage William has over her. Kate will always care enough to make sure the fridge is full of food and the airing cupboard full of clean linen and the beds changed regularly and the carpets swept and the dishes washed and the lunch cooked and the rats and the lice and the assorted nasties consigned to the dustbin of history.

This is what is so irritating. Kate knows that deep down it is *all her fault*. A more ruthless woman would have sorted William out long ago. A more ruthless woman would have let the whole place slide into chaos until he learned to do things for himself. Except that he probably wouldn't even have noticed.

And she would.

This is the disadvantage of being well brought up.

William and Kate have been married for nine years and known each other for sixteen. They met when they were both at university. She was attracted to him partly by the little-boy-lost quality which she now finds so infuriating. That puppy-dog expression of one who has been up to mischief and is worried you will find out but knows you will forgive him anyway.

She knows a lot of men like that and has heard of more, but it does not reconcile her to having one herself.

She sighs, but peeling the taters is having its usual calming effect. Kate likes taters. There is something about taters, something deeply satisfying, even in the peeling of them.

Kate puts this down to the peasant in her.

Kate's family came over from Ireland a long time ago and their closest contact to the soil is the odd spot of weekend gardening, but Kate associates closely with the dispossessed peasantry of old Ireland, and anywhere else for that matter, and taters brings out the culchie in her. One day soon when she has a garden again, she will plant taters of her own, whole rows of them.

In the meantime she must Plan. Something must be done about William, and soon. William had better watch out. As an historian

12

he should know that peasants, when pushed too far, have been known to revolt.

'*Toxicara canis*,' said Preston, profoundly.

'Excuse me?' said William, poised over the carrots, sugar-glazed and dripping as Kate likes them.

'That's the name of the worm I was telling you about,' said Preston, 'the one that lives in canine excreta. Apparently the soil of every park and common in the city is infected with it. Hundreds of children go blind from it every year.'

William glanced up at him sharply.

'Do they?' It seemed to remind him of something. 'Is that so?'

His expression took on its normal abstracted, slightly troubled, look.

'Do you think we can change the subject,' said Kate, sweetly, 'while we're eating?'

'Sorry,' said Preston. 'It's just that you do get rather obsessive about them in the city. I'm not against dogs in the country at all. I quite like them there. Like sheep and cows and . . .' He sought desperately for other examples, but the best he could come up with was, 'Things.'

'Ah, the country,' said Kate. It was a small poisoned dart aimed at William, but if it went in there was no visible sign of agitation.

'Do you miss it?' enquired Preston, politely. Hens, he thought, geese, turkeys, pigs . . . It all came back once he began to think about it. He hoped Kate wasn't offended. He rather thought of Kate as a country person. He could easily imagine her in wellies with a basket of grain or something, throwing it about the yard for Things to peck at. Not William, though.

'Sometimes,' said Kate. 'Days like this I do. Are you with us, darling?' she enquired of William, watching with interest as his mind returned, startled, from whatever journey it had been on, the glazed eyes focusing, with puzzlement at first, then dawning recognition. It took the merest instant, but as a process it never ceased to fascinate her. She used to wonder where he'd been in the meantime, but not any more. She'd given up.

'Carrots?' he said. 'More lamb?'

Kate sighed.

'It'll be better when we get our own place,' she told Preston, 'and our own things around us.'

The move from a fenland cottage to a rented London flat had been far too abrupt for Kate, and she was sufficiently self-aware to acknowledge that this was a large factor in her current sense of alienation. Yet, like so many other things she later regretted, it had been her own decision. She could have stayed on in the country, until they found a place of their own, or even permanently, with William coming back at weekends. But within a few weeks of William's appointment she had applied to three different London boroughs for a job – any job – in social work, taken the first one she'd been offered, fixed up the flat, put the cottage on the market, found a school for Edwin, and fled from the last five years of her life with almost indecent haste.

Panic, that's what it was.

The feeling that if William went now, by himself, and she stayed, that would be it. And she wasn't ready for that. Not quite. Not yet.

She had to give it at least one more try.

'Well, it's good to see you,' said Preston. 'I missed you both.'

Kate smiled but inwardly doubted. They had seen little of Preston in recent years. He and Polly and the twins had been to stay at the cottage once, that was all, for a weekend. She had found him a bit too inclined to enthuse, like a tourist visiting some primitive culture, while Polly was 'tense'. But she felt sorry for him now. There was a look about him, as if he'd recently returned from the Front.

So she smiled and said, 'Well, it will be good to see some of our old friends again. You tend to get a bit buried in the country.'

She felt a small tug in the maternal breast which she knew she must resist. The wounded-bird or stray-cat syndrome. It was strong in Kate and she knew if she was not careful she would be offering him refuge, sorting out his problems, arranging his life for him. She was aware, too, that certain couples tend to acquire single men like Preston, or women for that matter, like pets, almost as a kind of catalyst for their own uneasy, brittle relationships. She was not sure she really wanted to acquire Preston just yet.

'William said you've started a new job, too,' she said.

14

He looked surprised.

'Me? No.'

William spoke.

'You said you'd been transferred.'

'Oh, that. That was some time ago now. I moved from Women to God,' he explained to Kate.

She nodded sagely, but was in fact unenlightened.

He realised the ambiguity and laughed, shaking his head, as if at some private, bitter joke.

'I mean programmes,' he said. 'I used to do women's programmes but I was moved to the God slot. As a kind of punishment.'

Preston was one of the few male friends William had who did not teach at a university. He was a television producer at the BBC. But she wasn't sure what that *meant* exactly.

'The God slot?'

'Religious programmes. I produce them. Well, some of them. I don't know why we still call it the God slot. We spend most of our time trying to pretend it's not about God at all. In case people switch off. God hardly gets a look in. We try and slip him in on the sly when we think we've got them hooked. I'm doing the Devil at the moment.'

'Satan, you mean?'

William was momentarily deflected from his frenetic attack on the meat and two veg, which was doubtless how he described it to himself. William normally ate as if food were some sort of obstacle between him and the next vital task, an obstacle which had to be demolished in as short a time as possible. Then, when he had finished, he would sit there, fidgeting, until everybody else had. Kate, who enjoyed the ritual of eating as much as the food itself, had been known to find this irritating, also.

'Same thing isn't it?' said Preston. 'Satan. The Devil.'

'No.' William assumed what Kate thought of as his tutorial manner. 'There's lots of other devils. Or different versions of the Devil. But I thought you meant Satan, people usually do. What are you doing about him?'

'Oh, you know, how he became part of popular mythology, what he's supposed to represent . . . I've only just started on it.'

He felt embarrassed, suddenly.

'Interesting,' said William. 'People should know more about devils.'

'Why?' demanded Kate.

It came out more aggressively than she had intended. They both looked at her. Then William shrugged and said, ''Cos it's interesting, that's all,' and picked up his fork again. But Preston felt constrained to answer.

'Well, if Satan is the opposite of God it seems to me that we know very much less about him, and yet, his works are rather more evident, don't you think?'

'His works?'

'I mean, wars, famine, disease . . .'

'You seriously think they're caused by the Devil?'

'Who do you think causes them?' William joined in again, rather abruptly, as if he wanted a fight about it. But Kate didn't. It would be like arguing about fairies, she thought, and while that might appeal to William, as an academic exercise, it certainly didn't to her.

Kate had been brought up as what her father called 'a healthy heathen', or at least as much of one as the English state school system would allow. Neither of her parents were church-goers and her father had so far lapsed from his native Catholicism as to despise and detest 'the whole primitive priestly caboodle', as he called it. 'Give me a child at seven,' he'd mock, 'and I'll fill its head with so much gibberish and superstition I'll have it scared of its own shadow for the rest of its life.'

He was a deeply pragmatic man, a doctor with a group practice in a Midlands market town, and Kate was, in most things, her father's daughter. She spent the greater part of her working life trying to understand people's needs, but the need for a God who would comfort and console and right wrongs – in the next life if not in this – although she might understand it, was something she could not uphold. Belief in supreme beings of whatever creed or breed seemed to Kate to constitute an evasion of personal responsibility. Belief in some prancing horned beast who conjured up all the mischief in the world strained her tolerance to the limit.

'The Devil's greatest success has been in persuading people

he doesn't exist,' William was saying. 'In the Middle Ages he was just as real as God was. People saw them as two opposing dynasties, with their courtiers and generals and secret agents, and even jesters . . .'

Kate sighed and reached for the wine.

'Everything had an opposite, you see. Every force for Good was matched by a force for Bad. God and Satan. Jesus, Lord of Heaven, and Beelzebub, Lord of the Flies. The Holy Ghost and Dagon, the Devil's almoner . . .'

This could go on a long while, Kate thought. She inclined her ear to the opposite end of the table in the hope of more mature conversation, but the disease had spread . . .

'What kind of ghost?' Edwin was enquiring.

'The Holy Ghost,' said Anna, with disturbing authority.

'What's that?'

'It's a kind of bird,' said Daniel, learnedly, 'like a kind of pigeon what can do magic.'

Where did they get it from? Preston? School? Surely not Polly . . . She'd have to have a debriefing session with Edwin when they'd gone. She began to clear up plates.

'. . . Asmodeus, the Devil's banker' – William was still working his way through the forces of Good and Evil – 'who was also the Maker of Bad Marriages . . .'

'And when it speaks,' said Daniel, 'flames come out of its mouth.'

'What about when it poohs?' asked Edwin, who knew anything to do with pooh usually got a laugh. It did this time, too.

Oh the joy of dining, thought Kate, the flowing wine, the flowing wit. The taters.

She carried the empty plates out into the kitchen.

'How's things at home?' William enquired of Preston, over coffee in the sitting room.

'Home?' Preston looked puzzled.

'I meant with your mum and Auntie Ethel,' said William hastily.

'Oh. That home. Fine.' He considered. 'At least I think it is. I haven't been back since I told them about me and Polly. Couldn't

17

take the tight lips and the heavy sighs whenever they looked at the twins.'

'I was up there last week,' said William.

There was something in his tone, something a little too carefully casual, that put Preston on his guard.

'Oh yes?' he said, warily. 'Everything all right?'

'Oh, fine.'

That word again.

'Mum's doing all right for herself – with the shop. Grandad seemed a bit down, though.'

One of the few but important things Preston and William had in common as children was the dominant role of women in their lives. They had both lost their fathers in the same year, Preston's having fallen victim to leukaemia, William's to the charms of Another Woman, and this had left William's grandad as the only adult male presence in both households. He was a big, shambling, shy man, more than a little soured by life, but he had taken the two boys under his wing and Preston had loved him. He felt a sharp twinge of guilt now for not taking the trouble to visit, but William's family had moved to a better neighbourhood when William's mum had made her first million, and Preston had gradually lost touch.

'What's the matter with him?' he asked. He had frozen the image of William's grandad in his late fifties, but he must be nearer eighty now.

'Oh, he's fit enough, for his age, just a bit morose, that's all.'

An uncomfortable pause while he sat forward on the sofa holding his coffee cup in both hands and gazing into it as if he was waiting for some kind of chemical reaction.

'He keeps going on about the murder.'

He looked up at Preston then and it was Preston who looked away. One of the cupboard doors had creaked open and he didn't want to see inside.

'It must be nearly thirty years ago,' he objected.

'Twenty-five,' said William. 'We were nine or ten at the time. Remember?'

Preston said nothing, but he remembered.

'He keeps on about Barry Moxton,' said William, 'and how he must be out of prison now . . .'

And the door was wide open and the bones rattling away in the shadows.

'He must have been let out years ago,' said Preston. 'What's a life sentence these days? Fifteen years?'

'I had a feeling he'd been committed to an asylum. For the criminally insane. They can keep them in there for ever.'

Preston shrugged, trying to cast off the memory.

'Well, I don't know what happened to him. I haven't given him a thought for years . . .' It was almost true. 'What made your grandad worry about that all of a sudden?'

'I don't know,' said William. 'Probably just his age.'

Kate came back from the kitchen and the ghosts cringed back into their corners.

Preston glanced at his watch.

'I suppose I'd better be going then.'

'I'll walk with you across the Common,' offered William.

But Preston wasn't going back across the Common. His time was up.

'I'm going straight to Polly's,' he said, 'with the kids.'

Polly's, he thought.

Formerly known as Home.

4

The Beast of the Underground

Preston took the tube to Polly's, an experience which the twins anticipated with rather more enthusiasm than he. Preston did not like the tube. Awful things happened to people on the tube. Preston had read the headlines. He'd seen the movie.

It was one of those Made-in-the-Fifties horrors bought up in bulk by the television studios to show in the early hours of the morning to night-workers and insomniacs like Preston, and it pandered to all his worst fears and fantasies about the London underground.

It opened with a lone commuter waiting for a train late at night. He begins to pace restlessly up and down the platform, his pacings taking him nearer and nearer to the tunnel at the end. He peers down it irritably, then with hope. Is that a noise? Is it a train? It is a noise. But not a train. It is the noise of a foul and loathsome beast which emerges from the tunnel and drags him screaming into the darkness and eats him alive.

For those who stayed with the film, like Preston, it turned out that the underground was infested with such creatures. They had once been commuters themselves but they had waited so long for trains they had taken to living permanently in the tunnels, skulking in the darkness by day and emerging late at night to devour unwary travellers. Preston thought this a bit far-fetched, but only a bit. He was prepared to believe almost anything of the London underground.

Only last week one of the 'free' newspapers which regularly infested his hallway had reported a spate of knife attacks by gangs

20

who 'worked' the lines, preying on travellers late at night and early in the morning, robbing them of their valuables and occasionally, to relieve the monotony, stabbing them to death.

This seemed to Preston only a degree or so less deplorable than a tube system inhabited by ghouls.

It seemed to Preston that if you avoided being stabbed to death by terror gangs, you stood an even chance of being burned to death by sudden conflagration, or pushed on to the live line by a psychopath lurking among the rush-hour crowds, or struck down by a heart attack brought on by the extreme rage and frustration of trying to understand a platform announcement.

Preston avoided travelling by tube as much as possible, but sometimes it was forced upon him. Part of the 'deal' struck in the course of his recent marital separation was for Polly to keep the family car. Preston normally travelled by bicycle or, if he was really pushed, bus. But the former was impossible with the twins in tow and the latter unthinkable given the length of time he'd have to wait for one on a Sunday.

He briefly considered lashing out on a taxi, but only briefly. The current state of Preston's finances put taxi rides across London among the long list of temptations he would have to put behind him for a while.

He marched the twins in the direction of the nearest station and prepared for a long, boring wait.

Preston had a long association with railway stations. His own name had been inspired by a brief interlude at Preston station in Lancashire where his parents had changed trains one Sunday afternoon on their way to Blackpool for their honeymoon. They had 'liked the sound of it'. Preston, who didn't, sometimes wondered if there was more to it than that and he'd actually been conceived there, in the waiting room of some remote platform or in the empty carriage of some forgotten train. It was hard to imagine, but then he couldn't imagine his mother Doing It anywhere. She herself, when pressed, indignantly refuted the suggestion. If copulation had indeed been the cause of Preston's subsequent arrival on this earth, and she was far from admitting the connection, it had more than likely occurred in the seaside boarding house that was their eventual destination.

'But we couldn't very well call you Blackpool, could we?' she had remarked once to Preston with somewhat suspect logic.

Preston might have preferred to have been called Blackpool, all things considered. Blackpool Moody had a certain ring to it. People might have thought he was a blues singer in an American jazz band.

But, whatever the truth of the matter, this pre-natal adventure had done little to increase Preston's regard for stations as an institution. He viewed them universally as dismal, dirty, draughty places where unpleasant incidents frequently occurred, especially on Sundays.

He was marginally cheered by a sign near the ticket barrier warning that Dogs Must Always Be Carried On Moving Escalators. 'Otherwise,' an authoritative hand had inscribed, in Biro, below, 'they can get their paws ripped off.'

This seemed to explain one of the few advantages of the underground network to Preston – the fact that it was comparatively free of Rottweilers and pit bull terriers. Doubtless the prospect of carrying eighteen stone of solid muscle and jaw up a moving escalator was something of a disincentive. Though given the number of escalators actually working it probably wouldn't be for long.

Preston tried to keep his fears from the twins but he also kept them as far from the edges and ends of the platform as he possibly could in case of beast attacks.

He wished William hadn't told him about Barry Moxton. He'd almost forgotten about him. But no, that wasn't true. Barry Moxton had been lurking there all the time, just below the surface of his consciousness, waiting to spring out at him.

He peered uneasily down the dark tunnel at the end of the platform and remembered something else from their past: Mother Bernie and her holes in the universe, the holes that let the Evil in.

William used to go to Mother Bernie, too. They used to go there together, on Saturday mornings, or Thursdays, after school. For catechism. It was another one of their common inheritances. They were both Catholics in a world of black Proddy dogs. Preston Moody and Billy Quirk. United in adversity, if in little else. The shared misfortune of an alien religion, a fatherless family, and a peculiar name.

Education had been the final tie that bound them, and forever parted them from their contemporaries. And now William was the last surviving friend of his childhood and they met as dissidents who have escaped the Gulag but left their roots behind and need each other to share the memories. Or was it to exorcise them?

The arrival of the train recalled Preston to more immediate concerns. He shepherded the twins aboard without losing either of them down the gap and found seats for them in the same row. So far, so good. Now to keep them occupied for the journey. He drew their attention to the route map on the opposite wall and set them to counting how long it took between stops, a favourite exercise that was considered by the twins to be the height of intellectual prowess but risked serious brain damage to everyone within hearing distance.

Preston sought anaesthesis in the colour supplement he had brought with him and was distracted for a while by a feature on Great Journeys undertaken or contemplated by the Rich and the Famous. None of them seemed to include the tube in their itineraries, but there was some useful advice on how to secure the best berths on a Nile river cruiser and an interesting complaint about the lack of leg room on Concorde which assured him that the R and the F of this world had to contend with life's little niggles just like everybody else.

He was startled out of this sombre reflection by the sudden awareness that something was Not Quite Right.

He detected it at once. The counting had stopped. The train was still moving between stations but the twins seemed to have lost all interest in knowing how long it took and relaying this information to the rest of the carriage. Instead they were staring with considerable fascination at a fellow traveller who was reclining, fortunately with his back turned, a few seats down from them. He wore a black leather jacket heavily embossed with metal studs and his legs, which were stretched out into the aisle, were wrapped in an assortment of rags and torn denim. But the feature which Preston knew had so captivated the twins was the great crest of

23

plumage rising from the centre of his otherwise shaven skull and gelled into sharp canary yellow spikes.

Preston, whose coming of age had coincided with the New Wave, mentally categorised him as a Punk and, therefore, Harmless. Punks were not normally aggressive, and though he adhered to his normal practice of avoiding eye contact in public places he was fairly relaxed about them. But apparently the twins had never seen anything like this before. Anna tugged at his sleeve to bring Preston's ear nearer to her mouth and enquired in a stage whisper, 'Daddy, is it a bird?'

Preston was amused. He appreciated that the literature favoured by the twins made little distinction between people and animals.

'Yes,' he whispered back. 'It's a chicken.'

'What did he say?' Daniel wanted to know.

'He said it's a chicken,' Anna replied, matter-of-factly, and in a voice loud enough to carry. Preston, now less amused, shushed her urgently. A small black lady smiled indulgently from the opposite seat. She wore a large white straw hat and looked as if she'd just been to church.

The train slowed down as it reached the next station and the Punk stood up and came down the aisle towards them. The crest of hair added about a foot to his height but he was no shrimp without it. His leather jacket was adorned with the face of a screaming woman symbolising, according to the caption below, Chaos, and his own blunt and pitted features suggested to Preston not so much those of a bird as of a pit bull terrier with acne.

Preston was aware that the twins were taking in all this with wonder and admiration, and as the Punk drew level with their seat, Daniel remarked in a reverent but not hushed tone:

'*BIG* chicken.'

The Punk stopped. Preston froze.

Eye contact became unavoidable.

'Did 'e call me a fucking chicken?' the Punk enquired.

It wasn't really a question but Preston corrected him, politely.

'A *big* chicken,' he said, smiling what he hoped was a disarming smile. 'He didn't mean to be rude. He prefers chickens to people, actually.'

This did not go down as well as he might have hoped.

The doors shut and the train began to move out of the station.

'You made me miss me stop, you fucker,' said the Punk.

Preston began seriously to question his information on the non-violent nature of the beast.

'Now look . . .' he began. He had a number of set speeches which he frequently rehearsed for such occasions. The content varied according to the imagined circumstances but it invariably contained the information that he was a magistrate, an exponent of the martial arts, or someone who had recently been diagnosed as HIV positive and would have no hesitation in biting if attacked. In one version he combined all three.

But before he could select the right tone and story-line for these particular circumstances, there was a diversion. The small, elderly lady opposite leant forward and poked the aggressor in the thigh with a delicately gloved forefinger.

'Don't you be using words like that in front of them children,' she instructed him fiercely. 'You oughta be shamed.'

Preston stared at her with mingled hope and alarm.

On the one hand he was glad of an ally; on the other he would have preferred someone a bit more the Punk's size. He looked around the carriage to see if there were reinforcements to hand, but it did not look promising. If there was anyone large, male and under sixty, he was hiding under the seats. When he looked back, the Punk had taken the woman's straw hat off and looked as if he might be about to eat it.

Preston realised he would have to Take Action.

He was not, in fact, an exponent of the martial arts, but for a few short but character-forming weeks during a university summer vacation he had boxed a kangaroo called Cobber in a travelling circus. He had never been able to hit the animal but he knew how to throw a punch, and the Punk wasn't such a good mover as Cobber.

What he hadn't counted on was how much it hurt.

5

Polly and the Tube Hero

'Where on earth have you been?' demanded Polly when she opened the front door. 'I've been worried sick.'

Preston raised his bandaged wrist in its sling.

'Sorry,' he said. 'Had an accident. Tried to ring you but couldn't get to a phone.'

'Daddy had a fight with a chicken,' Daniel announced proudly.

'Then the police came and took it away,' said Anna, 'and we all went to hospital.'

'Preston,' said Polly, when she came down from putting the twins to bed and in a tone he had come to recognise over the years.

'Polly,' he said, smiling the same kind of disarming smile that had failed to disarm the Punk.

Polly appeared to be no more susceptible, but then his expectations had not been high. He was suspicious of her motives in inviting him into the house – he usually got no further than the front doorstep. It was possible, of course, that she wanted to dispense tea and sympathy, but he had his doubts.

They were quickly confirmed.

'I'm sorry, Preston,' she said, 'but I just don't think you're behaving very responsibly at the moment.'

'Oh, I don't know,' said Preston. He pointed out quite reasonably that defending an old lady from assault on a tube train could conceivably be described as extremely responsible behaviour and doubtless would be by most right-thinking members of society, Polly's opinion notwithstanding.

'But what if he'd had a knife?' she said.

26

Preston shrugged, as one did who had just single-handedly dispatched a Beast who Rode the Underground. He could see the headline now: 'TUBE HERO FLOORS MUGGER'.

'I mean, you've got the twins to think about,' Polly insisted. 'Couldn't you have talked your way out of trouble like most people with any sense?'

'I *was* thinking about the twins,' protested Preston. 'And I *did* try to talk my way out of trouble. I only hit him when the situation looked like getting out of hand.'

'And look what happened.'

Polly pointed triumphantly at the sling.

'All right, I sprained my wrist,' Preston admitted, 'but you should have seen the other bloke.'

The other bloke was being sat on by three other passengers, including the little old lady in the straw hat, while Preston hopped around moaning and clutching his wrist, but he did not tell Polly this. He was rather proud of the Punch that had floored the Punk, and he wasn't having Polly make mock of it.

'I'm not saying you shouldn't have hit him,' said Polly patiently, who was, after all, the daughter of a trained killer (Squadron Leader, RAF, Ret.) and not unduly given to pacifism. 'Maybe you didn't have much choice in the matter, but you do have a habit of getting into situations like this, don't you, Preston?'

Preston denied this with some zest, pointing out that it was the first time he'd thrown a punch at anyone since his days in the ring with Cobber the kangaroo.

'I don't mean fighting,' said Polly. 'I mean situations.'

Preston decided not to pursue the subject. He knew that if pressed to give examples Polly could, and would, produce a long and depressing list, complete with times, places and personalities involved. He sighed and looked at his watch. Twenty-five past nine. And he'd meant to watch the God slot.

'Anyway,' said Polly, 'that's not what I wanted to talk to you about.'

She sat down opposite him at the kitchen table and fixed him with the kind of look that usually preceded a full eighteen-round contest.

'How's the wrist?'

27

'Oh, fine,' said Preston, surprised. 'Well, it's . . .'

'Not hurting?'

'No, no . . . they said it might later, but . . .'

'Good,' said Polly, with satisfaction, as if she needn't worry now about pulling any punches. 'Well, what I wanted to talk to you about is this flat of yours.'

'Oh?'

Preston was momentarily relieved.

'I mean, when are you going to get yourself a decent place to live?'

'Ah.'

'I mean, you can live where and how you like, it's no business of mine, but there's the children to think about.'

The relief evaporated and was replaced with a profound anxiety.

'Anna says it's filthy. She says there's no carpets on the floor or anything. And there's no garden.'

Bloody women, Preston thought. And she was only five.

'And you know how particular Daniel is about the bathroom. He says it's absolutely freezing in there, and there's hardly ever any hot water.'

'The guyser's a bit temperamental . . .' Preston began.

'The geezer?'

'I think that's what I mean. The thing you light and it heats the water up.'

'Good God, I thought those things went out with the ark. They're very dangerous, Preston, don't you know? They blow up on people. Haven't you got a boiler – central heating? What kind of place is this? Daniel says it's the kind of place poor people live.'

'The little shit,' said Preston.

'Preston.' Polly reproved him sharply. Preston modified his tone.

'It's only temporary,' he wheedled. 'Until I buy somewhere.'

'It's been temporary for six months now. You haven't spent the mortgage money, have you?'

This stung.

As compensation for Polly's keeping the house, Preston had received the sum of twenty thousand pounds to put down on a small flat. Not wishing to live in south Durham and commute daily, this had presented something of a problem for him.

'I'm not asking you to buy a palace,' said Polly. 'But if you could just find somewhere they'd feel a bit more comfortable, that's all. You've just got to get your act together. Go and look in cheaper areas.'

'Yes, well, I'd already crossed Belgravia off the list,' Preston confessed.

'And another thing we've got to talk about – it's not really fair that you have them every weekend. I've got a full-time job now, I hardly get to see them during the week.'

'All right, then, let's alternate,' said Preston, reasonably. 'I'll have them every other week and you have them every other weekend.'

Polly had to think about that.

'And how will you get them to school in the mornings?'

'I'll just have to get up a bit earlier, that's all.'

But he could see what was coming.

'And travel halfway across London? On the tube? Like tonight?'

Preston threw in the towel before it went the whole distance. He could have come back on that one, if he'd really tried, but sometimes it was much easier to lie on the floor and watch the lights on the ceiling and listen to the count going on.

'Okay,' he said. 'You have them next weekend and I'll look for a house.'

He trudged back to the tube station on his own. His wrist was beginning to hurt, he had a headache and he was depressed. He'd have quite liked to have spent the night on the couch in Polly's living room, as he had for the last few months of their marriage, but it had not been offered as an option and he supposed it was just as well. That part of his life was over. He had to get used to the new arrangement.

But it still depressed him.

In his mind's eye, Preston saw himself as the daddy in one of the twins' bedtime books. It was called *Are We Nearly There?* and it was about a little boy who was on a journey with his father. Only at the end of the story do you realise that his parents are separated or divorced and that the journey is to return the child

29

to his mother after an access visit. The picture on the last page shows the father walking off alone along the darkening street, leaving the brightly lit house behind him. Preston always found the story deeply distressing, but the twins seemed to like it.

Preston took full responsibility for the breakdown of his marriage. He had compounded a number of venial failings with the mortal sin of adultery. Worse, he had been Found Out. It followed as naturally as night followed day that he should now be punished for it. That was how it worked. Mother Bernie had said so a long time ago and all Preston's life's experiences since then had born it out.

Mea culpa, mea culpa, said Preston to himself, as he had said aloud as a child at Mass with neither thought nor understanding then, *mea maxima culpa*. He understood now, all right, and there was some comfort in taking on the complete burden of guilt, a kind of purgative sense of martyrdom, not unrelated to self-pity. In another age Preston would have been out there with the self-flagellants, scourging away for all he was worth.

But from somewhere in the fog of received wisdom and what passed for it, struggling to be heard above the sound of cracking whips, a persistent and unrepentant voice relayed a subversive message.

Bullshit, it said.

Preston identified it at once. It was the Voice of Reason, and it perched on the opposite shoulder from the Voice of his Conscience, and it was frequently on his side.

Preston's marriage had been ended, as the official record, Polly and his conscience would have it, by his adultery with Carla, rising star of the modern spoiled-brat school of journalism and presenter of *Shrews at Ten*, a women's magazine series which Preston had produced and which had achieved a certain dubious fame before ending in tears, tantrums and Preston's demotion to the God slot.

But the Voice of Reason argued that Preston's marriage, and his career, were demasted, holed and rudderless a long time before they foundered together on the rock of Carla. Carla had done a fairly professional job of staving in the rotten planks, that was all. The modern *femme fatale* in baggy trousers, sloppy T-shirts and Doc Martens. Every broken marriage, every wrecked career must have one, in some form or another, and doubtless career and marriage might have drifted aimlessly on together for a few more years if the sea had been clear of Carlas, but it would have ended some time or other, and possibly with a lot more pain than there was now.

He kept on remembering the good bits, that was the trouble. He kept seeing them over and over in his mind, like an action replay of a not very good football match that only showed the goals. He saw clips of them with their heads together across a table in a wine bar, or making love in the garden of a cottage they had once rented in the New Forest, or building a sand castle with the twins on their first family holiday together at the seaside.

He knew the bad bits existed, but he had edited them out. He didn't want to look at them. And so when he talked to Polly now, and when she talked to him the way she did, it depressed him. He could not reconcile it with the images he had preserved.

He was too depressed even to care about travelling back on the tube with his right wrist in a sling during a period which the *Tooting Guardian* had described as a peak time for knife attacks. Or to worry about the thin but penetrating drizzle that greeted him when he finally emerged from the subway.

He was only jolted out of his misery when he approached the front door leading to his much-maligned flat and, as he struggled to pull his keys out of his right pocket with his left hand, a voice spoke to him from the shadows of the front porch.

'Preston,' it said. 'At last.'

6

The Corsican Connection

The figure stepped out from the porch and the light from the street lamp spilled on to its face. Preston started to breathe again.

'Emily!' he said. 'Jesus Christ.'

'Sorry,' she said. 'Did I startle you?'

He felt his heart.

'Oh God, I'm going to die.'

She put her arms up to embrace him and noticed the sling.

'What happened to your arm?'

'Never mind that, what are you doing skulking in my porch?'

'I wasn't skulking, I was sheltering from the rain. Where've you been? What happened? Is it broken?'

'Emily, what are you doing here?'

'Well, charming,' she said, stepping back a pace. 'If I'd known I was that unpopular . . .'

'It's not that,' Preston assured her. 'I just thought . . .'

What had he thought? That it was the Angel of Death? Certainly that, though, curiously, an image of Carla had also flashed across his mind. *Preston. At last!* And he'd been braced for the knife lunging out of the darkness. But why? Why should he fear Carla? It was all over months ago and, as far as he knew, with no hard feelings.

Obviously his conscience was not so sure.

'Well, if that's how you feel, I won't trouble you any further,' said Emily, and she made to push past him.

But not very convincingly.

Preston stopped her without much trouble with his one good arm.

'Here, take the key,' he said. 'Open the door, let's get out of the rain. I'm sorry, I've had a bad day.'

The flat felt colder than it was outside, but at least it was dry. Preston put the fan heater on in the kitchen and produced a bottle of brandy.

Emily perched on a stool, biting her bottom lip. She looked as if she was fighting back tears.

'What's the matter?' said Preston, more gently now, but with an ingrained wariness.

He wasn't quite sure how to treat Emily. They were at that stage of going out that wasn't yet a Relationship. Or at least, that was how Preston saw things. He wasn't certain that Emily hadn't forged ahead a stage or two.

He'd met her at work, which was about the only place where he did meet people these days. She was a production secretary attached to a programme in the same series as Preston's 'Who is the Devil?' documentary. She was twenty-four and rather beautiful in a pale, pensive, studiously Pre-Raphaelite way, with a glint of hennaed gold in her curly hair and large, solemn eyes.

Unfortunately she was also crazy.

On their first date she had shown Preston, with nonchalant pride, the scars where she had slashed her wrists a few days after her nineteenth birthday.

'Most people try to kill themselves when they're nineteen,' she'd informed Preston. 'I didn't feel very loved.'

It was surprising, now he came to think of it, that this hadn't scared him off, but he'd been lulled by her flippancy. It was all part of the mad social whirl that young women of her age had to endure. Suicide attempts ('Not that it was serious,' she told him, 'just attention-seeking'), anorexia, the odd abortion (only one in her case, but she gave the impression this was well below average) and messy affairs with married men.

'I had a lot of emotional problems when I was younger,' she told him, 'but I'm fine now. Quite boring in fact.'

Preston had given the expected response and they were off and running.

Even Preston had to admit it was fun at times. She showed an enthusiasm for sex and a lack of inhibition which was entirely alien to Preston's recent experience. He felt that, given time, he could really get to like it. If only he could stop worrying about the consequences.

One of these was Getting Involved. Preston wasn't sure he wanted to. Not with Emily, not with anyone, at the moment. The bruises left by Polly and Carla were still too sore.

Another was the horror stories.

Emily had a way of launching casually into an anecdote about some fix she'd got herself into in the past and Preston would listen with increasing alarm, wondering just what *he'd* got himself into. What bothered him most was that the past seemed to get closer and closer to the present. It appeared that for two years after the wrist-slashing incident she'd been in and out of mental hospital. At the same time she'd had 'this disastrous affair' with a married man that led to her pregnancy and a late abortion. ('I couldn't make up my mind whether I wanted it or not, and then I just panicked.') There had been 'complications' and she'd been told she couldn't have children.

And that was intimately connected with the other problem.

They were making love without contraceptives.

Preston was astonished at himself for letting it happen, but when he'd first suggested wearing a condom Emily had said, 'You don't have to,' and told him the story about her abortion, and he'd felt too sorry for her, and too embarrassed, to insist on doing so for health reasons.

He looked at her now, sitting there like a bird with a broken wing, and was torn between wanting to give her a hug and a kiss, as he would with Anna when she'd fallen and hurt her knee, and a rather more powerful instinct for self-preservation that urged him to climb into the airing cupboard and pull the door shut after him.

Unfortunately there was no airing cupboard. Only a guyser. Alleged by his wife to be dangerous.

'Come on,' he said, 'what's up?'

'Only after you tell me why your arm's in a sling,' she said.

Preston told her why his arm was in a sling. She was impressed, also sympathetic. Preston warmed to her. They kissed. They took

34

the brandy into the sitting room and lit the gas fire and curled up on the sofa.

'It could be very cosy here,' said Emily, cuddling up to him and shivering, and clutching her brandy, 'with a bit of effort.'

Preston looked around the room. Objectively, he could see why his treacherous brood might be moved to complain. There was a cold, unlived-in, unloved feel about the place. The walls and ceilings were all painted the same insipid magnolia and there was rush matting on the floor which trapped bits of food and stuff and hurt if you walked on it with bare feet. He had rented the flat through an agency and had no idea who owned it, only that he was male and single and working abroad for a year. Preston, in the idle early hours when he wasn't watching fifties horror movies, sometimes speculated on what kind of person he was and what he did for a living. The place itself provided few clues, only that he must be entirely devoid of imagination and not overly bothered by cold and lack of comfort. He'd decided he was most likely an agronomist attached to an Antarctic survey team.

He was upset about the kids. He would have to find somewhere they would like. He wondered if he should move out of London. Buy a caravan with a horse, maybe, and try and make it into an adventure. Or a narrow boat on a canal. But he'd always hated horses and he knew nothing about boats. And whatever he did it would probably be wrong.

'There doesn't seem much point,' said Preston. 'I won't be here that much longer.'

She looked up at him, anxiously. 'Oh, why's that?'

But Preston didn't want to go into his domestic problems. He wanted to know what Emily was doing adding to them.

He found a more tactful way to put it.

'So what brings you here? Great though it is to see you.'

'Well,' she said, 'I kept getting these phone-calls.'

'Oh, yes?'

'You know. When no one answers and there's just silence at the other end, but you know someone's there.'

Preston regarded her uneasily.

'How often?' he said.

'Oh, about four times last night. Then I left the phone off the hook. But it started again this evening. Three times in one hour. Brenda's away until tomorrow so I was alone in the flat. And when I went out yesterday I had this horrible feeling someone was watching me all the time. I didn't think I could cope with another night in that flat all alone.'

'Someone watching you?'

'Yes.'

'You saw someone?'

'No.'

Preston thought about this and came to no satisfactory conclusion. Like most people who are themselves paranoid, Preston had difficulty in taking other people's fears very seriously, unless they could be directly related to his own. He had not himself suffered from mystery phone-calls and silences on the line. In Preston's experience the problem came from people he knew extremely well screaming down it at him.

'It was just a feeling I had,' she said.

'No idea who it could be?'

'Well . . .' A longish pause. He shifted so he could look at her. Whenever Emily started to screw her face up like that it invariably preceded some appalling confession.

'Emily?'

'Well, I think it might be my husband.'

'Your *what*?'

The screw turned a little tighter.

'Didn't I tell you about that?'

'No.'

'Oh. I thought I'd mentioned it.'

'I think I'd have remembered if you had.'

'It's something *I'm* trying to forget.'

Preston untangled his arm from around her shoulder and reached for the brandy glass.

'How long ago was this unmemorable event?'

'You're not upset, are you?'

'Me? No. Not at all. A little surprised, perhaps, that's all.'

'That was why I left university. I met him during the summer vac. In Nice.'

Preston nodded to himself. It all fitted. At some stage during

36

her crisis-strewn life Emily had gone to the University of Lancaster to study French but she'd never completed her course. Preston had not liked to ask why. Or else he'd been too afraid of the answer.

'I thought he was French,' said Emily, 'but he turned out to be Corsican.'

'Was this before or after you were married?'

'You *are* upset, aren't you.'

'No, no, I'm not. I promise you I'm not upset.'

'Then why have you got that sort of stiff look?'

Preston was looking stiff because he was braced for another horror story. He felt he needed more brandy, but the glass was nearly empty and the bottle was in the kitchen.

'Sorry, I'll try to relax,' he said. 'Go on.'

'He was in the tourist trade. It was a family business. Quite big. He ran the office in Nice. But the rest of the family were in Corsica.'

The juxtaposition of those two words, 'family' and 'Corsica', rang serious alarm bells in Preston's mind. He concentrated hard.

'He was quite a bit older than me. He'd been married before. But his first wife died. In a car crash.'

Preston drained his glass and decided to go for the bottle in the next interlude.

'The day before I was due to go back to England he asked me to marry him. I still don't know why I said yes. Except that I was all caught up in it, the romance and everything and the sunshine. We had this balcony and I used to sit out there sunning myself with no clothes on. Some days I didn't bother to get dressed at all. Others I'd just throw on a cotton frock and a pair of sandals to go out shopping.' She giggled. 'I never used to wear any pants. I felt like Betty Blue.'

Preston felt a moan coming on, from deep inside.

'And he was very good-looking. And very . . . well, I'd better not say any more about that. I was just in love with being in love, you know what it's like, I loved the image of myself being in love in that kind of careless, easy way. Haven't you ever felt like that?'

'Not when there's been sunshine as well,' said Preston. 'Excuse me, I'm going to throw up.'

'What?'

'I mean, top up. The glass. Sorry, I don't know why I said that.'

He fled to the kitchen and brought back the bottle.

'Anyway,' she said, 'we went over to Corsica for the marriage and that's when things started to go wrong. The family weren't exactly wild about me – at least the women weren't –'

No, they wouldn't be, thought Preston.

' – and then it turned out they wanted him to stay on over there. I was dead against it, but he always did what the family wanted. I soon sussed that out.

'They owned this kind of enclave on the coast just outside Ajaccio – like a kind of tourist village – that's where they kept the women, really, while they were away on business. So there were people to keep an eye on you. And the babies. All those babies. I nearly died when I saw them. That's what you did, you see, if you were a wife, you had babies. Well, I suppose that would have been fine if I could have gone along with it, but I wasn't quite ready for that. Certainly not on those conditions. I knew what those men were like. They were off running the travel business and having affairs with all those couriers and secretaries and people while the wives prayed and cooked and had babies.'

But Preston had spotted a hole in the plot.

'But – hadn't you told this, what's-his-name, you couldn't have babies?'

She looked guilty. Or was it coy? Or was it both?

'Well, actually, I wasn't sure I couldn't then. I mean, the doctor had told me, but I'd kind of shut it out. It was only when I didn't, and we'd been making love without contraceptives for months and months, that I decided he must have been right.'

'So you wouldn't have minded having one?'

'I didn't have much choice, did I. He *wanted* me to have babies. He wasn't going to wear a condom and I didn't have anything. And I didn't know where to get anything from. Everything was so *controlled*. The doctor was one of his uncles, for God's sake.'

'So you still didn't tell him?'

'I couldn't by then. It got to be such a strain, though. And all those women and babies. My God, you felt like a leper without one. And then there was *him*. He just changed completely once he got back with his family. He was a real chauvinist. And so jealous. He had these terrible rages. Once, just because I wasn't wearing any knickers – and he used to love it in Nice.'

The fire had at last begun to warm the room up a bit, and the brandy was warming him up inside, and Preston was suddenly feeling terribly, terribly randy. He wondered how difficult it would be to make love with his arm in a sling. He lifted his wrist experimentally to see what it felt like without the support. It hurt. He winced.

'Is this very painful for you?' Emily enquired.

'No,' said Preston. 'I'm fascinated.'

That was the trouble with Emily's stories. You had to get to the end of them. You knew it was going to be awful, but you had to *know*.

'Finally I couldn't stand it any longer, so I left him.'

'That can't have been easy.'

'No, it wasn't. I had to steal a car and . . . all sorts of things.'

Preston nodded. He didn't mind skipping a bit. Especially 'all sorts of things'. He wanted to get to the phone-calls.

'So you never got divorced?'

'I didn't want him to know where I was.'

'No. So what makes you think the phone-calls are from him?'

'Because he tried it once before, when I was working up in Manchester. The phone kept ringing and no one there, and then he turned up on the doorstep. I had to pretend I wanted to go back with him. Then I gave him the slip and came to London.'

'So he does want you back?'

'You needn't sound so surprised about it.'

'Oh, I'm not. I'm sure he does.'

'Well, if you must know, I think it's because he just doesn't like the idea of *me* leaving *him*. It hurts his pride. You know, all that male machismo.'

'I've heard about it,' said Preston, absently. He was worried now. Even if only half the story were true, he was still worried.

39

'You didn't feel watched on the way here?' he asked, trying to make it sound light-hearted.

'Preston, I was two hours waiting for you in that porch. I think I'd have noticed if someone was watching.'

'That's true,' he said. But he had to restrain himself from leaping up and switching the light off and peering out into the street from behind the curtains.

He no longer felt randy.

But Emily apparently did.

'I can't do much with this wrist,' Preston pointed out.

'You don't have to,' Emily assured him. 'Not with your wrist at any rate.'

It was a novel experience for Preston, going out with somebody who wanted him for his body. That part of his body, anyway. Carla had been opposed to penis penetration on political grounds and Polly had never once achieved orgasm during intercourse. Emily, however, was one of the minority featured in the *Hite Report* who invariably did. Either that, or she was a very good actress.

So Preston put his reservations behind him and his wrist in front and lay on his back on the sofa while Emily *bounced* on him. It was her preferred position, slings notwithstanding. She liked to *ride* him, as she put it, and the ride was accompanied by a kind of commentary, as if she was urging a horse along in a steeplechase.

This was the main problem about sex with Emily. In Preston's experience there was always something and with Emily it was the commentary.

'You're doing fine,' she'd say. 'That's great, that's just fine. No, no, easy, easy. Not too fast. Hold it there, hold it right there. Don't you dare come. Now, a bit faster . . . a bit faster . . . Perfect.'

If Preston kept his eyes shut and his mind on something else, they occasionally achieved simultaneous orgasm, but it took energy, it took stamina. Most of all it took discipline. Not infrequently he wished his penis didn't have to take the entire responsibility for the success or failure of the operation.

Once he'd achieved erection the trick was to keep it up without coming but without losing rigidity. He normally managed this by allowing himself a few seconds of pure indulgence in sensation and then thinking of something neutral for a while and, if this didn't work, something really horrible. Then, when it started to go down, he'd open his eyes and concentrate on Emily for as long as his self-control would allow. Thirty seconds was about the limit. Sometimes it was much less.

Tonight he tried to imagine what the Corsican looked like in a rage. This worked for a while. It even made him groan a bit, which Emily liked. It also made him feel sick, which wasn't so good. He thought about the incident in the tube train, but this almost induced total decline. So he resorted to an old favourite, which was to imagine himself as a First World War fighter ace engaged in an aerial duel with an enemy pilot.

He concentrated hard. He was in a Sopwith Pup, or was it a Camel? The other man was in a Focker Triplane, a Tripehound. No, not a Tripehound. An Albatross. A bright yellow Albatross with Maltese crosses. It was behind him, lining him up in the sights. *Dadadadada* . . . Bits of wings falling off. What could he do? The Immelmann Turn. A difficult manoeuvre named after the pilot who had invented it. A German, one of the Baron's men. It was a kind of loop and roll that dodged the pursuing aircraft and brought you up behind it. Then, a quick burst of the twin Lewis guns. *Dadadadada* . . .

He was halfway through the Immelmann Turn when he became aware that Emily's commentary was rising to a peak. He opened his eyes and cleared his mind of Camels and Albatrosses and Pups and Tripehounds, cleared his mind of everything but the thought of her beautiful body and the beautiful things she was doing with it, and for the next minute or so they were almost flying.

'You're a very solid person, Preston,' said Emily, surprisingly, and with a sigh, when she cuddled up to him afterwards. 'I feel very safe with you.'

He meant to check the street for signs of the Corsican before he went to bed but he was so tired he forgot. He only remembered when he heard the scream.

7

Terror in the Night

He thought it was part of the nightmare at first, though up to then there'd been nothing much to scream about. He only classed it as a nightmare because of the head, and even that had more farce to it than terror.

He was a mechanic in the Royal Flying Corps in France during World War One and he had to patch the planes whenever they got smashed up or shot down. It wasn't a role he was particularly keen on – he'd rather have been a pilot.

As usual, William was in the dream, and *he* was a pilot.

He came into the hangar where Preston was gluing bits of plane together and told him he was taking one of the new chaps up for a spin.

The new chap looked about eight years old, but then, so did William.

'Get the machines ready,' he told Preston.

But they didn't have any machines. Not ones that could fly, anyway. They were all in pieces. They had to pretend.

They stretched their arms out to make wings and Preston swung an imaginary propeller and they made engine noises with their mouths and ran out of the hangar.

Preston went back to his pot of glue.

Moments later there was an almighty crash and a head flew in through the door of the hangar and bounced across the floor.

That was when Preston realised he was in a nightmare. He was not unduly alarmed. He'd had nightmares featuring William before and they invariably ended with someone being beheaded or disembowelled or otherwise mangled in an unpleasant manner. He knew, deep down, that this was something to do with Barry Moxton and the murder, but he didn't wake up sweating and shaking the way he used to when he was younger. He just picked the head up from the floor and wiped the blood off a bit and looked at it. It was the head of the new pilot, of course. He still had his flying helmet on but the goggles were smashed. You couldn't see his expression, but Preston knew it would be anxious.

He put it on a shelf at the back of the hangar with the rest of the heads. Then William came back.

'Lost the new chap,' he said. 'Crashed on take-off.'

'I know,' said Preston. 'He's dead.'

William sighed. 'S'pose I'll have to write to his mother,' he said. 'And he didn't even have any medals I could send her.'

Preston felt angry then. Bastard, he thought. He wanted to smash William's teeth in, he wanted to kick him all round the airfield.

But he stayed very calm.

'I've got his head here,' he said. 'You could send her that.'

William looked surprised.

'D'you think she'd like that?' he asked, doubtfully.

Preston took the head down from the shelf. I'll show him, he thought. I'll show him who's chicken. *Big chicken*.

'She'd love it,' he said. 'I'll give it a bit of a clean up. I'll get a new pair of goggles for it. She could put it on her mantelpiece.'

He thrust the head at William.

'Stop it,' he told him.

He didn't shout. He didn't even raise his voice. He was just very firm.

'Stop doing this. Stop filling my hangar with bits of corpse.'

It was then that he heard the scream. And there was something about it that froze the blood, even before he woke up and knew it was real.

'No,' he yelled, reaching for the baseball bat he kept by the side of the bed for intruders and finding he couldn't move his arm. It seemed to be tied to his neck.

He flung the bedcovers off and stood up, shaking and staring wildly into the darkness, trying to identify the threat, knowing it had to be the Corsican and bracing himself for the shotgun blast that would cut him in half, disembowel him, blow his head off, send it bouncing across the floor of the bedroom.

But there was no intruder, no Corsican, no shotgun.

Just Emily. Still screaming.

He felt for the bedside table with his left hand, remembered why the right one was all bandaged up, and switched on the light.

Emily was rolling almost rhythmically from side to side in the bed with her arms crossed over her breasts and her eyes wide open and staring. She looked terrified.

'Emily?' He reached out to touch her. 'What's the matter?'

She stopped screaming then and began to sob.

And Preston sat there beside her, patting her ineffectually on the shoulder, saying, 'It's all right, it's all right, really, it's all right,' until finally the sobbing stopped, too, and her eyes closed and she gave a great, shuddering sigh and slept.

If she'd ever been awake.

Preston sat there for a while stroking her and then, when he was sure that she was sleeping soundly, he crossed over to the window and lifted a corner of the curtain and peered cautiously out into the street. It was still dark, and he could see the rain slanting down in the light of the street lamps.

There was no sign of anyone watching the house. Was that what he had expected? A solitary figure standing there in a trench coat under one of the street lamps? The Corsican come to claim his own? He didn't know his name. But 'the Corsican' sounded better than a name. More sinister.

Was he the cause of Emily's distress? But it seemed more primitive, less articulate than that. As if there was something locked deep inside her that she just had to let out.

It was just after three in the morning, and there were no lights on in any of the houses and nothing moving on the street. It was somehow reassuring to see all those houses, those solid Victorian terraces in the rain and the soft yellow light of the street lamps. But it was depressing, too, because he did not know a single person who occupied them. He hardly knew the people in his own house, only to exchange a casual greeting if he met them going out or coming in. Perhaps they had heard Emily screaming. If so they had done nothing about it. He might have murdered her.

44

He found himself wishing he was at home again, at Polly's home, and could creep stealthily into the twins' room and sit there as he sometimes had at night, on the floor among their discarded toys and cuddly animals, with his back to the wall, listening to the sound of their breathing. Like a watchdog. No, not a dog, a bodyguard stationed there to protect them from evil.

But he couldn't.

He couldn't go into their room and he couldn't keep the evil out.

It was a three o'clock in the morning thought, negative and self-destructive.

So he went back to bed and slid in beside the now silent, still figure of Emily, and nursed his throbbing right wrist with his left hand and imagined himself as one of those recumbent stone knights you sometimes see in churches, stretched out with arms crossed at the breast, cold and grey and dead, feeling no pain.

And closed his eyes and tried to sleep.

8

The Prince of Darkness

'Jam on your toast?'

Preston opened his eyes.

Emily was sitting on the edge of the bed in one of his shirts, holding a tray. He smelt coffee.

'Sleep well?'

So he had obviously slept.

'What time is it?' he said.

It was eight o'clock. His last memory was of a rather half-hearted dawn chorus outside the grey windows, so he'd probably slept for about two hours. Not well.

Emily, however, looked as if she had. Her hair was tied in a ribbon and she looked positively chirpy.

He eased himself up on the pillow and examined the breakfast tray. Orange juice, coffee in a pot, toast, butter, jam, marmalade. Did he really have all that in the kitchen or had she sent out for it?

The curtains were half drawn back, it had stopped raining and there was sunshine.

Preston felt foul.

'Just butter,' he said. 'Thank you.'

He took the orange juice and observed her warily while he drank and she spread.

'So how are you,' he said, 'this morning?'

'Fine,' she said brightly. 'Much better than last night.'

So she wasn't going to mention the screaming. Perhaps it was like sleepwalking and she wasn't aware of it. Perhaps it would be dangerous to tell her.

He took the toast and bit thoughtfully. Crumbs fell on his sling.

'D'you want me to come back with you tonight?' he asked her.

Meaning did she plan to come back with him?

But she shook her head.

'I'll be all right,' she said. 'Brenda will be there tonight.'

Brenda was her flatmate. A New Zealander. Not easily intimidated.

'Besides,' she said, 'I don't think it was him now.'

'Oh?' Preston was surprised. 'Why not?'

'Well, I've been thinking, why should he ring and ring like that and not come round? He'd ring once to make sure I was in and then he'd be at the front door, wouldn't he?'

Unless he was driving across France, Preston thought, and ringing every time he stopped for a break, to make sure she was still there. He'd probably be on his way across the Channel now and waiting outside her flat just as she got home from work.

He did not mention this possibility to Emily.

On consideration it did not seem likely.

But it still left the question of who *had* been ringing her.

Assuming she hadn't made the whole thing up.

'If the phone rings again I'll get Brenda to answer it,' she said. 'She's got this whistle thing she holds next to the receiver and it blasts your eardrums out.'

'Wonderful,' said Preston. 'Does she ask who it is first or does she just use it as soon as she hears a man's voice?'

Preston wasn't sure about Brenda. He thought she had an attitude problem. Towards men.

Emily chuckled. She looked very nice in his shirt. She looked very young and girlish and normal.

He had to ask her about the screaming. He couldn't just leave it like that.

'You know you were crying out in your sleep?' he said.

He thought that was tactful. Then she could always pretend it was a nightmare. Perhaps it *was* a nightmare. Perhaps she had nightmares with her eyes open.

'I wasn't asleep,' she said. 'Not properly. I wasn't properly awake either. It's just something that happens in my brain.'

'Were you scared about something? Him?'

She shook her head.

'It's not as rational as that. I'm scared but I don't know what of. I feel as if I'm drowning, or as if the room's closing in on me. I feel as if I'll die if I stay where I am but I'm scared to get up and go somewhere else. It's awful, I can't explain it. Poor Preston, did I scare you?'

'I was worried about you,' he said.

They took the same tube into work but walked apart on the final stretch to the office in case anyone saw them together and jumped to the right conclusion.

There was a note on Preston's desk.

'Call William,' it said, 'soonest.'

And a number.

Preston stared at it for a moment, frowning. He'd never had a call from William at work before. He wondered what it could be that was so urgent, and why he hadn't mentioned it yesterday over lunch.

He dialled the number.

'Preston. It was good to see you, yesterday.'

'It was good to see you,' said Preston, cautiously.

'I was just thinking when you left – I've got an idea that might interest you.'

'Oh yes? For a programme?'

'No. No, nothing to do with television. Look, are you free for lunch and I'll tell you about it?'

'It would have to be this side of town,' said Preston. 'I've got a meeting that'll probably go on until one at least.'

He could see the vultures gathering already in the executive producer's office.

'That's fine,' said William. 'Anywhere you like.'

Preston gave him directions to a small and inexpensive restaurant not far from the studios and put the phone down thoughtfully. He wished he could feel easier with William. More than that, he wished he could put his finger on why he didn't. There were plenty of

48

individual reasons. He could tick them all off, one by one, the petty misdemeanours and misadventures of childhood, starting with the trespass on the railway line and ending, of course, with the murder at the Turk's Head. But it was none of these, nor the sum of them. It was something else, some element in William himself. He was dialling the restaurant to book the table for lunch when it came to him. It was a facility for unleashing chaos.

Of course, he'd long since grown out of it. It was a childhood thing. He was a university lecturer now, a family man, respectable, boring, even. His life was ordered, there was not even a hint of chaos in it now.

But it was a surprising and disturbing thought, all the same, and no sooner had it presented itself than he had another, even more surprising and disturbing. *Emily had it, too.* Only with her, it was still very much an ongoing thing.

She was there at the departmental conference and he included her in the general nod and smile as he entered the executive producer's office, but his eyes were guarded, and not just on her account.

The conference was to discuss the programmes currently under production as part of the documentary series. Although Preston still referred to it privately as the God slot, as he had indicated to Kate it made little or no reference to the Almighty. The Almighty was something of an embarrassment to the BBC of late, ever since He had ceased to be the exclusive property of the Church of England. He now came in so many shapes and sizes they didn't know quite where they were with Him. It was almost as if, after years of stolidly predictable behaviour, an old and respected great-uncle had declared himself to be a Buddhist or a Muslim or the follower of some obscure Eastern mystic, and, instead of keeping it to himself, insisted on dressing up in a variety of different-coloured kaftans and talking to people loudly about The Meaning of Life at drinks parties. It was not the sort of thing you did in polite company. It was certainly not the sort of thing you did at the BBC.

It was best to ignore Him. To pretend He didn't exist.

The traditional God slot early on Sunday evening was now given over entirely to sing-songs, and the late-night documentary series concentrated on moral issues.

The first three films in the new series were about mercenaries, murderers and adultery. Preston's was the only film that even mentioned God, and that was only in connection with his opposite number.

Preston had been quite keen when he started the project but now he felt a bit shamefaced about it. If God was an embarrassment, a politically suspect and rather quaint anachronism, how much more of an absurdity was the Prince of Darkness?

This film was obviously going to be yet another stage in Preston's own decline and fall as a BBC producer.

He wouldn't have minded so much if there'd been a rise somewhere along the line – a moment of triumph, no matter how brief – but he'd gone from children's programmes to women's programmes to the Devil in one slow, unspectacular but continuous slide.

He looked around him at the other producers and researchers. All bright young things, on their way up, or looking as if they were, with their murderers and their mercenaries and their adulterers. He caught Emily's eye on him and looked away quickly. Adulterers. That's what they both were, technically speaking. He'd never really thought about it before today. Before he knew about the Corsican.

He suddenly noticed everyone was looking at him.

He blushed guiltily, but the small part of his brain that had been vaguely monitoring the discussion alerted him to the fact that he had been asked a question by the executive producer.

But not, unfortunately, to what it was.

'Sorry?' he said, startled.

'I was asking, Preston, how you were getting on with the Devil.'

William was already there when he arrived at the restaurant, and halfway through a bottle of wine.

'Sorry,' said Preston. 'It went on longer than I expected.'

'That's all right,' said William. 'Have a drink.'

'I need it,' said Preston.

'Problems at work?'

'It's my film about the Devil,' said Preston. 'No one will take him seriously.'

'Ah,' said William, absently, 'that's where he scores.'

Preston looked at him curiously.

'Do you?'

William was studying the menu. He looked up.

'Excuse me?'

'Take him seriously. The Devil. All that stuff you were telling me yesterday. Beelzebub and the Devil's Cabinet and Amadeus . . .'

'Asmodeus. Well, I'm not saying I see it quite like that, I mean, that's the mythology . . .'

'But you believe in him? As a supernatural being?'

William wriggled.

'Honestly, how can I say? Theologians have been arguing this for two thousand years . . .'

'But what do you *feel*, William, what's your gut reaction to this?'

But he could never get a straight answer out of William, not nowadays. Perhaps he didn't have gut reactions any more. He'd spent too many years being an historian, analysing things.

'Well, it always seemed to me that the Cathars had got pretty close to it,' he said.

'The what?'

'Cathars. The Albigensians.'

'I'm sorry, William, you've lost me.'

'After Albi. The city in Provence. But it spread through most of southern France during the latter half of the twelfth century. Have you never read *Montaillou*?'

'No, no, I haven't.'

William was always doing this to him. He talked about events in the Middle Ages as if they'd happened yesterday and been fully aired on the nine o'clock news. He was always surprised that no one else had the faintest idea of what he was talking about.

'It was a religion, a heresy. Cathars believed there were two co-equal powers, God and the Devil. God was the Good One, the Lord of Light, the ruler of the spirit world; Satan was the

Lord of Darkness and ruler of the material world. He tried to corrupt people by the desires of their bodies . . .'

'So he had a lot going for him.'

'Exactly. That's why the world is so corrupted. The Cathars believed you had to forgo earthly pleasures. You were forbidden to take life of any sort. Couldn't eat meat. Couldn't have sex . . .'

'I take it this didn't exactly catch on?'

'Oh, on the contrary. Among the common people it was very much the thing. There was a let-out – only the *perfecti*, the priests, had to obey all the rules. Everyone else was allowed a lot of latitude, particularly in sexual matters, and then just before they died they took the *consolamentum* which permitted them to enter the life of the spirit.'

The waiter was waiting to take their order.

'Italian sausage with potato and beans,' Preston ordered. He felt like nursery food after the pummelling he'd had during the meeting and that was the nearest thing to it on the menu. Afterwards he would have a pudding. His consolation.

'So you could have your cake and eat it,' he said. 'I can see why that went down big in the South of France. What happened to them?'

'Oh, the Catholics persecuted them,' said William, as if it was obvious. 'Don't you remember? Simon de Montfort led a crusade, massacred them by the thousand . . .'

'The Parliament chap?'

'No, no, no. His father. I thought you read history.'

'Modern history. I didn't go that far back. So what was it the Catholics objected to? The sex bit, or not eating meat?'

'Oh, there were all sort of political reasons. They didn't like the competition. Also, of course, they didn't like this idea of Satan being God's equal. They were locked into this idea of God being omnipotent. If you ask me, they should have incorporated Catharism into their own theology, it would have filled in a lot of holes . . .'

'How do you mean?'

'Well, they've always been pushed to explain why an omnipotent God permits Evil . . .'

'The Fall of Man,' said Preston. 'Original sin. Free will.'

'Yes, well, I always thought Augustine was a bit simplistic in his ideas,' said William, waspishly, as if he was talking about a rival academic. 'God's great apologist. Always trying to blame it on Man, as if God had nothing whatsoever to do with it. You know why, of course?'

Preston shook his head.

'Fear. Trying to make up for his misspent youth. Thought if he sucked up to God enough he'd get away with it.'

'Wasn't he the holes in the universe chap?'

'Excuse me?'

'Remember Mother Bernard and the holes that let the Evil in?'

'Of course. Fancy you remembering that. Yes, she was rather struck on Augustine, wasn't she. A lot of nuns are, of course. Rather more of a sex symbol than Jesus.'

Preston was shocked.

'Poor old Mother Bernie,' said William, shaking his head. 'She had theories, too, you know. Quite a theologian in her own eccentric way, was Mother Bernard. Remember her theory about Hell?'

Preston frowned.

'It rings a vague bell. Go on . . .'

'She reckoned it was like a department store, don't you remember?'

'That's right, I remember. Mary Ann Evans's. Before your mum bought it.'

It all came back now. Mary Ann Evans's, the oldest, poshest store in town, which was always, out of respect, called by its full name, never simply Evans's, and which in those days still had the old-fashioned lifts with wood-panelling and carpets and concertina doors, and uniformed attendants who called out the wares on each floor.

First floor: ladies' lingerie knitwear maternity garments bedlinen swimwear and ladies' separates . . .

And the attendants would wait with their expressionless faces while some people got out and others got in, and then they'd press a button and off you'd go again.

Second floor: menswear children's wear sportswear toys electrical goods and gents' toilets . . .

53

It was almost as good as a ride at the fun fair.

'And when you die,' said William, 'according to Mother Bernie, you get in the lift and if you're in a state of mortal sin the Demon who works it takes you down instead of up . . .'

Preston remembered.

Going down, first floor: gluttons drunkards lechers blasphemers debauchees hooligans and defilers of religious relics . . .

And you had to get out on the floor that catered for your particular dominant moral propensity, and stay there for the whole of Eternity.

'And on the very bottom floor,' William reminded him, 'was the Adultery Department. Except that it was for adulterers, *and* murderers. They were on the same floor.'

Preston stared at him. 'I don't remember that,' he said.

William grinned and Preston saw the schoolboy again, full of mischief, with the devil in him. That Billy Quirk, as Preston's Auntie Ethel called him, a child too advanced for his years.

'You probably didn't know what adultery meant,' he said.

'No,' said Preston.

William would have known, though. Or pretended he did. Throughout their infancy, and into early adolescence, William had been Preston's sexual consultant, advising him on all technical and ethical complications. He invariably had some spicy piece of information to impart that would add to Preston's meagre understanding. Unhappily, he did not so often get it right. It was William who had convinced Preston at an impressionable age that little girls, as they grew up, also grew 'two tits and a willy', a fantasy which Preston had accepted as gospel for at least two years and which he sometimes thought still influenced his relations with the opposite sex. It was William who had given Preston the first *believable* explanation of how you made babies. According to William, the man and the woman took all their clothes off and climbed into the bath so the woman was sitting with her back to the man, and the man peed into the water. Then little invisible tadpole things in the pee swam through the bathwater up the woman's bottom and laid eggs, and six months later she had a baby. He'd even got the gestation period wrong, but given the rest of it this was a minor consideration.

Preston sometimes thought that Mother Bernie and William between them had ruined whatever chance he'd ever had of a normal sex life. Whatever that was.

He emptied the rest of the wine into their glasses and wondered if he should order another. He had to try and rescue his documentary from the mauling it had received during the morning conference, so it might be wise to keep a clear head. On the other hand, it might be even wiser to get totally pissed. It was always difficult to tell.

He ordered another bottle.

'What was this idea of yours?' he said.

'Oh, that,' said William, as if it had completely slipped his mind and he'd have been quite happy talking about Satan and Hell and related matters for the rest of the afternoon.

'It's a house,' he said.

'A house.'

'A big house. Kate found it.'

'Oh. You mean to live in? You're going to buy it?'

'We'd like to. Only it's too big. So we had this idea of getting other people to buy it with us.'

'I see . . .'

'There's already one other couple interested but I'm not sure it's such a good idea to have just two couples. We thought . . . well, maybe you'd be interested as well.'

'And divide it up, you mean? Into flats?'

'Well, not necessarily. It would depend. Kate thinks it might be good to turn it into a sort of commune.'

'A commune? These days?'

'Well, that's the point. Kate thinks it's time for a revival. She says things have gone too far the other way. She says the way the world's going we could use a bit less individualism and a bit more collective responsibility.'

It sounded like the sort of thing Kate would say, Preston thought. He wasn't sure about Kate. He wasn't sure Kate was sure about him.

'So this is all Kate's idea?'

'Well, more or less.'

'And who suggested bringing me in?'

'Well, I did. I thought we needed a single person as a sort of
. . . catalyst. What do you think?'

Preston was suspicious.

'I don't know,' he prevaricated. 'Who's the other couple?'

'Old friends of ours. Well, more Kate's than mine. Louis and
Tess. I don't think you've met them.'

Preston shook his head.

'Well, think it over,' said William. 'I mean, I'm not so ideological
as Kate, but I just think it makes sense for all sorts of practical
reasons. Like pooling our resources and that. And the price of
big houses like that has really plummeted in the last year. It's a
bargain.'

'How big is it?'

'Come and see for yourself. We're all going to look at it tomorrow
night.'

'Well, I'll think about it,' said Preston. 'Where is it, anyway?'

9

The House

It wasn't far from where he lived, just a stop further on the tube, but he'd not been to the area before. Nor, from the look of it, had the developers. No wonder it's cheap, he thought.

The first thing he saw when he came out of the station was an antiquated sign on a lamppost saying, 'Stand for 6 licensed hackney cabs'. No cabs, of course, hackney or otherwise. Just a tired row of shops opposite and a seedy-looking pub on the corner and a disused laundry with boarded-up windows and a For Sale notice. It felt closer to Dickens's London than to Preston's.

But perhaps that was the fog.

Not quite the fog of Dickens, or even his own childhood. They'd cleaned it up since then and taken the soot out. The poisons it contained were less visible now. But it was still a proper fog, a city fog, with a whiff of brimstone in it, a hint of the old sinner it used to be. It crept round the corners of the buildings and hung in the doorways and fled in ragged wisps from the car headlights.

He turned right out of the station, according to William's instructions, and then right again, and saw the viaduct.

Come and look at the place, William had said, *it's like everyone's dream of a Victorian childhood.*

And here it was, the nightmare.

It spanned the road ahead, the brickwork streaked with dark tears and three black holes in the middle, one for the traffic and two smaller ones on each side for pedestrians, and they looked to Preston like mouths, or nostrils, breathing fog.

It was the monster of his infancy, lying in wait for him all these years, or a warning sign, saying, Go Back, make your excuses and leave, exert your free will . . .

But he was older now and in another city, and besides, the wench was dead.

So he shook off the ghosts and walked on, his footsteps muffled by the fog, shivering from a chill that wasn't just in the air, until the nearest mouth engulfed him.

It was a real Fanny-by-gaslight relic of the old city, redolent of gin and vomit and brutal crimes, and the fog had crept in like an old friend and made a dripping urinal of the walls. Only the graffiti was of the present, but even that had its roots in ancient hatreds. Troops Out of Ireland. Keep Britain White. Bring Back Hanging . . .

They should never have abolished it, hanging's too good for him. A life sentence. He'll be out in ten years . . .

Committed to an asylum for the criminally insane . . .

For a moment he thought he saw a figure at the far end, waiting, but that was from the nightmare, too, just a trick of the light and the fog.

There was a significant improvement on the other side of the viaduct, a Victorian class divide that had survived the years, and within two blocks he was walking down a tree-lined avenue composed of tall, detached houses set back from the road behind fair-sized gardens. He could see from the number of bells beside each door that they'd nearly all been turned into flats now, or dentists' surgeries, and some were in urgent need of renovation, but they still retained some of their former grandeur, or was it pretension? The make-believe pomp and affected circumstance of the people for whom they'd been built, the doctors and lawyers and merchants and administrators of Empire who all, in one way or another, made their money out of trade but built houses like miniature castles, or palaces, to reassure themselves that they were closer to the Barons than to the Peasants, and safe from both.

Preston was fascinated by them. As a very young child he had learned to read from picture books that showed children living in houses like these, in nurseries with sloping ceilings and toy yachts and teddy bears on the floor and solid Papas and gentle Mamas and a view through the window of rooftops and spires, and if there was a cloud across the moon it was in the shape of a sailing ship. As an adolescent and well into his twenties he had affected to despise the whole fairy tale – the people, the properties, the false virtues, the false security it represented. But now he was of an age and living in an era whose insecurities craved the reassurance of nursery images, the illusory solidity of Victorian values which, if they had never existed, could always be invented. He was confused by a barrage of conflicting ideologies. The sneer had turned into a lump in his throat. The contempt into envy.

The house that William had found was down one of the side streets and not so majestic, but it still had a fair bit of the Gothic about it, and the brass knocker on the front door had the face of an ogre.

Preston lifted it and knocked.

Kate answered the door but he heard William's voice, shouting down the stairs.

'Is that Preston? Come in, shut the door on the fog.'

It evoked some distant memory but he couldn't quite pin it down.

He stepped into the hall.

'Bloody hell,' he said. 'Take some heating, this.'

He stamped his feet on the tiled floor. Original by the look of it, and so were the banisters, but someone had painted them a kind of snot green.

'What do you think of it?' William bounced down the stairs, a grinning schoolboy again, and he could hear other voices somewhere in the upper reaches.

'He hasn't seen it yet,' complained Kate. 'Give him a chance.'

'He's seen the outside. Wait until you see the fireplaces.'

Preston couldn't remember when he'd last seen him so enthusiastic about anything.

'Wait until you see the soot,' said a sardonic but unseen voice, and then a woman emerged from one of the downstairs rooms off the hallway.

Preston stopped stamping his feet.

She was stunning. She had tawny blonde hair down to her shoulders and a rather thin face with high cheekbones and a wide mouth. She wore a leather coat and boots and his first thought was that she looked Slavonic, a Russian or a Pole. His second was that she was from the estate agent's. His third that he was in love.

But he was mistaken. She wasn't Russian or Polish, she wasn't from the estate agent's, and if he was in love, it was the worst mistake of all.

'This is Tess,' said William. 'Louis' upstairs with the kids.'

Her handshake was cool and firm and her eyes were grey.

But Preston had stopped looking.

'They're bloody choosing the rooms already,' said another voice, deep and loud, and from somewhere above ceiling level, and Preston looked up and saw the man who must be Louis, hanging over the banisters on the landing.

Was this the ogre? Preston's glance took in the broad shoulders, a black beard, a lean, dark face and a big nose.

'Bit premature, isn't it?' said Tess.

And there was a small, uncomfortable silence, or so Preston imagined, and a chill in the air, but that could have been real.

'Preston, Louis,' said William, and he was half bent at the waist, like a supplicant monk, rubbing his hands and smiling, nervously. He is nervous, Preston thought, he wants us to like each other.

Louis came bounding down the stairs. He was as tall as William and half as wide again, and he exuded a genial, gregarious energy. He looked, at closer quarters, less of an ogre, more like a Victorian explorer, but was this an improvement? And yet Preston *did* like him, instinctively, and without his usual reserve. More than that, he wanted Louis to like *him*, but he didn't know why.

'Come and look at the fireplaces,' said William, and they filed dutifully into the room Tess had just come out of. Preston looked at the fireplace. A steel grate like a suit of armour, a long time unsquired, and what looked like a tile and marble surround, it was difficult to tell, the snot-green artist had been busy here, too.

'We'd be able to have coal fires,' said Kate.

'They only allow smokeless fuel these days,' said Preston.

He knew what he was doing but was incapable of stopping it. It was the same thing that made him physically shrink into his scarf and his leather jacket. He felt he was being drawn out of his comfortless hole into something altogether more vast and impressive and alarming.

'Well?' said William, when they'd seen it all and adjourned to the pub opposite the station, an old waiting room of a pub that had not yet been converted into a wine bar or a theme park and was consequently empty. The three children were at a separate table, grudgingly tolerated by the landlord.

'Well it's . . . big,' said Tess.

'Big?' thundered Louis. 'Is that all you can say? It's fantastic.'

'Fourteen rooms, three bathrooms, a hundred-foot south-facing garden . . .' William intoned.

'You sound like an estate agent,' said Tess.

William looked stricken. Tess relented.

'Sorry, but it's a bit . . . overwhelming, really. The work we'd have to do.'

'That's why it's so cheap,' said Louis. 'My God, woman, you were the one who said we needed more space.'

'I said we needed a playroom for the kids and a bit more garden – not a damn great manse at the arse-end of the Northern line with its own private wilderness . . .'

'Where's your sense of adventure?'

'I exhausted it on you, darling.'

Preston kept his head down and his nose in the beer.

'So, I take it we look elsewhere,' said Kate, flatly. She sounded disappointed.

'Is it the house – or the whole idea?' William demanded. He looked so crestfallen Preston felt sorry for him. He wished he could say something encouraging, but he didn't *feel* encouraged. He was on Tess's side.

She sat crumbling a beer mat between her fingers. She looked more out of place in the shabby pub than any of them.

'I really like it,' said Kate plaintively. 'I think we could do an awful lot with it. And think of the advantages of sharing. Sharing the shopping, babysitting . . .'

'Decorating?' said Tess. 'Mending the roof?'

'We'd get builders to do that.'

'Oh God, you mean we'd have to live with builders as well?'

61

'There's nothing wrong with the roof,' said William. 'Not as far as I know . . .'

'Anyway, I think we should be more positive,' said Kate. 'We have to *make* it work.'

'Maybe it's just the fog,' said Preston. 'And seeing it at night . . .'

But no one was listening.

'She's just a bloody pessimist,' said Louis. 'Always looks on the dark side. I think it's great. I think the house is great, I think the idea's great. My God, we're all victims in this fucking city. They're all out to screw us. Plumbers, builders, estate agents, the government, the council, bloody thieves . . . We've got to fight back. Otherwise we're just prey.'

Preston stared at him in astonishment. Anyone less like prey he couldn't imagine. He looked as if he'd make a Rottweiler pause for thought.

'Consumers,' said Kate, with a shrug, 'that's what we are. And they use the whole sham of our so-called individualism to make it easier to manipulate us. Buy what they want us to buy, live the way they want us to live. We have to learn how to live collectively again. I know it's not exactly fashionable at the moment, but it's the only hope we've got.'

'Exactly,' said Louis. 'Collective security. Fuck the bastards. Especially burglars.'

He banged the table with his fist and the glasses jumped and the drink spilled. The landlord glared.

Preston wondered where the burglars came into it. His face must have registered his confusion.

'We had a break-in last year,' said Tess. 'That's what this is all about really.'

'Bollocks!'

Tess was undaunted.

'The house is full of weapons,' she complained. 'It's like we're preparing for Armageddon.'

'What kind of weapons?' said Kate.

'Well, on the hallstand we have a set of those ball things Argentinian cowboys swing round their heads and jump in and out of . . .'

They looked at her blankly.

'You know, for bringing down runaway cows.'

'I shouldn't have thought you were troubled much with runaway cows,' said Kate, mystified. 'Not in a first-floor flat in Clapham.'

'For intruders,' explained Tess. 'Rapists, murderers, burglars. It's for throwing at them as you retreat into the living room. He's got it all worked out, he calls it Defence in Depth. We have regular drills.'

Louis was glowering over his beer. William looked embarrassed.

Preston was impressed.

'And then in the living room we've got an umbrella stand with two stout walking sticks and a Samurai ceremonial sword, and on the Welsh dresser in the kitchen there's a lemon squeezer full of ammonia, and on top of the wardrobe in the bedroom he's got an air pistol that fires steel ball-bearings . . . Knock out a rabbit at fifty paces, they told him in the shop. We're not sure about burglars but we think it might have a deterrent effect.'

'Good God,' said Kate, 'what about the children?'

'Oh, they've just got plastic bows and arrows,' said Tess, 'but we reckon that if a burglar's been squirted with ammonia and slashed with a sword and pelted with ball-bearings and wooden balls his resistance is going to be pretty low by the time he reaches the kids' bedroom, don't you think?'

'I didn't mean that. I meant, aren't you worried about the kids playing with them?'

'Speaking personally, yes, this is a point of concern, but Rambo here seems to consider that's one of the things we have to live with if we're going to beat the baddies.'

She smiled at him, tauntingly, and raised her glass of dry white wine.

'Isn't it, darling?'

'Clever bitch,' he said. 'I don't notice you laughing when I have to go away for the night. It's chains and bolts on the door, the telephone next to the bed, all the lights left on . . .'

Tess flushed, ever so slightly.

'All right, I don't like being alone in the house with the children, I admit that . . .'

'Well, you wouldn't be,' said William, 'if we all shared.'

He looked quite flushed, too, Preston noticed. He had a feeling this was all getting rather out of hand. But perhaps they were always like this.

A catalyst, he thought. My God, I'd have my work cut out with this lot. He didn't quite understand the chemistry yet, but it looked complicated. He glanced at the other table. At least the kids seemed to be getting on.

'Preston, you're not saying much,' said Kate. 'What do you think?'

10

An Evening with Emily

'I think it could be great fun,' said Emily. 'I think you've got the wrong attitude.'

'So what's the right attitude?' Preston demanded. People had been telling him he had the wrong attitude since he was potty trained. Probably before, if only he could remember.

'You always see the obstacles in everything. You're so cautious. Sometimes you've just got to take a chance and dive in.'

Like you? Preston thought, crabbily, though he knew it was true. Emily saw herself as the Elephant's Child in the *Just So Stories*, drawn by her 'satiable curiosity to partake of all new experience. Constant messy encounters with crocodiles seemed not to have deterred her.

'I don't like rushing into things until I've thought them through,' he said, reasonably. This was the first time they'd been out together since the alleged phone-calls, and if there'd been any more since then she hadn't mentioned it. Yet. They were in a wine bar not far from the studios, and every time the door opened Preston looked up nervously in case it was one of their colleagues, or the Corsican with a sawn-off shotgun.

'What you don't like is commitment,' said Emily.

Preston knew what this was about now, or thought he did.

'I don't mind commitment,' he said, mildly. 'Once I know what I'm committed *to*.'

Was this true? He'd never really felt committed to Polly, even after six or seven years of marriage. Nor to any woman. He'd always held something back. It seemed only sensible.

'I've only just met these people,' he said. 'How do I know what they're like to live with?'

65

'I thought you'd known them for years. I thought this bloke was your oldest friend.'

'William, yes. I'm talking about the other couple. And I'm not that mad keen on the house, either.'

Their glasses were empty and he took them to the bar for a refill. It was Emily who had suggested this 'drink after work', and he knew it would lead to more than that. Either a row or bed, or both. It was over a fortnight now since they'd last met, outside the office. He told himself he was 'trying to take the heat out of the relationship' but he knew he was running scared. He watched her covertly in the mirror behind the bar. She looked very sexy, dressed all in black, with one of those tight little ribbed skirts and her long legs crossed . . . If only it could be *uncomplicated*.

'What are they like?' she asked when he came back to the table. 'This other couple?'

Preston considered, choosing his words carefully.

'Well, I quite like Louis. He's very open and extrovert and . . .' Reassuring? *You need a reassuring presence in your life, Preston*. Who'd said that? Probably Carla. But it could just as easily have been his wife. At some period during his affair the distinctions between the two had become a little blurred in Preston's mind. Carla, however, usually had the edge when it came to put-downs. He chose another word.

'Big,' he said.

'Friendly?'

'Yes,' he said, more cautiously. 'Sort of.'

'A Big Friendly Giant. Nice. I could do with one of those in my life.'

Preston recognised this as a personal criticism and felt it was unjustified. Also it was the wrong analogy. Louis did not at all resemble Dahl's amiable dream dispenser as Preston remembered him from the twins' illustrated paperback. He sought alternative images from his nursery reading.

'More like Beorn,' he said, 'the skin-changer in *The Hobbit* who could turn from a man to a bear.'

And who could turn nasty if the mood took him, who could turn dangerous.

'What does he do?'

'Well, from what I can gather he makes up fantasies . . .'

'I meant for a living.'

'That's what I meant. He designs fantasy games. You know, *Heroes and Dragons*, *Lost in the Labyrinth*, that sort of thing. It started as a kind of hobby, now it seems to be his main source of income. He taught sociology before that. William met him at university.'

'And what about her?'

Preston frowned. 'I don't know what she does. They've got a couple of young kids, four and five, so she's probably got her work cut out with them. Only . . .'

'Only what?'

'I just don't see her as a full-time mother . . .'

He was on dangerous ground here. Carla would have taken him to the cleaners for that. The chance remark that revealed his deep-rooted chauvinism and basic male insensitivity. She'd have had him back to the manufacturers for radical restructuring. Or melted down for soap. Either way it wouldn't have been pleasant. Preston had more or less given up being a New Man since Carla – it was so difficult to get it *right* all the time and they kept moving the goalposts – but he still liked to make the right noises. The problem was they kept coming out as grunts.

Emily was looking at him curiously. Or was it with suspicion?

'What does she look like?'

'Oh . . .' Preston pushed his bottom lip out as if he had never really considered the matter but that anything in the range between plain and repulsive would just about cover it.

'Bit thin,' he said in the end, 'but she's got . . . quite a nice dress sense.'

He was irritated with himself for being so pathetic. Why didn't he just say she looked absolutely wonderful? What was he so afraid of?

Emily sighed.

'I wonder how you'd describe me if someone asked you,' she said. 'Nice body, no brain, that's what you'd probably say.'

'That's not true, Emily. Emily, what is this?'

'Could you ever see me as a full-time mother?'

Preston groaned.

'I'm sorry, Emily.'

'Sorry for what?'

Sorry you can't have children. Sorry you want them. Sorry you don't have a career to compensate. Sorry you don't want one. Sorry you're so low on self-esteem. Sorry I don't love you.

'Just sorry,' he said.

'It's not your fault.'

No. So why did he keep blaming himself? *It's a form of conceit, Preston.* That was Carla, too.

Be open with her, he urged himself, tell her . . .

What?

I'm sorry but I just don't want a relationship right now. I'm about to get divorced. I'm scared stiff I'm going to lose touch with my children. I don't know what I want. Except . . . somewhere safe. Something with four solid walls that won't blow down in the first puff of wolf's breath. I need a refuge. What I don't need is a love affair with a woman who's on the run from her past, her husband and God knows what else I haven't been told about yet.

Any of that would have done. Or even, just, *Well, see you next week.*

The one thing he shouldn't have said was, 'Let's have supper.'

Emily chose the restaurant. A franchise bistro near her flat where the food came straight from the freezer to the infra-wave and the waitresses were on their way to something better and wanted you to know it. Emily had a post-anorexic's lack of interest in food and anything to do with it. She picked listlessly at a plate of Sole bonne femme while Preston ate something called a Scampi provençale in a kind of nervous frenzy. They both drank a lot. And it was clear, some way into the second bottle of Frascati, what was going to happen next.

Or perhaps it had been clear a long time before that.

She lived on the fifth floor of a pre-war block, and when they went up in the lift she casually passed him her handbag and said, Hold this, and started to take her clothes off.

Preston began to panic.

'God, Emily . . .'

But he could only watch, alarm contending with excitement and coming out about a nose ahead.

'What if someone gets in?'

And the mouth pouting, eyes full of mischief, and the breasts popping out under the sweater as she tugged it over her head.

And the lift still moving up through the floors, and no one else getting in, yet, and a voice in Preston's brain chanting tunelessly . . .

Second floor: ladies' lingerie bridal garments maternity wear murder and adultery . . .

When it stopped she wore only her shoes and stockings and Preston had an armful of clothes.

He followed, gibbering, down the corridor to the door of her flat.

'What if Brenda's there?'

'Give me my coat then,' she said. 'If you're worried about it.'

Preston bundled her into her coat and tried to hide the rest of her clothes inside his jacket.

But Brenda wasn't there.

Emily walked into the sitting room, let the coat fall to the floor and sat down on the couch, crossing her legs as she had in the wine bar, and watching him coolly as he stood there in the doorway. She hadn't even drawn the curtains.

'What if she comes in?' hissed Preston. He still had his arms wrapped round his jacket to stop her clothes from falling out.

'Don't worry about Brenda,' said Emily.

But it wasn't that easy. Brenda was very particular about keeping the place clean and tidy. She didn't really like Preston being there at all. She didn't like him sitting on her cushions or dirtying her nice clean towels or weeing in her water closet or dripping on her bleached oak vinyl tiled floor. Once Preston had entered the bathroom to find a sign hung there that said: 'PLEASE WIPE SURFACES AND SURROUNDS AFTER USE.' He knew it was directed at him. He had met women like Brenda before. He knew that when she looked at him she saw a leaking penis.

Preston quailed at the thought of being caught by Brenda in an act of passion on the sofa without a box of tissues to wipe up the drips.

Emily put her feet up and stretched out and closed her eyes. Putting her hand between her legs, she began to stroke with an expert finger.

Preston stopped worrying about Brenda. He stopped worrying about the curtains and the tissues and the drips. For a while he stopped worrying about anything.

But only for a while.

It came back, like a pain, temporarily dulled by drugs, in the terrible early hours in Emily's bed where he lay, awake and fretful, scourged by his conscience or his sense of preservation, or whatever it was he had so recklessly ignored, tensed for another screaming fit and wondering how he would explain to Brenda that it wasn't his fault.

But Emily lay beside him, sleeping peacefully. Tonight, only Preston was in torment.

He lay awake through the night wishing he could go home or into the sitting room and watch a horror movie, and then, as the room paled with the threat of day, he drifted into an uneasy sleep, finally waking in full light with a foul taste in his mouth and the disjointed memory of a dream in which he was trapped in a lift dressed in women's underwear and wondering how to explain it when the fire brigade finally came and rescued him.

He sat up and groped for his watch on the bedside table.

It was nearly eight o'clock.

He leapt out of bed and began to search for his clothes.

'What's the matter?' Emily rolled over and squinted up at him. 'Where're you going?'

'I've got someone coming to see me at nine,' he said.

They did not speak again until he was dressed and ready to leave.

'Well,' he said, 'better be off, then.'

She still said nothing.

'I expect I'll see you in the office,' he said.

She muttered something into the pillow.

'Sorry?'

She turned round to face him and he thought that she had been crying.

'I said I won't be in the office,' she said. 'I've got an appointment with the pregnancy advisory service.'

He didn't understand at first. He thought it was some research she was doing. But she wasn't a researcher.

'I'm having an abortion,' she said. 'Next Tuesday.'

11

The Man Who Let the Evil Out

'But I thought you said she couldn't . . .'

'I did,' said Preston. 'Or rather she said. But she was wrong. She can. Apparently.'

'I used to rehearse what I'd say to my students if they came to me with a problem like this,' said William, 'but no one ever did. I don't know if it was because it never happened, or because they didn't think I was the right person to talk to.'

He sighed.

'You're not,' said Preston. 'If there was anyone else I could possibly talk to about this I would. I'm beginning to think I'd be better off talking to my Auntie Ethel.'

They were in one of the pubs near William's college. A typical students' pub, full of old beams and smoke and noise. And students. It took Preston back fifteen years. Like the problem. It was a problem of youth, not of approaching middle age. Except that, ironically, it had never happened to him then. He'd always taken precautions. Or someone had.

William seemed to be obsessed with the fact that he hadn't.

'Quite apart from the risk of pregnancy,' he said sententiously, 'weren't you worried about . . .' They were in a corner, speaking low, but he lowered his voice even further. '. . . Aids?'

As if the mere sound of it would send students screaming from the premises.

'Yes,' said Preston. 'Yes, I was. Only . . .' He put his hand up to his eyes and squeezed them together. He felt very tired. Perhaps it was the smoke. Perhaps it was William. Perhaps it was life. 'She's got this thing about me being so bloody cautious about everything.

72

Not diving in and all that. For God's sake, William, I know. But what am I going to do now?'

William looked around the bar, with a slightly hunted expression. Preston waited. He'd desperately needed to talk to someone about this and when he'd thought about it, William was the only person he *could* talk to. This had been a shock.

'And I thought you wanted to talk about mortgages,' said William.

'I expect you did,' said Preston. 'Sorry.'

'No, no,' said William, hastily. 'It's quite all right.'

He had a drink of beer.

'What do *you* think you should do?' he said eventually.

Preston studied him curiously.

'Is that what you rehearsed?' he said. 'I mean, when you were a moral tutor, was that the first line? I mean, did they train you to say that?'

William was stung.

'Well, it's a reasonable question, at least to start with. You don't expect me to tell you what you should do, do you?'

'It's not a question of me,' said Preston. 'It's Emily. It's what she should do.'

It disturbed him that she hadn't broken the news by saying she was pregnant. *I'm having an abortion next Tuesday*. It felt like they'd missed out a stage or two.

'All right, I'm sorry,' said William. 'I was just a bit taken aback, that's all. Are you saying she doesn't want this abortion?'

'Oh, I don't know. I think she feels she has to, but she'd rather not. She was shattered when she was told she couldn't have children. Now she feels it's a bit like looking a gift horse in the mouth.'

'But you don't want her to have it?'

'How could I? We're not even going out, really.'

It sounded ridiculous.

'I mean, we're not . . . committed in any way.'

'Then it's probably just as well. And it *is* her choice.'

That old chestnut, thought Preston.

'I keep trying to tell myself that,' he said, 'but I know she wants me to say, Have it. I did say, If you really want it, I'd help with

73

the money and things. I wouldn't leave her in the lurch. But she wants more than that. She wants commitment. And I can't give her that.'

'You mean she won't have it unless she has you?'

'I think that's what I mean, yes.'

'Then there's really nothing you can do. It is her decision. Not yours. All you can do is be supportive . . .'

He sat back as if that was the final word on the matter. Next student, please. What's your problem, old boy? Examination, Matriculation, Accommodation, purple lesions on the skin or just another female in the family way?

'I know that,' Preston said, irritably. 'But . . .'

'Is it the Catholic thing?'

'I don't know. Maybe.'

'You still believe in all that?'

Preston sighed.

'I didn't think I did. But when it comes to something like this, there seems to be a lot of left luggage lying around.'

'Funny, that's what Grandad used to call it,' said William. 'Left luggage. Well, baggage, really. Remember? All that baggage they pile on you, he said, and you're going to have to carry it round with you for the rest of your life.'

William's grandad had fought a lonely war against the priesthood – and the grandmothers and mothers and aunts who were allied to it – but he'd lost every battle so far.

'We still have this idea that if we do something morally wrong, or what *They* said was wrong, there'll be some kind of Divine Retribution,' said William. 'Some sudden thunderbolt from Heaven. Or Hell. It's ingrained. We can't shrug it off.'

'I'm not worried about Divine Retribution,' said Preston. This wasn't true, but he didn't want to get dragged into one of William's theological discussions, not just at the moment. 'I'm worried about Emily.'

But there was no stopping William now, he was off on one of his tangents.

'Did I ever tell you about the Man who Let the Evil Out?'

'No,' said Preston, in the tone of voice which would have convinced most people he didn't want him to. But not William.

74

'It was some research I was doing at Cambridge into the Black Death,' he said. 'There was this village, it was wiped out by the plague, no one was left except the priest. He tended to the people while they were dying, gave them the Last Rites and everything, buried them. But he never caught it. Everyone else died but not him. And in the end, when the last of them was dead, he went into the church and hanged himself.'

There was a moral in there somewhere but Preston wasn't sure if he'd cracked it yet.

'He left a journal,' continued William. 'A kind of confession. He'd committed adultery with the wife of the local steward – the land agent for the lord of the manor. He thought that was why the plague had come. It was all his fault.' He leaned forward across the table, fixing Preston with eager gaze. 'His sin had let the Evil out.'

'I see,' said Preston, after a moment. He waited to see if there was any more, but there didn't seem to be. William sat back and finished his drink with apparent satisfaction.

'So you think I should hang myself, then?'

'Excuse me?'

'Or wait until we see if there's any adverse effect first. I mean, a sudden leap in the statistics for people dying from Aids or some disease they haven't put a name to yet.'

'I only offer it as an example of the Catholic guilt complex,' said William, looking hurt.

'Ah,' said Preston. 'Well, thank you very much. It's been good talking to you. I feel a lot better for it.'

They walked to the tube station together. It was the tail end of the rush hour.

'I said we'd go away together for the weekend,' said Preston. 'Somewhere in the country.'

'To talk it over?'

'Not really. I don't think there's much to talk over. No, more as a kind of . . . consolation. A treat before the pain. You know, like your grandad and the elastoplast.'

When they were little, whenever they had a cut or a graze and had to have the plaster taken off, which was painful, William's

75

grandad used to give them a treat first. A chocolate bar or an ice-cream, or sometimes he'd just take them for a walk. The two boys and the grandad. They'd walk round the block and along the side of the railway embankment as far as the viaduct where the line crossed the road, and then they'd turn and walk back. Preston used to love these walks, far more than the chocolate bars and the ice-cream, though he favoured having all three if William's grandad could be pushed that far. He loved the ritual and the quiet sense of harmony between them as they walked along, and the things they talked about.

He especially liked them when it was William who had the plaster that had to be taken off.

'I used to hate it when they yanked it off,' said Preston. 'I always wanted to ease it off, even if it prolonged the agony. But they were ruthless, those women.'

Those women. Five of them, there were. William's nan and his mum and Preston's nan and his mum and his Auntie Ethel.

And just the one grandad.

No wonder he kept losing the battles.

'I don't suppose you've thought any more about the house,' said William.

'Not really,' said Preston, 'it's been difficult. You'd better count me out. Sorry.'

'That's all right.' He seemed to hesitate for a moment. 'We thought we'd go ahead anyway.'

'Just you and Kate?'

'No. Louis and Tess are coming in.'

Preston was surprised.

'She didn't seem too keen,' he said.

'Well, Louis must have persuaded her. Anyway, we won't look for anyone else a while. So if you do decide . . .'

'Okay,' said Preston. 'Thanks.' But he thought he'd already decided.

They took the same tube for the first few stops.

'Where're you going away to,' William asked, 'for this weekend?'

'I don't know yet,' Preston said. 'Haven't really thought about it. Some country house hotel, I expect. I'll have to look through a guide book.'

'You could stay at our place if you want.'

Preston thought he meant in London. He tried to say it wasn't quite what he had in mind. But William meant the house in the country, near Cambridge.

'I thought you'd sold it,' said Preston.

'Well, we've had an offer and it's going through the system, but it's still ours. And all the furniture's still there. All you have to do is turn the electricity on.'

'Are you sure?'

'Of course. We keep going back ourselves so it's quite lived in. We'd be back this weekend only we're staying with Kate's parents in Sussex.'

'Well . . .'

'It's very pleasant.' William seemed almost anxious for him to accept. 'Remember? You came there with Polly and the twins . . .'

12

The Picture

Preston remembered. A weekend in May and the fields full of blossom and the twins a little short of their third birthday.

It was unthinkable, of course, to take them this time, but it was a wrench leaving them behind with Polly. It's started, he thought. He was on his way to becoming a statistic, one of the sixty per cent of fathers who lose all contact with their children within five years of divorce. And he wasn't even divorced yet.

He hired a car for the journey because the cottage was difficult to reach any other way. His wrist still throbbed from his fight with the Big Chicken but it seemed to be the only part of him that still had feeling; the rest had retired bleeding but numbed into some secret cave of its own.

They set off early to beat the traffic, and instead of blossom there were dead leaves on the pavement and a thin white mould of frost. Emily's mood was sombre. They listened to tapes throughout the journey and hardly spoke until they reached the cottage.

'But it's lovely,' said Emily, with surprise, as if it was the last thing she had expected. 'How could they bear to leave it?'

It did look good from the outside, even at this time of the year, an eighteenth-century fenland cottage, half-timbered and thatch-roofed, originally built as a home for the man who worked the sluice gates. But Preston wasn't sure about it. On his previous visit he'd been full of gushing enthusiasm, trying to banish, or at least mask, the strange sense of unease it evoked.

It was partly the proximity to the fens, for though they'd long since been drained and farmed, all the fields were bound by ditches and dykes and he felt as if the land was oozing bog water, or sinking imperceptibly into some primeval slime. And though the cottage was pretty to look at, it was rather poky inside with small, dark rooms and low ceilings.

But the worst of it was the paintings.

They were prints from some medieval Book of Hours that William had had framed and stuck up on the walls. There was one of Adam and Eve being tempted by the Serpent, another of them being kicked out of the Garden of Eden, and three others depicting Heaven, Hell and Purgatory.

And there was one other that Preston liked least of all. It was in the kitchen and it consisted of three panels side by side. The first panel showed people in a tavern, indulging in various forms of merriment, otherwise known as self-abuse, such as eating, drinking, carousing, kissing, cuddling, squeezing the barmaid's tits and fucking under tables. In the second panel the same people, considerably sobered and looking as if they had a serious hangover, were being led away by the classic medieval figure of Death, a grisly skeleton in a black robe and cowl, who rather reminded Preston of an old schoolmaster he had known called Mr Pilkington. In the third panel they were in Hell, stark naked and having various sharp instruments poked up them by a load of chortling demons.

It wasn't the kind of thing that grew on you.

He couldn't believe, now, that he had brought Emily here. Was it just to save money, or had he imagined the atmosphere would perhaps induce a miscarriage? Either way, it seemed to be the latest in a long line of crass decisions.

But Emily seemed quite cheerful about it all, now she'd arrived. She went from room to room, praising the decor, and if she noticed the paintings they didn't appear to do her any obvious mischief. There was a pile of logs and some firelighters and paper in a large basket in the hearth, and Preston started to pile them in the grate while she continued her explorations in the garden. He had quite a cheerful blaze going by the time she came back, with an armful of twigs and berries which she arranged artistically in a vase on the table. Then she came over to where he was kneeling by the fire and put her arms round him from behind and pressed her cheek against his.

'Thank you for bringing me here,' she said. 'It's nice.'

For a moment, Preston thought it was going to be all right.

They made up the double bed in William and Kate's room, which was the best room in the house, overlooking the back garden and mercifully free from images of death, destruction and eternal torment, which presumably meant that William had been kept out of it, at least so far as the decor was concerned. The walls and ceiling were papered with a print of forget-me-nots and there were original water-colours of the fens on the walls and a large portrait of Christ. Not the Sacred Heart sort Mother Bernie and his Auntie Ethel tended to go for, but a post-Renaissance Rembrandt Christ, serene but human. He bore a calm, gentle, sort of all-knowing but all-forgiving look. Like a sixties' hippie, Preston thought irreverently, halfway to getting stoned. It wasn't the sort of thing he would have put on the wall next to his bed but it was a lot more acceptable than Mr Pilkington in a black cowl.

They went to the village pub for lunch. It was called the Eel and Boot and it had a large sign outside with a welly covered in slime and an even slimier serpentine creature peering irritably out of the top of it like Ridley Scott's alien in one of its earlier manifestations.

But it was an improvement on William's taste in art and they served a good pint of bitter, and Preston might almost have settled back to enjoy it if he'd been able to forget their reason for being there and if Emily hadn't kept on at him about William and the Black Death.

She'd seen one of his books in the cottage and Preston had told her that William was a leading authority on the subject. He thought now it might have been a mistake.

'But why did he choose *that*?' she wanted to know.

'I don't know,' he shrugged. 'Maybe he just kind of drifted into it.'

'You don't drift into things like that,' she said. 'He must have had a reason.'

'Well, he's always been a bit into death and destruction,' Preston conceded. 'He's a Catholic.'

'So are you,' Emily pointed out.

'Not any more,' said Preston, shuddering. He didn't like the way the conversation was going.

'Even so . . .' She looked thoughtful. 'What else have you got in common?'

'Nothing,' said Preston, firmly. The thought of having anything in common with William horrified him.

'Then what made you friends with him?'

Preston shrugged again.

'My Auntie Ethel said I had to mind him,' he said.

'Mind him?'

'Look after him. You know. Be his Minder.'

'Why? Was he much younger than you?'

'No, but he was kind of . . . strange. Vulnerable. His mum married an American. An airman from this base near us.'

As if this explained everything.

'My dad's a Master Sergeant,' William used to tell them, with a swagger in his voice, which was not wise in that neighbourhood.

Hank the Yank, they called him, or Quirk the Jerk.

'My mam says he's prob'ly in prison or run off with a bit of stuff,' said one of the hostiles in the playground one milk-break. 'That's why he ain't around.'

And William in there with fists flailing and Preston inevitably drawn in, too, as the fight spread until they were hauled off to the headmaster's study for retribution; he was a caning head and it was two strokes on each hand for a fight in the playground, four for the classroom.

It was no picnic being William's Minder.

'He's gone to look for a house for us,' William would tell Preston on their way home from school. 'He doesn't want us to come until he's found somewhere nice.'

And Preston, embarrassed, saying nothing.

The mystery of the missing Master Sergeant kept them all embarrassed for the best part of a year. The story was he'd left the USAF and gone to America to find a job. William and his mother were supposed to be going to join him later.

In the meantime he sent back parcels full of toys to keep William's spirits up; wonderful toys like an electric train with

81

a cowcatcher and a working headlight on the front and models of Liberators and Mitchell bombers and a replica of a Colt Peacemaker in a real leather holster.

They did nothing to improve William's popularity in the neighbourhood.

And then the toys suddenly stopped. And Preston knew that William knew what the rest of them had known, or suspected, for some months: that he and his mother were never going to America and that the Master Sergeant was never coming back.

'He's found another W-O-M-A-N,' Preston heard his Auntie Ethel tell his nanna. 'Apparently she's having his C-H-I-L-D.'

Preston's Auntie Ethel didn't seem to think Preston could spell until he went to university.

'Elaine sent him a letter telling him to stop sending the T-O-Y-S and things. She says it only unsettles him.'

Preston's Auntie Ethel and William's mother, Elaine, had been best friends at school, which was why Preston had been detailed as William's Minder – another one of Auntie Ethel's great ideas, like the newspaper that could defend you against muggers.

'They were a grand lot for rallying around in a crisis, my family,' Preston told Emily. 'It kind of brought out the best in them. Mind you, they'd had a lot of practice.'

The male Moodies had a long history of accidental death.

Preston's maternal grandad, his Great-Uncle Eddie and a cousin called Pete had all died from having things dropped on them from cranes down the docks. Preston's father had decided to vary the tradition by volunteering, whilst in the Royal Navy, to be bombed by a low-flying aircraft with bags containing radioactive dust.

The idea, as subsequently explained to Preston, who was naturally curious, was to test its effect on steel deck planks. No one, in those early days of nuclear weaponry, seemed to have anticipated the adverse effect it would have on the men sheltering below. There was still no public admission of a connection with the leukaemia from which most of them, including Preston's father, had died.

'The one thing I do have in common with William,' conceded Preston, 'is that we both grew up knowing the heavens might open at any moment and drop a load of shit on our heads.'

And if there was any risk of their forgetting it, there was William's grandad to remind them, who had a lifetime's experience of dodging flying effluent, not always with complete success.

William's grandad had been a surrogate father to both of them and some small counterweight to the preponderance of nans and aunts and mothers.

'I think that's why William and I stayed friends,' Preston told Emily. 'Because I loved his grandad.'

They spent the rest of the afternoon shopping in Ely for food and wine – and a pair of thigh-length boots which Emily said she wanted to wear 'about the house'. Without anything else.

But there didn't seem to be much of a demand for thigh-length boots in Ely. They certainly couldn't find any in one of the four shoe shops.

'Perhaps you could try waders,' suggested Preston.

But in the end she settled for a pair of thick black stockings that she said would have to do.

She then announced that she wanted some cream cakes.

This seemed a little out of character.

'I want you to eat them off me,' she said. 'On the rug in front of the fire.'

Preston looked over his shoulder to see if anyone had heard. But no, Ely High Street went about its normal Saturday afternoon business without any visible sign of outrage. The towers of the cathedral did not crumble and fall, the choir in the precinct outside did not falter in their fund-raising performance for the Conservation of Rural England.

Emily led him to a cake shop and he viewed the selection in the window like a naughty schoolboy surveying a stack of girlie magazines in a newsagent's.

'Does it have to be real cream?' he asked her.

'That's up to you,' she said. 'You'll be eating them.'

But in the end she had to choose for him. He said he was too embarrassed. He said he was sure the shop assistants would know what he wanted them for from the way he asked.

She chose a chocolate éclair and a dairy cream sponge with strawberries and kiwi fruit.

'The messier the better,' she said, as they were leaving the shop.

Preston drove back to the cottage in a state of high nervous excitement but with some serious reservations. This seemed to be developing into a regular pattern in his dealings with Emily. Perhaps it would be good for him. He wasn't sure about the rug, though.

It began well. They ate, they drank, they took their clothes off, Emily put on her stockings and Preston piled more logs on the fire. And then Emily fetched the cream cakes in from the fridge.

They were quite a success, too, at first.

Preston was in such a state of arousal that he stopped worrying about the rug. He managed to eat most of the cream, anyway, and Emily seemed to absorb the rest. Also, he found that by glancing occasionally at William's medieval illustrations he was able to prolong the actual phallic performance to well over half an hour, a personal best, even deducting the time taken to eat the cakes.

But afterwards he felt depressed, and a bit ill, and there was a nagging pain in his chest which could either be indigestion or the start of a heart attack.

He recovered sufficiently to make love once more before they went to bed, but it wasn't as frantic or as demanding and he fell asleep afterwards on the sofa.

He couldn't remember the transition from sofa to bed, but he must have made it because he woke up there in total darkness with a headache and a blocked nose and a sense that something was not quite right.

There was a noise in the room, like the breathing of some large animal.

He felt for Emily, but she wasn't there.

'Emily?' He sat up in bed.

The noise grew louder.

He felt for the light switch.

Emily was curled up in a foetal position, naked, on the floor, sobbing.

Preston stumbled out of bed and tried to give her a hug, but she fought him off as if it was an attack. It seemed to be another fit like the last one, only worse.

'It's the drink,' he said, desperately. 'It's just the drink, we shouldn't drink so much.'

It was very cold on the floor with no clothes on. Emily must have been there some time. Her body felt cold as death.

He pulled the duvet off the bed and tried to wrap it round her, but she reacted violently, as if he was trying to suffocate her.

After a long period of soothing and occasional stroking he managed to get his arms round her. She was shuddering uncontrollably, either from cold or terror, or both.

He tried to warm her with his body but he was so cold himself he didn't know if it would work. He kept trying to make calming noises but his teeth wouldn't stop chattering.

Finally he was able to coax her, half carry her, back on to the bed. He began to chafe her with his hands to get some warmth into her, and suddenly, and to his complete astonishment, they were making love.

Or at least Emily was.

At first he thought she was attacking him. And it *was* a form of attack, a 'frenzy of passion'.

He'd always thought of that as a cliché before he met Emily.

The body that had been racked with sobbing was now pressing into him and moving in an altogether different rhythm. She was covering him with kisses, her nails digging into his back.

But Preston's mind couldn't cope with it, and nor could his body.

'Emily,' he said. 'Please . . .'

He tried to hug her again, comfortingly, but she wouldn't have it. She started to moan and pull at his limp penis. Her face was wet with tears, her eyes open but without expression.

He didn't know what to do.

He kept stroking her.

Then, over her shoulder, he caught sight of the reflection in the glass of one of the picture frames. The picture itself was so dark he could only see the image of Emily in the glass, naked and moving wildly, her buttocks pumping urgently against him.

Preston felt an immediate response from that part of his body

85

which was most necessary to the occasion. His brain still felt numbed.

They both came together very quickly, and Emily fell asleep almost immediately, her breathing regular, her body still.

But Preston stayed awake, staring at the picture on the wall.

The Rembrandt face of Christ.

Had he been truly ignorant at the time of what it was? Had he known, but refused to acknowledge it? And did it make any difference, theologically speaking, whether he knew or not?

These were the kind of questions they never gave you in catechism.

'Preston?' said Emily, in the morning, standing by the bed with a glass of orange juice.

He took it gratefully and drank. He caught Christ's eye on him and flinched.

What could you say?

But it can't have happened. It was all a dream, or he wasn't properly awake. Or the picture had been transformed, temporarily, into a mirror.

Or it was just some seventeenth-century Dutch hippie paid to sit still for a few weeks in a dark robe in a cold studio.

What would Mother Bernard have said? My God, did the lift go down low enough? I did it for the girl, he protested. But Adam had taken that line and it hadn't done him much good.

Emily sat on the bed beside him, smiling, and running the back of her hand along his cheek.

'Sorry about last night.'

He nodded, and took her hand and kissed it.

'At least we had a nice love,' she said.

Then the phone rang.

Emily jumped and spilled her juice.

'It's all right,' said Preston, but he'd been shaken, too. 'He said it was still connected.'

They were like a pair of burglars, he thought, making free of someone's house while the owners were away on holiday.

It was William.

'How are things?' he said.

'Fine,' said Preston, wondering.

It was just after eight.

'No problems?'

'No.' Preston glanced guiltily towards the rug by the fire but he couldn't see any stains, not from here at least.

'Anything you want me to do?' he enquired.

'No, no, I don't think so.' A silence.

Preston knew then that something was wrong. Perhaps he'd known before, as soon as the phone rang.

'I've just had some bad news,' William said. 'I thought you'd want to know. About Grandad. He had a heart attack . . .'

And Preston's heart, too, seized and violently squeezed, and then released so the blood pumped wildly.

'They got him to hospital, but then he had a second attack. He died in the early hours of this morning. I'm going up there now. I knew you'd want to know.'

The fire was cold, the ashes piled up in the grate. They'd left the plates lying around and the wine bottles on the floor, and there was still a bit of wine left in one of them. They'd have a fair bit of tidying up to do before they left.

Preston opened the back door and stared out into the garden. He couldn't see the hedge at the far end. There was an early morning mist rising from the fens.

Come in, lads, come in and shut the door on the fog.

He remembered who had said it, now.

'Preston?'

He turned and saw Emily watching him from the bottom of the stairs with his leather coat wrapped around her. She looked very sexy.

'Who was it?'

'It was William,' he said. 'He wanted to tell me that someone's died.'

13

The Marmot and the Black Rat

William sat by the phone for a long while after he had called Preston, wondering if he'd done the right thing.

He couldn't help wondering if he'd interrupted him in the act of copulation.

Copulation. Now why did he call it that, rather than making love?

And why did it matter if he had?

But William knew why it mattered.

They had both, from an early age, made the sinister connection between sex and death, and he didn't want Preston to make it now. He didn't want him to feel guilty.

Sex and death, where d'you get that from? He could hear his grandad's scornful retort. *The poor mad nuns down the convent, I suppose.*

William had loved his grandad, but he'd never really listened to him. Never really accepted his reasoned view of life and history. It was too simple, too enlightened. William was invariably drawn to the darkness, finding a deeper, more complex truth in the world of myth and superstition; to the 'poor mad nuns down the convent'; to the world of Mother Bernard and her visions of Hell and Damnation; to the demons and the shadows . . .

When he was a child of about ten or eleven, William used to play a kind of game with his shadow, except that it wasn't a game, really, it was deadly serious.

At night, when he was getting ready for bed, he would switch on his bedside lamp and stand with his back to it so he could see his shadow against the far wall. Then he would make a pair of horns with his hands and step slowly backwards, and the closer he got to the bedside lamp the bigger the shadow grew, so that finally it outgrew the wall and spread across the ceiling and towered above him, a vast and terrible Demon.

And then, when he couldn't step back any further, he would walk forward, watching the shadow shrink before him until it ended up as a small and pathetic figure beneath his feet.

He was never quite sure why he played this game. It was partly because he got a weird buzz out of scaring himself half to death, and partly because he felt it was a kind of exorcism, to convince him he had control over his fears – and the horrors that were waiting for him round the corner of sleep.

William suffered greatly from nightmares as a child. Many of them were predictably connected with the murder at the Turk's Head and what he had seen, or thought he had seen, one night on the railway embankment that ran behind it. But the two he remembered in the clearest detail, well into adulthood, were a crazy, terrifying patchwork of the history he learned at school, or at his grandad's knee, who was a great, if not unbiased, teacher, and of his own personal history.

One, frequently occurring, featured his father. He and William were working in a field covered with snow. William was never very clear what they were doing exactly; picking sticks, perhaps: two peasants in a Brueghel winter landscape gathering fuel for the fire. William was nervous because he'd been here before and he knew what was going to happen next, but his father kept smiling at him cheerfully, a strong, reassuring presence by his side. William could see the village where they lived and the smoke from the fires rising straight up into the air and the dark tower of the church rising above a cluster of stark trees, and because he was nervous he wanted to work his way in that direction, so it would not be so far to run, but because his father was beside him, smiling his reassuring smile, he didn't. He just kept on working in the field. Until, as he had always known they would, the horsemen appeared, giant figures in steel armour, much larger than life, with great crested helmets dark against the sky. And suddenly his father wasn't there any more. He just disappeared, as if he'd never been there at all. And the horsemen came riding down with their horned helmets and their lances and William was running, screaming, towards the village, but it was always too far away.

The other nightmare he remembered in detail was the one about the Black Death.

It started with William standing alone in the middle of a street in a typical medieval city. There were houses all around but all the doors were closed and the windows shuttered and there were great heaps of what looked like garbage in the dark, shadowed alleys between them. William could see darker shadows moving on the garbage heaps and he knew these were rats and that the garbage was composed of rotting corpses and the rats were eating them, gorging on the swollen, putrefying bodies of the plague victims. And as he watched, not really wanting to see but unable to tear his eyes away, he heard the death cart coming, trundling through the empty streets with the hooded ghouls of the burial squad walking along beside it tolling their bells.

And William began to run from the approaching cart, which was piled high with the bodies of the plague victims, and as he ran the streets became the familiar streets of his childhood and he knew that all the time he was running from the terrible cart he was getting closer and closer to the dark house by the railway embankment with its shuttered windows and its locked door, and that this was more terrible to him than anything in his history books.

When he was a bit older and more rational, William wondered if his interest in the darkest periods of human history was an attempt to exorcise these terrors of his childhood; to look at the worst of them, coldly and analytically, and not be afraid. But his friends just thought he was a crazy obsessive with an unhealthy fascination for the macabre.

Either way it was the inspiration for the academic success that took him faster and further from the streets of his childhood than even his mother's success in business had.

And made him one of the leading authorities on the fourteenth century, which was arguably the most terrible century that had ever been, at least until the present one.

His grandad was proud of him. 'The Professor,' he called him, or, more often, 'Young Bamber Gascoigne there . . .'

But it didn't impress his mother.

He knew that as far as his mother was concerned it was like painting fairground panels, it was like keeping whippets.

It wasn't Real.

'What you going to do with a degree in history?' his mother asked him when he graduated with a first.

'How about taking me on as a lift attendant?' William suggested, because she'd just bought Mary Ann Evans's and was always talking about the trouble she was having finding good staff.

But his mother didn't think that was funny. She was thinking of getting rid of the lift attendants anyway.

'I'm going to do a PhD,' he told her, 'on the Social and Economic Consequences of the Great Plague of 1347 to 1350 on Rural Parishes in the South of England.'

'My God,' said his mother, 'and on the taxpayers' money.'

It should have been on *her* money but William was on a full grant at university. His mum had a good accountant and technically she was running at a loss.

'Why don't you do the social and economic consequences of the Great Plague of the Twentieth Century?' his mum wanted to know.

She meant the trade unions.

But William wasn't interested in the trade unions. He was interested in the story of the Manchurian marmot.

'Once upon a time,' he would begin his lectures, 'in the remote marches and forests of Central Asia, near a lake called Issyk-Koul in the province of Semiriechinsk, there lived a small, pretty squirrel-like creature called the Marmot . . .'

His students thought he'd finally flipped and started telling fairy stories, but this was no fairy story, this was a real Gothic Horror.

For thousands of years the marmots had lived on the banks of the lake in Central Asia where they played host to a flea called *xenopsylla cheopsis* and a tiny bacillus, or disease, called *pasteurella pestis*, with no dramatic consequences to any of them, and not the slightest impact on the rest of the world.

And then something happened to disturb the marmots.

William didn't know what it was – flood or earthquake, drought or famine, or a combination of all four – but they moved, and they took the fleas and the bacilli with them, and somewhere in their travels they encountered the black rat *rattus rattus*, and the drama began to move along a bit, because *rattus rattus* was a vagabond and a great little mover. *Rattus rattus* moved all over Europe and Asia, hitching rides on camel trains and on waggons and particularly on ships, and the fleas deserted the marmots and attached themselves to the rats, and the bacilli went with them.

William didn't know why the fleas left the marmots for the rats. Maybe they liked the taste better. Maybe after a few thousand years of marmot for breakfast, dinner and tea they fancied a change. Maybe they had a sense of adventure. Maybe they knew this was their big moment, their chance to make history.

Or maybe they had no choice. Maybe, as William strongly suspected, this first communion between the rat and the marmot had not been without violence and *rattus rattus*, being the little fucker he was, had savagely copulated with the small, pretty, squirrel-like creature – and then torn her throat out. Or not necessarily in that order.

Sex and death, the guilty violent coupling; an ongoing historical theme. He must write a paper on it some day.

But if this were the case, then the fleas had taken a terrible revenge for the loss of their erstwhile companion through history, their life-support system. Because unlike the marmots, the rats had no resistance to the disease that the fleas carried. And when they died and the fleas had finished feasting on their blood, which was by then putrid and crawling with the bacilli, the fleas looked round for another host, and if they could not find another rat, or any small hairy creature to their liking, they settled for the next best thing, which was usually human.

What really fascinated him was the idea that it was such a small thing, in such an obscure corner of the world, and between two such insignificant creatures. The world did not stop in its tracks when it happened, it did not pause for breath, it did not miss a heartbeat. People continued to go about their daily lives, make their plans, take decisions, eat, drink, love, pray for a good harvest, pray for rain, in complete ignorance of the dramatic effect this far-off encounter would have on their lives.

'History is the story of humankind's attempt to impose order on chaos,' William told his students. 'Feudalism was the process by which individuals bartered their personal liberties in return for protection. They traded freedom for security; or, rather, the illusion of security. For chaos was the natural state and there could be no protection against the chance encounter of the Manchurian marmot and the black rat.'

And nor is there now, he might have added, because William was obsessed with the idea that it might happen again; that it might be happening now, the next chance encounter between the marmot and the rat – or whatever their modern equivalent. The first link in the chain of events that would unleash chaos on the world.

14

The Devil in the Corner

'Seamed stockings,' said Preston's Auntie Ethel. 'Those were his last words on this earth. Seamed stockings, he said, and then he died.'

Preston winced. He'd always had a thing about Famous Last Words. Before his own grandad had died he was alleged to have remarked, 'By, that wind's a killer,' seconds before it blew the crane that dropped the crate that smashed his head in.

Whenever Preston said anything that sounded remotely like Famous Last Words, he always said something else quickly, something so trite and meaningless that it could never tempt Fate. But could you ever be sure of making it trite and meaningless enough?

'Seamed stockings' seemed to be a pretty safe bet on the face of things. But perhaps he'd been over-excited.

'He always thought they were sexy,' Preston mused. 'He said it was because the seams looked as if they were going some-where . . .'

'It had nothing to do with That,' said Auntie Ethel, sharply. 'Trust you. It was because she'd just started to sell them at the shop. It was too much for him after all that business at the stocking factory.'

Preston knew who 'she' was, and it wasn't the cat's mother. It was William's. Auntie Ethel's old schoolfriend, Elaine, not so popular now that she was Rich and Successful.

'But they closed the factory twenty years ago,' said Preston. 'It couldn't still be bothering him.'

'These things do,' said his mum, 'especially as you get older.'

'And it was the last real job he ever had,' said Auntie Ethel. 'I don't count that stuff with the fairs.'

They drove to see him at the Chapel of Repose. He was wearing a navy blue suit Preston had never seen him in before, and his long wispy white hair had been combed back and slicked down with something to make it neat. Preston would have preferred him in his cloth cap with the old woolly cardigan he used to wear, or the long grey mac. He didn't look anything like he remembered him.

'Come in, lads, come in and shut the door on the fog.'
On a chair in the scullery in his cardigan and his cap and his bad leg stuck out to one side, and his tins of paint on newspapers all around, and a big panel of wood propped up against the wall with a picture on it of a battleship in a stormy sea.

And the two of them shuffling in with the hoods of their duffel coats over their heads and their school scarves pulled over noses and mouths like a pair of monks doing the rounds during the Black Death.

They always knew things were bad when they came back from school together to William's house and found William's grandad painting battleships. It meant he'd been laid off again at the stocking factory.

Whenever this happened he'd get his paints and brushes out and start on another panel for Uncle Titch, who had the contacts with the fairground people. It kept him occupied and brought a bit of money in, but not much, because fairs were going through a lean patch, too. William's grandad blamed it all on the Television, like most things, the cathode god, the new opium of the masses.

William's grandad, Samuel Morris Epstein, was a communist and an atheist and a Jew. He saw no contradictions in this. To be a Jew was to be a member of a tribe, even if you'd stopped dancing round the totem pole. He was an outcast among outcasts and proud of it; it didn't mean he had to believe in all the mumbo-jumbo. Communism had been his religion, the romantic, revolutionary communism of 1917 and Petrograd and the streets full of soldiers and sailors and workers and red flags and armoured cars that looked as if they were made of galvanised steel buckets, and the cruiser *Aurora* out on the river with its searchlight blazing – now there was a fairground panel he could have painted if only he could have got away with it – but it wasn't the same any more. It had grown stale and ugly and he'd left the Party the first time they sent the tanks in, but he didn't stop believing in the dream, the illusion, the *myth*, any more than he stopped believing in the Devil just because he didn't think there was a God.

He painted, as required, the scenes of Britain's imperial past: red-coated soldiers and turbaned Sikh lancers, and white hunters and gorillas, and aborigines and kangaroos, and Baden-Powell and battleships. But being a rebel at heart he always modelled the battleships on the *Potemkin*, and in the corner of every panel he painted a little red devil with a pitchfork and a knowing grin.

'It's my trademark,' he told the boys. 'I like to remind people he's always there.'

It was Grandad's basic contention in life that whenever you were cycling downhill with the wind behind you and the sun on your back and never a care in the world, some little bugger nipped out of a bush and stuck a spike in your spokes.

Though a committed atheist and dedicated opponent of the Catholic Church, William's grandad maintained a healthy respect all his life for the power of Satan.

'Where's the funeral?' Preston asked on the drive over to William's house. They lived in Woolton now, since his mother's move into the merchant classes.

'At St Oswald's,' said his mum, who was sitting next to him, prim and nervous in her best hat and coat which was only proper for a visit to Woolton.

'Really? But I thought they only allowed you to bury Catholics there.'

A small but significant silence. He heard Auntie Ethel sniff in the back seat. He looked at her in the driving mirror.

'Well?'

'They had him baptised before he died.'

'What?'

'Keep your eyes on the road,' said his Auntie Ethel. 'You nearly went into the back of that bus.'

96

'Well, it can't do any harm, Preston,' said his mum. 'And it might have done him a bit of good.'

'They had him baptised while he was *dying*?'

'Not *while*, Preston,' said his aunt, in the tone of voice she used when she wasn't going to take any nonsense. But there might have been a hint of defensiveness there, too.

'Well I presume they didn't wait until he was dead?'

'No, but you make it sound as if it's a bit tasteless.'

'A bit tasteless? My God, it's gross. How would you fancy having a heart attack with a priest and a couple of altar boys hopping round throwing cold water all over your head? Jesus Christ . . .'

'It wasn't like that – and don't take the name of the Lord in vain.'

'Well, what *was* it like?'

'Well, they don't use altar boys for a start, and they did it between attacks.'

'Oh, wonderful. I bet that helped his survival chances no end.'

The poor old man. He'd always predicted it. Lying there helpless as a babby, paralysed and drugged and dumb while they fetched the priest to him. *Don't let them do it, boys*, he'd said to them. *If you're anywhere near, keep them away from me.*

But they hadn't been near enough.

'Anyway, I thought it was the Last Rites they gave you when you were dying, what d'you call it, Extreme Unction?' That was the Catholic name for it and it had always seemed very appropriate to Preston, conjuring up visions of an unctuous priest dripping oil and glib assurance. 'Or did they get two for the price of one?'

More silence, brittle with self-righteousness. Auntie Ethel sniffed again. As they reached the outer suburbs it began to drizzle slightly and Preston switched the wipers on. Big new detached houses on either side of the road with gardens and garages and Georgian colonnades made of plastic. The odd bit of woodland, neatly railed and labelled and no wolves allowed, and Dogs Must Be Kept on a Lead and Not Be Permitted to Foul the Footpath Penalty £50 and Quite Right Too.

'Whose idea was this, anyway, his wife's or his daughter's?'

But he thought he knew the answer to that one already. William's mum had never been too bothered about the Church; she had other gods to propitiate.

'He did promise her, you know,' said his own mum, 'before they ever got married. He said he'd convert and he never did.'

'Only because he wanted to get his leg over.'

His mum giggled.

'Preston!' Shock waves from the rear seat. 'That's no way to speak of the Dead. And don't you be laughing at him, our Nell. It only encourages him.'

'That's what he told me,' said Preston.

I'd promise anything for a leg over in those days, he used to say, *but I've got more about me now.*

'And it's not as if he had any convictions of his own,' said his Auntie Ethel.

'What do you mean he didn't have any convictions? He was a communist.'

Not strictly true, he was a *lapsed* communist, but Preston meant it to be provoking and it was.

'Rubbish,' snapped Auntie Ethel. 'I hope you're not going to make a nuisance of yourself, Preston, because if you are it would have been better if you hadn't come.'

'Thanks for coming,' said William, formally, and he squeezed Preston's arm.

He was wearing a suit, too, a grey one. Preston felt depressed. It seemed as if everyone was going to conform to this funeral except him.

'I wanted to pay my respects,' he said, equally formal.

But he didn't want to go to the bloody thing, not after what they'd done to the poor old man. He would hang about outside and then go up to the grave afterwards and pay his own quiet tribute.

Did William know about the forced baptism? Had they dared to tell him? Would he care?

'Did they tell you about his Last Words?' Preston asked him instead.

'No.' William looked puzzled. 'Mum said he got up in the middle of the night to go to the toilet. Then she heard this crash. She didn't say anything about any Last Words.'

Preston told him what his aunt had said.

William stared at him.

'My God,' he said, 'after all those years.'

'He always said Fashion would be the death of him,' said Preston.

'Fashion,' he'd rant, when they sent him home on short time from the stocking factory. 'It's all part of the Great Capitalist Conspiracy. They're just trying to cut labour costs.'

That was when they first changed over from seamed stockings to seamless ones and started laying off the skilled knitters and bringing in the women.

'Fashion, my arse,' he'd rave. 'You don't need a skilled knitter to spin seamless stockings, that's what this is all about. A trained monkey could operate them new machines – or a woman.'

They learned a lot of things at the twisted knee of William's grandad, and one of them was misogyny.

'Grandad was never very good at spotting trends,' said William. 'He had a knack of jumping on roundabouts just when they were coming to a dead stop.'

This was true. Ever since the horses.

'My grandad was a bronco buster when he was younger,' William used to tell them at school, and they'd scoffed, even Preston, who was meant to be his Minder. It was just Quirk the Jerk spinning another yarn.

But he wasn't. Not that time. Though they weren't the rangy mustangs they took him to mean.

'Great strapping brutes they were, with backs on them like the deck of a ship,' William's grandad said, who'd been thrown off both and knew. 'One kick of them hooves and you'd be in the middle of next week.'

He'd been brought up on a farm and had a way with horses, and his first job when he left school was working for a brewery breaking in the big black cobs they brought over wild from Ireland and put to use as cart-horses dragging the great heavy drays full of ale.

But they got rid of the lot for a couple of Ford motor trucks, and William's grandad with them.

'The first job I was robbed of by Progress,' he told the boys, but added darkly, 'and the Yanks.'

It was the beginning of a remarkable career.

'The jobs I've been in and out of would tell the history of the twentieth century,' he'd say.

Preston didn't know the half of them, only the big ones. Even wars had a way of making William's grandad redundant. He'd joined the International Brigade just before Franco's final victories and been sent back when he was on his way to Cardiff to catch the potato boat to Bilbao.

'I knew right away we'd have to start preparing for the next one,' he told the boys, who were the only ones who'd listen to him by then, in the home at any rate.

So he dug a bomb shelter in the back yard, which was fine for his wife and little daughter, William's mum-to-be, but not so convenient for him when he joined the Merchant Navy and found himself out on Atlantic convoys with the wolf packs at his heels.

They didn't make him redundant this time, they just sank the ships he was on. The third time he was eight days in an open boat before they picked him up, near dying of exposure, and his nerve gone. They sent him to a nursing home to recover, deep in the English countryside, well away from the war.

'In the middle of bleeding Lincolnshire,' he said. 'If there was anywhere safe in England in 1943 you'd have thought *that* was.'

But he was badly informed again and hadn't calculated for the Americans. They were flying the Liberators in for the big daylight raids on the Ruhr and one of them flew straight into the field where Grandad was working, planting carrots for the war effort.

'They said it was engine failure,' he said. 'But I reckon they just mistook it for a runway. Bloody Yanks.'

William's grandad was deeply prejudiced against Americans, even before the Master Sergeant.

'Where were they when we were running down U-boat alley?' he used to demand, and the boys would shake their heads dutifully, and William with some embarrassment on account of being half American himself. U-boat alley was the gap in mid-Atlantic where they didn't have air cover from Britain or Canada, but Preston always imagined it a bit like the alley at the back of their houses

100

with a U-boat at each end firing torpedoes at Grandad as he hopped and scuttled down it on his way to the Turk's Head.

But he wasn't hopping when the Liberator exploded. He was sprinting for dear life across a carrot patch and doing quite well until one of the pieces caught up with him. They identified it afterwards as the seat off the chemical lavatory.

'And that was me, crippled for life,' he used to say, 'knee-capped by a Yankee flying bog.'

'There's nothing glamorous about war,' he'd tell the boys years later when he found them watching yet another Great American War Movie on the TV. 'It's all shit and blood, so don't go believing any of the rubbish on That Thing. And don't tell your nan I said shit.'

When he came out of hospital they fixed him up with a job in a parachute factory, but he'd just finished the training period when the war ended, and they didn't think they'd need so many parachutes for the next one.

But when he got the job in the stocking factory he seriously thought it was for life. They'd always be wanting nylons, he thought, he'd seen what they'd do for them during the war. Nylons were part of the US strategy for world domination. Nylons for the women, Coke for the kids and guns for the men to go on fighting 'Germins' or 'Reds' or whoever happened to be next in the firing line, that was William's grandad's uncluttered view of world history.

'They didn't reckon on us making our own nylons,' he gloated. 'It's the Boston Tea Party in reverse.'

Like Marx, William's grandad went in for the broad dialectic of history and wasn't too fussy about the fine print.

He should have read the writing on the machine they gave him to spin the golden thread. Made in Reading, Pa., it said.

But William's grandad was too busy working to notice or care, riding shotgun to a great clattering brute of a knitting machine that reminded him of the Irish cobs he'd broken in for the brewery; he could knit thirty fully fashioned stockings an hour, sixteen hours a day.

'Twenty-two yards long it was,' he'd tell the boys proudly, during their consolation walks before the elastoplast came off. 'The length

101

of a cricket pitch, and you had to move as fast as Denis Compton, believe you me, to get from one end to the other and pull them levers.'

Why the machine had levers at each end was a mystery never satisfactorily explained to the boys, but it created another alley in Grandad's life, the alley between one machine and another, and though there were no U-boats shooting at him, it was hard going with his bad leg.

But William's grandad had a system working for him. He had an alley mate, the man on the next machine, who pulled the levers for both of them at one end while William's grandad pulled for them both at the other. The only problem was, they were supposed to be on piece work, and it meant working at the same pace. The foremen didn't like that; it smacked of syndicalism.

'They didn't want us to work together,' William's grandad said. 'They wanted us to work *against* each other. Divide and rule, that was the policy.'

So they kept changing the man on the next machine, and until he could talk him into using the System, William's grandad would have to lurch down machine alley every few minutes, heaving his stiff leg behind him like Long John Silver and cursing like his parrot.

But it was good money most of the time and he loved his machine. He fed it lots of oil and wiped at it all the time with an oily rag so it shone. Black Beauty, he called it, on the good days. And on the bad days, when he didn't have an alley mate, Black Devil.

But like the dray horses its days were numbered, and so were Grandad's.

'They must have known when they sent them over,' he raged when he first went on short time. 'Dumping their old rubbish on us.'

The Pa. stood for Pennsylvania, and the machines had been sent over as part of the Marshall Plan to get Europe back on its feet and wearing nylons just like the Americans. But within a few years the Americans were using new machines, a fraction of the size, that an unskilled woman could operate for a fraction of the pay, and upon which she could spin as many stockings an hour as the Black Beauty – and without seams.

'What's the matter with seams?' William's grandad would roar. 'Men *like* seams. Seams *go* somewhere.'

'That's enough of that, thank you,' William's nan would say. 'In front of the boys.'

She was careful what was said in front of boys, especially William. She knew he had the Master Sergeant's genes and she was worried he'd grow up to be an adulterer, just like his dad. But it was Preston who'd become the adulterer, not William.

'Where's Kate?' said Preston. 'Did she come up with you?'

But William shook his head.

'Something happened at work,' he said. 'She couldn't get away.'

But he seemed a bit tight-lipped about it.

'Will you help carry the coffin?' he asked Preston before he left. 'He was as much your grandad as mine, really.'

'Yes,' said Preston. 'I'd like to.'

But if he was going to carry the coffin he had to go to the funeral service, so the Church had him by the balls again, as it had, more or less, since he was born.

'Did your grandfather have any favourite hymns?' the priest asked William before the service.

'I don't think so.' William looked helplessly at Preston.

'He was very fond of "Here We Go, Here We Go, Here We Go",' said Preston.

It was the battle hymn of the striking coalminers in 1984, and the old man used to sing it while he watched them fighting the police on the television, but it turned out to be another lost cause.

'Takes you back, doesn't it?' said William as they went into the church. Preston wondered if he really didn't know about the deathbed pantomime. Or was he just pretending to be ignorant? That was the trouble with William. You never really knew what he knew.

'Have Mercy, oh Lord, on the soul of thy dearly departed servant Samuel,' they all incanted dutifully in the crowded church. Except for Preston, who had his own one-way dialogue with the Almighty.

'I don't seriously believe it had anything to do with That Business over the picture,' he informed his silent Saviour on the cross above the altar. 'I honestly don't think your mind works like that and I don't suppose you thought it was a very good likeness anyway, but was it the Adultery?'

He didn't think it was a case of God's being vindictive, more a case of rules being rules and God having to administer them, like a caning head, and where there was Adultery there was always a Death, that was the way it was. Or else he, Preston, had inadvertently torn a hole in the fabric of the universe and the Evil had come seeping through.

But even as he prayed he could hear the voice of William's grandad berating him from under the lid of the closed coffin. The Voice of Reason.

I was seventy-five years old, you daft bugger, d'you seriously think it was your fault, just because you got your leg over some Judy? This is the daft nuns they sent you to all them years ago and your head's still full of the rubbish they crammed into you.

He'd fought a long battle against the boys' religious indoctrination. There wasn't much he could do about Preston except shout abuse across the garden fence at his nan while she was putting the washing out, but he managed to persuade her it would be a mistake sending him to a Catholic school.

'You don't want him growing up different from the rest of the kids in the street,' he said cunningly, because he knew this was a weakness of Preston's nan. And when William came back from Germany and a decision had to be made about his education, he argued that it made sense to send him to the state school, the same as Preston.

'He'll look after him,' he said. 'He'll stop people from picking on him for being different.'

There was a terrible fear of Being Different in those two houses. Maybe it was a reaction to William's grandad and his wicked flaunting of convention. Maybe it was because they thought it was dangerous to stand out in any way from the crowd, in case fate was tempted to drop a crate on their heads.

So both boys went to the state school in spite of Father Michael at St Oswald's, but it was a hollow victory because twice a week, once after school, once on Saturdays, they were sent to the Convent to learn catechism off the nuns so they would grow up good Catholics after all.

'I might have failed where you're concerned,' said William's nan, grimly. 'But I won't with the boy.'

It was part of the feud they fought over his refusal to convert.

'And the promises he made me, Father, when he asked me to marry him,' she complained to Father Michael. 'And you, too, remember? And never once has he been for Instruction.'

'Remember our Lord was a Jew,' said Father Michael, piously, but he remembered and did not forgive.

But William's grandad reckoned the real reason they had it in for him was because of the name.

Mary Teresa Epstein, what kind of name was that for a good Catholic girl, orthodox to the core? There was a joke to make the Devil laugh, nasty smirking face in the corner of the picture.

So William and Preston were sent for the Instruction that William's grandad had so artfully dodged. 'Like lambs to the slaughter,' he said, sorrowfully, thinking of the rubbish they'd be taught and wondering how to counter it.

'They'd do the same to me, if I was ever helpless enough,' he'd say. 'But when the pair of youse has got enough sense you can fight them off for me and all the damn priests and nuns they'll bring along with them.'

'I can see by those here present that Samuel did not lack for friends,' said the priest who now filled the place of Father Michael. 'And I am sure that a mighty host awaits him in the Next World.'

But he cleverly avoided being specific about the geography, Preston noted, obviously not convinced that the late baptism had done the trick. He might not have been able to dodge the water, but they'd never pinned him down for the Instruction.

He was right about one thing, though, that priest. William's grandad had a lot of friends, unless they were there only to make sure he was safely laid to rest, where he couldn't get up to much more mischief.

'I've never seen the church so crowded for a funeral,' said

105

William's nan proudly, though there was a hint of suspicion in the eyes that gazed around the congregation. She was looking for communists and ex-lovers.

Preston didn't see any he could put in either category, not at first. He didn't know many of the people there. In the last few years of his life William's grandad had finally found employment in a growth industry – he was a volunteer with the Victims Support Scheme, and a lot of the mourners were people from the office, or victims of muggings and burglaries that he'd helped to put on their feet again. But Preston found he was scanning the crowd at about the right height for an eight-year-old child, and it was only after a while that he realised he was looking for Uncle Titch.

He was waiting for the crowd to disperse from the grave so he could say his own private farewells when a respectable old lady with a blue rinse came up to him and said, 'You don't remember me, do you, I'm Mrs Flaherty.'

Preston did a double take.

'Not *the* Mrs Flaherty,' he said, wondering if it could be her sister.

But it was *the* Mrs Flaherty all right, of Flaherty's Famous Funfair and the Wall of Death Riders and Flaherty's Flying Horses.

She'd lost a few stone since the last time he'd seen her and put on about half a ton of make-up.

'What happened to the Flying Horses?' Preston enquired, thinking they'd probably been put down years ago, but the Flying Horses were alive and kicking and in at least as good a shape as she was.

'People like a good old-fashioned merry-go-round,' she said. 'We've got five of them operating now. We do functions mostly, college balls and barbecues and company outings and that. I've got a bright young thing working for me does all the bookings and the publicity, can I give you a brochure?'

She took one out of her handbag. Take a ride into the past, it said, on Flaherty's Flying Horses.

It took Preston back, looking at it. All that gold, all that scrolling, all those teeth and glaring eyes.

'People like the old gallopers,' said Mrs F. 'They like a bit of

106

the old nostalgia. Don't like the present, you see, and can you blame them?

'*He* knew that,' she said, inclining her head towards the grave. 'And Titch, bless his heart, but it came too late for them.'

She took a white lace handkerchief out of her bag and dabbed a corner of it carefully at the corner of her eyes before the make-up ran.

'I often wondered what happened to Uncle Titch,' said Preston. He saw William looking at him curiously across the crowd and then detach himself from the group he was with and move towards them.

'Been dead for years now, has Titch, don't live to a grand old age as a rule, his sort, everything's compressed, you see, and he lived a lot longer than they usually do. I took him into the business with me, you know, after all that bother at the Turk's Head.'

All that bother.

'I didn't know that,' said Preston. 'He just disappeared.'

'Ah well, you were only a lad, they don't tell you everything do they.'

'What don't they tell you?' said William, smiling but curious.

'This is Mrs Flaherty,' said Preston, 'from the funfair. She was telling me about Uncle Titch.'

He watched William's face, wondering if he'd forgotten, or blocked it out as he appeared to have blocked out so much else.

But he remembered.

'So he came in with me, into the business,' said Mrs F., 'and brought the best part of a blessed fairground with him. All that stuff Sammy used to paint . . .'

All that stuff. All those panels with the *Battleship Potemkin*, all those scenes of imperial glory, all those horses and birds and lions and tigers and bears in the dark silent rooms covered with blood and the mad eyes glaring.

'It was Sammy got them out for us and loaded into the van,' she said. 'Titch wouldn't go near the place after what happened, and I was surprised your grandad could after what he'd seen.'

'Excuse me?' said William.

'Well, when he found the body.'

Preston's astonishment was reflected in William's eyes, and it didn't look feigned.

'Didn't you know it was him that found her? Well, perhaps you were too young, they didn't want to give you nightmares. Titch left him a key, you see, while he was away, so he could keep an eye on the place, or maybe if he wanted to do some painting, the way your nan carried on about him doing it at home – anyway, he went round there that night.' She shuddered theatrically. 'All that blood. I'm surprised it didn't give him a heart attack there and then. Mind you, he was younger in those days, and a fit man in spite of his leg.'

They stood there, shocked and remembering among the graves and the mourners filing past paying their respects.

'I'd better get on, I suppose,' said Mrs Flaherty. 'Your mam's invited me back to the house.'

They walked back to the cars together and Preston never did get to stand there alone.

'I've still got some of the things Sammy painted,' said Mrs Flaherty. 'You can always tell the ones he did, he used to put a little devil in the corner, do you remember that?'

15

Uncle Titch

Why had they never told him?

The graveyard was on a slope above the village, and from where he stood William could look down over most of the neighbourhood where he used to live. He could just make out the railway embankment from here, but not the station or the building that used to be the Turk's Head. He could see the stocking factory, though, or at least the shell of it. It had been turned into what they called industrial units but his mum said only half of them had ever been taken up. One of them made crochet toilet-seat covers that they sold at the shop. And beyond the factory he could see the bit of wasteland where Mrs Flaherty used to keep the Famous Funfair under tarpaulins for the winter. There was a car dump there now.

William felt no sense of nostalgia for any of it. He had never been happy here. He had never felt as if he belonged. At times, in the months following the return from Germany, he had actively hated it and all the people who did belong. Later, usually with Preston or his grandad, he'd felt a bit more at home, but not much. He was always an alien.

He heard his mother calling from the gate of the church. 'Come on, William, the car's waiting.'

He used to visit the graveyard sometimes when he was a child and just wander about reading the headstones. When he went up to Cambridge he met another American who'd been brought up in England, whose father was a journalist in the London bureau of the *Washington Post*, and he'd had a thing about graveyards, too. He said it was something to do with digging for roots, but William didn't know about that, he just liked graveyards. Graveyards, old churches, gargoyles . . .

He turned back to look at them, jutting out from the foot of the church tower. The usual menagerie of demons. He even knew the names of some of them: Grafficane, the doggish; Dragnignazzo, the fell dragon; Ciriato Sannuto, the tusked boar; Caynazzo, the snarler . . .

'William, are you going to stand there all day?'

'Okay, okay,' said William.

' "Where God erecteth his church, the devil in the same churchyard will house his chapel",' he quoted, as he joined her in the limo.

'The sandwiches'll be all curled up at the edges,' his mum complained.

William gazed out of the window as they drove through what used to be called The Village and was now just another suburban shopping centre. He could remember how strange it had seemed after the base in Germany. It felt strange now, but there were still a few shops that seemed familiar.

And then he saw the pet shop.

He twisted round, looking back at it.

The pet shop where his grandad had bought him his hamster called Hammer and his goldfish called Sickle and where his nan used to take them for resurrection when they died.

His grandad had told him about that, years later, when he was about fifteen.

'Your nan used to take you in there,' he said, 'with this dead hamster in a cage or the bloody goldfish floating belly up in the bowl, and she'd wink at him and say, It's very sick, can you take it in the back and make it better? Wink, wink. Daft bloody woman and you standing there gawping next to her.

'And he'd go away and chuck it in the bin or down the sink and come back with a new one. You never knew the difference. I went in there myself one day for a packet of sunflower seeds for the hamster, and he says to me, I don't know what I'm going to do, Mr Epstein, when she comes in here with you over her shoulder.'

William had been amazed. He'd thought he had the longest living hamster in captivity.

His nan was furious when she found out he knew, and who'd told him.

'It's like telling him there's no Father Christmas,' she sniffed. 'You'll take away all his illusions.'

'And a bloody good thing, too,' his grandad had told her, bold with rebellion. 'How's the lad ever going to come to terms with death the way you carry on?'

But there never was any coming to terms with it, not in William's experience. It made its own terms, and the best you could hope for was it wouldn't happen the way it had happened to Mary Moxton at the Turk's Head.

William peered out of the side window when they came to the crossroads but it would be too far away to see anything, even if it was still there.

'Let's go down the Turk's Head,' his grandad used to say, when it was still a treat for them both and not the stuff of nightmares.

And he'd wipe his brush on a rag soaked in turps and wash his hands in the kitchen sink and off they'd go, calling for Preston sometimes from next door, because he liked it, too.

The Turk's Head.

'Sounds like it ought to be a pub,' people used to say, but it wasn't a pub, it was a café. Grandad never went near a pub because of what he said they put in the beer.

'No wonder it makes people sick,' he said. 'The things I've seen in them vats when I worked for the brewery.'

One of the things he'd seen was cockroaches and the other was rats. Dead rats, floating in the brown swill of beer with teeth bared in a last deathly snarl. It was the first image William ever had of rats, and an enduring one.

So Grandad stuck to tea, and the occasional mug of Bovril when the weather was bad. You could get both at the Turk's Head, and coffee and Horlicks and Tizer and Eccles cakes and jam doughnuts. Not much else, though, in the way of refreshment, because the Turk's Head was only masquerading as a café. It was really a front for Uncle Titch and Grandad's Great Fairground Enterprise.

Uncle Titch was the proprietor, manager and sole occupant of

111

the Turk's Head, then. He was called Titch because he was a midget with a very large head and very short legs, and Uncle for reasons that were never satisfactorily explained to William, but then, not a lot ever was.

'Why did Uncle Titch never grow up?' he asked once when they were home having tea.

'Because he stayed in the bath too long and got shrunk,' said his grandad, who could never get into the bathroom when he wanted to because William or his mum were usually there, her in the bath or him on the lavatory reading a comic, which was one of his little pleasures in life.

'Because he was forever making dens in trees,' said his nan, who knew this was another, 'and one day a big crow flew up and scared him and he lost his hold and fell on to his head and stopped growing so let that be a lesson to you.'

You could rarely get a straight answer from any of them, they'd been dodging questions about his father for so long; evasion was a way of life with them.

One thing William did know was that Uncle Titch had once worked in a circus. He knew this not just because Uncle Titch said he had – you couldn't believe anything a grown-up told you, and Uncle Titch belonged to the world of grown-ups even if he wasn't – but because of the tricks he could do. He could do somersaults and cartwheels and he could walk on his hands carrying a plate of Eccles cakes on one foot. And that was only a fraction of the tricks he said he could do in his Heyday.

In his Heyday, Uncle Titch was a crowd puller, a roller-upper. Whenever the circus came to a new town he used to dress up in his costume and go out into the streets with a clown on stilts and do a turn. It invariably ended with Uncle Titch pretending to get cross with the clown on stilts and chasing him along the street on his fat little legs and trying to kick him up the bum and falling over backwards.

This always got a laugh.

'It couldn't fail,' said Uncle Titch. 'People love to see some poor sod making an arsehole of himself.'

Uncle Titch had a bit of a grudge against the world. He got his own back by playing tricks on it. He drove about in a horse and cart and one of his tricks was to whip the horse up into a canter and crouch down behind the seat so people would think it had bolted. When responsible citizens or policemen came rushing out into the road to grab at it and avert a disaster, Uncle Titch would leap up from behind his seat and pretend they just hadn't noticed him.

'Just because I'm a dwarf,' he'd shout, 'it doesn't mean I'm NOT HERE.'

Another one of his tricks was to lurk behind the counter at the Turk's Head so customers would think there was no one there, and then, when they were thinking of leaving or helping themselves to the jam doughnuts, he'd leap on to a wooden box to bring his large dome head just above the level of the counter and say, 'Can I help you?' in a very loud voice.

This was probably one of the reasons the Turk's Head didn't take a lot of custom.

The other reason was the location. It was hidden away down a dingy little cul-de-sac ending in a railway embankment and a station hardly anyone used any more.

'Not what you'd call a Major Thoroughfare,' said William's nan, who had a sarcastic tongue on her at times. 'Not what you'd call well placed for the passing trade.'

People who came to the Turk's Head really had to know what they were looking for.

It didn't even look like a café. It looked like a small, run-down Victorian railway hotel, which was fine, really, because that is what it had started off as, some time round the middle of the last century in an age of soaring optimism when all things seemed possible, or at least profitable, even the commercial success of a travellers' rest beside a branch line in the middle of nowhere.

No one could remember the last time anyone had stayed there, or, indeed, if anyone ever had. Most travellers with their wits about them and an eye for aesthetics would have preferred to rest at the Bates Motel.

It was a mad mongrel of a building, a Victorian folly lampooning the worst taste of several architectural ages. It looked as if the builder had started off with the plans of a Tudor manor house, swapped them for an Early English cathedral in mid-storey, and then suffered a total loss of confidence and tried to convert it into a Dutch barn. The end result was a kind of Gothic Wendy house.

The owner before Uncle Titch had been a retired seaman and he'd renamed it the Turk's Head, not after an Ottoman warrior, as most people thought, but after a special type of nautical knot that looked like a turban.

He thought it would give it a bit of glamour.

But it didn't.

Uncle Titch just shrugged and got on with the important things in life. He only used the ground floor as a café, anyway. The other two floors were devoted to the real business of the Turk's Head and Uncle Titch's particular folly.

'Fairground renovation,' he grandly called it.

'Mucking about with bits of junk,' said William's nan.

'If there's ever a fairground revival,' his grandad, who had a stake in the business, would insist, 'we'll be laughing all the way to the bank.'

'The only people doing any laughing are the gypsies that sell it to you,' she'd retort. 'Daft as a brush you are, the pair of you.'

She didn't have much time for Grandad's artistic flair.

'You ought to do something that'll bring some proper money in,' she told him, 'and take that stuff out the back where I'm not forever tripping over it.'

And if she'd married Vincent Van Gogh it would have been the same story. 'Get out from under my feet, out in the yard, and let's have none of your histrionics – you're dripping red stuff all over my linoleum.' Painting was a hobby, it wasn't a job, not something Real. It was like keeping whippets.

She had a strongly defined concept of what was Real and what was not, did William's nan, and some people were just playing at life.

'You stand as much chance of getting rich with that stuff,' she'd say, 'as I do scrubbing floors at the Liver Buildings.'

Though young and impressionable, and usually on Grandad's side, there was enough of the pessimist in William, even at the age of nine and a half, to concede that his nan was probably right. Whole rooms of the Turk's Head were taken over by bits

114

of fairground waiting for the revival that would send Uncle Titch and Grandad chortling off to the local branch of the Co-op. And while they were biding their time over a game of backgammon down in the café, William used to wander through the silent, cluttered rooms where their investment languished, gathering dust. Scenes of empires lost and won, Gordon at Khartoum and fuzzy-wuzzies at Omdurman, dreadnoughts and dreadlocks, gallopers plunging and rearing and lying on their sides with their legs broken, bears and tigers and great striding birds and British lions with Union Jack saddles. A battleground of historic events and a jungle of eyes watching him out of the gloom, bright eyes and eyes dulled from misuse, flaring nostrils and faded plumage and gaping jaws and once-golden beaks.

He was convinced they'd inspired his interest in history, those fairground animals, those famous scenes his grandad painted. They'd certainly coloured it. He was rare among scholars in being more interested in events than trends. He had a childish fascination for battles and revolutions and catastrophes. Dead horses lying in the dust.

'He ought to get rid of the lot,' his nan used to say. 'Burn it in the yard outside and take in lodgers.'

'Leave the man alone,' said William's grandad. 'He doesn't need you to organise his life for him.'

'It'll end in tears,' said Nan, and it did, but that was her fault as much as anyone's.

His mum had got the caterers in back at the house and there were great plates of sandwiches and cakes and even a couple of barrels of Tetley's out in the kitchen with the head waiter from the restaurant at Mary Ann Evans's dispensing from the tap.

William watched the murky liquid gushing out.

'She's done him proud,' said Mrs Flaherty, 'I'll say that for her.'

'Have you had a chance to talk to Nan?' he asked her.

'I gave her my condolences,' she said, properly, 'but that was as far as it went. We've never been what you might call close, me and your nan. I think she thought I had an eye on your grandad.'

She giggled into her glass of beer. 'And between you, me and the gatepost, she was right.'

William remembered her in the Turk's Head that time, looking twice the size she was now and wearing a pink suede jacket with studs in the sleeves and a pair of men's corduroy trousers tucked into silver and black cowboy boots. She'd been involved with fairs and circuses since the age of fourteen, when she'd run off with a Wall of Death rider on his motorbike.

He'd taught her the tricks of his trade until by her own account she was better at it than he was.

'You wouldn't know to look at me now,' she'd say, 'but I could hold them spellbound, the things I could do on that bike in a crash helmet and a pair of tights and a stars and stripes swimsuit.'

One of those held spellbound was the fairground owner, the Great Flaherty himself, who'd lured her away from her Wall of Death rider and made her his child bride and business partner.

'But I still used to pose on the bike for publicity purposes,' she'd say archly over her tea and Eccles cakes, 'until the varicose veins started to show through me silver tights and Flaherty said I'd better call it a day and let them find themselves another pin-up girl.'

Through the crowd round the barrels William saw the priest who'd officiated at the funeral and who'd asked him about the hymns.

'Would you excuse me a moment?' he said. 'I'd like to speak to the Father.'

The Father was a genial soul, and Irish with it.

'Nice drop of ale,' he said, raising his glass. 'I expect your grandfather liked his pint, did he not?'

'Never touched the stuff,' said William. 'The rats put him off.'

'Ah, yes. They would, they would.'

But he looked a bit uncertainly into the glass.

'My nan never said anything to you, did she?' William asked him. 'About what brought on his heart attack?'

'I don't believe she did, no. She was very distressed at the time, of course.'

William left him holding his glass up to the light from the kitchen window and frowning slightly.

116

He found his mum in the drawing room showing off her Inchbold original to a crowd of people he didn't know.

'Mum, can I have a word?' he said.

'Of course you can,' she said, taking his arm and walking him towards the bay window, but she kept one eye on the painting in case they were tempted.

'I've just been talking to Mrs Flaherty,' she said. 'Do you know, that woman's got five merry-go-rounds?'

'I know,' said William.

'And do you know what each of them's worth?'

'No. Mum . . .'

'Seventy thousand pounds, and that's just the insurance value. Nostalgia, William, it's what everyone's after these days.'

'Mum, what was it gave Grandad his heart attack?'

It was a test, really, to see if she said anything about the stockings. But she just stared at him.

'William, he was seventy-five years old, it does happen, you know, and he had terrible eating habits. You should have seen the butter he put on his toast in the mornings, I kept on at him but you know what he was like, he wouldn't be told. And you know what he'd have for a treat? Bread and dripping. Bread and dripping, I ask you.'

She spotted someone poking at her Inchbold.

'Don't touch,' she said, scuttling across. 'It's wired for burglars.'

William gave up, but he tried it on his nan later, when most people had gone.

'Was Grandad very upset about the seamed stockings?' he said, gently.

She looked at him for a moment as if weighing up the consequences of telling the truth for once. Then she sighed and nodded.

'He took it very bad,' she said. 'She gets them made in a factory in Hong Kong. I knew she shouldn't have told him. All the rage, she says, selling like hot cakes. Stockings and suspender belts, nostalgia and sex appeal, she says, you can't beat it. The madam.

'He went very quiet but I knew he was upset. Then, when we went upstairs, he says to me, Mary, he says, first time he called

117

me that in years, Mary, why is it all my life I've always got the timing wrong? Then a bit later when I was just nodding off he says, Seamed stockings. Those were the last words he said to me, apart from when he woke up and said he had to go to the toilet but you don't count that, do you.'

He knew Preston wouldn't have left. He found him out in the garden, sitting on a wooden bench by the pond.

'Have you got the car?' he said. 'Let's get out of here.'

'Where do you want to go?' said Preston.

'Anywhere,' said William. 'Let's just drive.'

16

The Murder at the Turk's Head

But, of course, they drove to the Turk's Head.

Or the place where the Turk's Head used to be.

'They couldn't sell it after what happened,' said Preston as they sat in the car together at the end of the cul-de-sac. 'They reckoned it was haunted and no one would buy it, and in the end it got in such a state they got the council to pull it down. That's what my Auntie Ethel said.'

Where the Turk's Head had once been there was just a piece of waste ground overgrown with weeds and used for dumping rubbish despite the sign that said No Tipping. The station had gone, too, and they'd shut the line down and taken up the rails. Only the embankment remained, and the tunnel they used to run through when they were kids, shouting to make the killer bats and the rats think they were bigger than they really were.

They didn't believe in things like that any more, but neither of them made any move to get out of the car. They just sat and looked.

'They turned the embankment into a nature walk,' said Preston. 'You're supposed to be able to walk all the way from here to the coast.'

Someone walked over Preston's grave and he shuddered. He knew William would know why, the thought of walking along that embankment, knowing what they knew.

'Did you know about Grandad finding the body?' William asked. Preston shook his head.

'They never told me,' he said.

'Seems there was a lot they never told us,' said William. And Preston felt embarrassed, thinking of the Master Sergeant.

There was a gang of kids playing up on the embankment, just as Preston and William had, junior hangers-on, rookie spear carriers in the terrible Derek Sumter gang which had once ruled the neighbourhood, so far as was tolerated by the greater power of the nans. Playing on the railway embankment was well beyond that tolerance. In those days, when the trains still ran, it was called trespassing and possessed the double attraction of being unlawful and dangerous. Do Not Trespass on the Railway Line. One of a long list of commandments, much more extensive than the original ten, that had circumscribed the exploits of Preston's youth. Yet another that he had broken.

'Remember the last time we went up there?' Preston said to William, knowing that he could not possibly have forgotten, whatever else conveniently slipped his memory. 'That night before the murder?'

But William just sat there, staring out of the car window at the waste ground where the Turk's Head had once been.

'She must have been about three or four months' pregnant,' said Preston, 'only it didn't show.'

And he had a mental image of Mary Moxton pacing the sparsely furnished room that Uncle Titch had given her, on the floor above the café, alone with her troubles.

In Trouble, that was the euphemism of the time. Mary Moxton's In Trouble. Except that they hadn't known how bad.

'She was always so full of life,' said William, suddenly. 'Much more than the rest of them. They thought she must be daft.'

The Daft One, Preston's nan called her, who had names for them all.

'She needs her head seeing to, that one,' she'd say. 'She's got so many screws loose it's a wonder it stays on her shoulders.'

She might have been daft in some ways, but she knew what was in and what was out, did Mary M. She knew the right clubs to go to. She was pretty and popular and she lived for the moment.

'I've got a long way to go before I'm thirty,' she'd say. 'Anything could happen before then.'

And she'd let her long hair fall around her face and shake it to some interior rhythm.

'"*Get your Mojo working*",' she'd mime. 'Get with it, girls, don't let the grass grow under your feet.'

They'd all grown up together on the same corpy estate, been to the same sink school, gone out with the same dreary lads. Elaine and Ethel and Nell and Mary – the Girls, as the two nans called them, fondly sometimes, but more often in despair of their ever growing up.

'They need to find themselves a decent bloke,' said William's nan once, presumably meaning four decent blokes as she was not a great advocate of polygamy.

'Or stop looking and make their minds up they're better off single,' said Preston's, who thought monogamy had its drawbacks, too.

They'd none of them been lucky with men.

Elaine's had run off and Ethel was still running after hers and Nell's was dead and Mary's a dead loss.

That was what they used to call him, the Dead Loss.

Or the Nose Picker.

Or the Queerfella, a widely dispensed sobriquet of Preston's nan, not knowing then how queer a fella Barry Moxton really was.

Barry Moxton was one of the shipwrecks of the area. Its endemic pessimism had got him by the balls and left him beached and burned out by his late twenties, unemployed, unskilled and unloved by all but his widowed mother.

And Mary Moxton, once.

'What the heck did she ever see in that one?' Preston could remember his nan asking on more than one occasion, and his mum shrugging and saying, 'She thought he looked a bit like Elvis Presley.'

But it had been years, even then, since Elvis was top of the Hit Parade, and if all he had to offer the world was slicked-back hair and a sulky pout, the Dead Loss was set to slip a lot further down the charts, and Mary wasn't going to be there to see it.

'She leads him a right dance,' the nans would say, during their daily exchange of news and analysis in the queue at the butcher's, until finally she danced off for good and all and left him with his mother and his clapped-out BSA and his jars of Brylcreem and his collection of 78 records and a lifetime's cumulation of unarticulated resentments.

'And what does the Queerfella have to say about it?' Preston's nan demanded when she heard that Mary Moxton was In Trouble and none of his making.

But no one seemed to know, or care, what the Queerfella felt about anything.

'I remember thinking for a long time afterwards that it must have been Uncle Titch's,' said William, and Preston stared at him in astonishment, shocked not so much by the thought of Uncle Titch and Mary Moxton in carnal embrace as by this sudden insight into William's dark imaginings.

'I suppose it was because she moved in with him,' said William, defensively.

'Oh, but that was the nans,' Preston assured him. 'They persuaded him. They kept nagging at him about all that space he had and how she'd got nowhere and her dad wouldn't have her back and her with a baby inside her. Your nan was always on at him to take in lodgers, remember?'

'So whose was it then?' demanded William. 'Did they tell you that?'

'No, but I knew.'

He felt a childish satisfaction in having that advantage on one who had claimed to be so well informed on such matters.

'I heard them talking about it.'

He could remember them discussing it over the ironing and himself on the floor playing with his soldiers behind the sofa and keeping very quiet about it because it was way past his bedtime. It was so clear in his mind, he could hear his nan's voice, even smell that strangely comforting smell of scorched linen as she pressed down on the iron, and yet he had understood little of their conversation at the time, hadn't understood, in fact, until years later.

'Whose is it then,' his nan had wanted to know, 'if it's not too much to ask?'

'She thinks it's one of the lifeguards at the municipal pool,' his mum said, and she must have sniggered because his nan came back at her very sharp.

'It's no laughing matter, madam. He might be a dead loss but he's still her husband and that makes it adultery in my book, and in the eyes of the Church.'

And Preston very tense behind the sofa, because when his nan called someone madam she meant business, and although he didn't know what adultery meant exactly he knew it was something smutty and another of the things the commandments came down pretty hard on. Even worse than Trespassing on the Railway Line.

'And what's he going to do about it then?' his nan demanded. 'This fella me lad?'

'Oh, he'd never admit it was his,' said his mum. 'He's married already.'

And the Tut was one of his nan's specials.

'Some people've got the morals of alley cats,' she said. 'It's a bucket of water they need, never mind swimming pools.'

His nan's abhorrence of the neighbourhood toms was legendary, and her punishment merciless when she heard them at it, raw-arsed and rampant, in the nightly flesh pit of the back yard. Many a time had Preston's youthful slumbers been disturbed by the sound of the deluge from Nan's bedroom window as it hit the corrugated iron roof of their garden shed and the wild feline howls as their coitus was so balefully interrupted.

'What's going to happen to the baby then?'

'She says she's going to have it adopted.'

No question of 'getting rid of it'. Not in those days, not for a good Catholic girl like Mary Moxton, who would only lapse so far, and abortion was a lot further.

The mystery of Mary Moxton's baby used to puzzle Preston, with his woefully inadequate sexual education. There was so much talk about it, so many furtive conversations, and yet no one ever saw it.

'Where is this baby then?' he asked his mum, boldly, one evening when his nan wasn't around.

'In her tummy,' said his mum.

And Preston very dubious, because she didn't look like she had

123

a baby in her tummy and experience had taught him to be very sceptical about any information his family gave out, especially on the subject of babies and where they came from.

'How did it get there?' he insisted, keeping his voice low because he knew having babies was something of an embarrassment, like some diseases you didn't talk about.

'She caught it at the public baths,' said his mum, with another one of her sniggers.

But Preston had thought that very plausible at the time. He'd caught a verruca once at the public baths.

'She should have worn her flip-flops,' he said, and was startled by the sudden explosion of mirth, but then his mother was always a bit prone to that sort of thing. Giggling Sheila his nan called her.

He never discovered how Uncle Titch was persuaded to give refuge to Mary Moxton and her hidden embryo. He must have put up a bit of a struggle, but they were a persuasive bunch, those women, and the two nans in alliance were practically irresistible. He could remember him complaining once in the café to William's grandad.

'I'll not have a babby in the place, I told them. I made myself very clear about that. Squealing and squawking and leaving its dirty nappies all over the show.'

'Oh, they've got that all sorted,' William's grandad assured him. 'Them and their precious Father Michael. He'll have it off her and into a good Catholic home quick as blinking, the poor little basket, and you'll not have sight nor sound of it, and nor the mother, I shouldn't think.'

Well, he was right about that, reflected Preston, looking across the site of the old café towards the abandoned railway line and remembering.

'And I thought he was the one who killed her, too,' said William, 'when they finally told me.'

'We all did,' said Preston. 'We all thought it was him. Except for Mrs Flaherty. And your grandad, maybe.'

Murder: he remembered the first chilling thrill of the word in the school playground, when it was still something to be excited about and before he knew who the victim was, or the chief suspect.

'Killed with an axe . . .'

'No, it wasn't, it was a meat cleaver, my mam said . . .'

'Cut into little pieces . . .'

'One of the policemen was sick . . .'

And the police up on the railway embankment when they walked home from school, and the tunnel fenced off so they had to go the long way round.

'They say he escaped along the line,' someone announced, 'because he was covered in blood.'

And by then they all knew who 'he' was, or thought they did.

'I'll never believe he done it,' said Mrs Flaherty, when she came round for a cup of tea and a slice of the action, 'not if he's convicted by a dozen juries, and don't tell me he'll get a fair trial in the current climate of opinion, not unless they pick twelve men the same size and true. I know, I've seen the prejudice of people, I know what they are.'

It was another image for Preston to carry into his dreams, or nightmares, of Uncle Titch in the dock and the twelve little dwarves grim and silent on the hard wooden benches.

And we find the accused . . .

'Harmless,' said Mrs Flaherty, 'harmless he is, harmless as a babby . . .'

And the last word hanging in the room and the awful silence until William's nan poured the tea.

'It looks bad for him all the same,' she said. 'How many sugars, Mrs Flaherty?'

And Preston trying to catch William's eye to share the wonder of it, for it was not the least of sensations to find Mrs Flaherty of Flaherty's Famous Funfair in William's nan's front room, taking tea.

Mrs Flaherty and the nans did not mix in the same circles. Mrs Flaherty was what the nans called the Wrong Element. Only Disaster could bring them together.

'It's not done him any good,' said Big Nan, 'running away like that.'

For Uncle Titch had scarpered, horse, cart and all.

There was a nationwide search out for them, it said on the television.

'Police state, he calls it,' said Nanna Epstein with a nod in Grandad's direction, very quiet in the corner, 'and they can't find a dwarf in a horse and cart – you're not safe in your beds.'

They kept the doors locked all the time now, and on a bolt and chain, and Big Nan had sewn Velcro round all the edges of the curtains so they'd stick together and no one be able to peer in.

'He'll be with fairground people,' said Mrs Flaherty, staring into her teacup as if she was reading the leaves. 'I hate to admit it, but they'll be sheltering him, they always stick with their own kind.'

She looked up and stuck her chin out. 'But I don't believe he done it, I don't believe he could do a thing like that and her with a babby inside of her.'

There was another awful silence then, because no one, not in Preston's hearing at least, had yet mentioned the babby inside of her. That was the trouble with Mrs Flaherty, you couldn't trust her not to say the wrong thing in company, that was one of the reasons why she was the Wrong Element.

'It was us persuaded him to take her in,' said Nanna Epstein. 'She'd be alive today if it wasn't for that.'

And the tears starting up again, and the boys quiet and solemn as only boys can be when there's a Disaster in the house and they're short on Information.

'Well, one thing's for sure,' William's grandad said, 'he can't have escaped along a railway line with a horse and cart, not even the po-lice are going to believe that.'

'They're not interested in details,' said Mrs Flaherty. 'They've made their minds up. He's the one that done it and they don't want to know no different.'

The next day they charged Barry Moxton with the murder of his wife Mary and there was a picture on the front pages of him being led away with a blanket over his head and another of a policeman coming out of his mother's house with a plastic bag that was said to contain his bloodstained and half-burned clothing, and a day or so after that Uncle Titch turned up in South Wales with his horse and cart where he said he'd gone after a merry-go-round and didn't know what all the fuss was about, didn't know about any murder, didn't read the papers and was generally believed, at least by the people on the estate, because it was typical of Uncle

Titch, and by that time the Queerfella who was queerer than any of them knew had made a full confession and it was all over bar the shouting and the trial, when he pleaded guilty and was sent down for life and everyone said he should have been hanged and pretended it had never once crossed their minds that it was Uncle Titch that done it.

But he knew, even though he never read the papers.

And the Turk's Head stayed shut with padlocks on the doors and the windows boarded up, and Uncle Titch went away and no one seemed to know where he'd gone to, not even William's grandad, and no one seemed to know whether he'd taken his fairground with him or whether it was still there behind the shutters and the padlocked doors in the dark rooms with the bloodstains still on the walls and floors.

Those rooms haunted Preston's dreams. He saw it all reflected in the eyes of those blood-spattered gallopers and bears and lions and tigers and ostriches, all frozen in mid-stride, helpless witnesses of the terror they could not run from, and Preston trying desperately to escape from it, as much in terror of the mutilated corpse of Mary Moxton as he was of her murderer, and running from room to room and pulling open the last door of the last room and out into the night and down the long black tunnel under the railway line getting closer and closer to the grey patch of light at the end until, on the verge of safety, the figure would leap out at him in its bloody clothes with the meat cleaver in its hands . . .

'I still had nightmares about it,' said William, 'well into my teens. Still do, sometimes, every now and then.'

Preston looked at him and wondered if they were the same nightmares he had. They'd be worse, probably. William always went that step further into life's nightmares, and he'd been closer to it, to start with. Mary Moxton had been his mum's friend more than anyone's, and Uncle Titch his grandad's, and it had hit them harder than most.

And then there was that night just before the murder when William came to him with his plan. If you went up the railway embankment at night, he said, you could look straight into the window of the room Uncle Titch had given her and see her getting undressed.

'Parading around in the Nude,' said William.

'She'll have the curtains drawn,' said Preston, who suspected it was another commandment they'd be breaking, even if he hadn't specifically been told about it. Thou Shalt Not Spy on thy Mother's Old Schoolfriends Parading around in the Nude.

'She doesn't have any curtains,' said William. 'She hasn't put any up.'

He'd noticed this when they were trespassing on the embankment one day, playing Robin Hood and his Merrie Men. She probably didn't think she needed curtains, with the room overlooking the railway line, not considering the ambition and initiative of a boy like William.

It was November and the nights drawing in, and they went after tea, telling the nans they were going to a friend's house to play with his electric trains.

But when they reached the embankment, Preston had second thoughts. It was too dark and he was too afraid, or his conscience troubled him, or it was a combination of the two and so he hung back. 'Chicken,' William called him, 'big chicken,' and went on alone, up behind the Turk's Head where the lights were on.

And came running back in stark terror a few minutes later as if all the hounds of hell were after him, and Preston, who thought they were, a half-length behind all the way back to the alley behind their two houses where they stopped to get their breath back before they went in.

'What did you see?' Preston asked him.

But he just kept shaking his head and wouldn't say, and the only thing Preston was sure he hadn't seen was Mary Moxton Parading around in the Nude.

'Come on,' Preston urged him now. 'What did you see?'

And William looked at him with an odd expression, and at first Preston thought he really didn't remember or was pretending he didn't, but then he smiled, even more oddly, and said, 'The Devil.'

And Preston frowned at him, half smiling himself, but he felt very cold suddenly.

'That's what I thought at the time, anyway,' said William, 'but

128

I think now it must have been Barry Moxton. He was just sitting there up the embankment among the bushes. I nearly fell over him and he turned round, but I didn't really see his face in the dark, or if I did, I blocked it out I was so scared. I just ran.'

Preston shivered. The night was drawing in and the kids had gone home and the tunnel under the embankment was deep in shadow. A black hole, waiting.

'We should be getting back,' said Preston, and he started the car.

'He used to watch most nights, apparently,' said William. 'I read it in a newspaper cutting about the trial that Grandad had kept. And the night of the murder something snapped. Or else the Devil *was* there, that particular night, sitting with him.'

'It was a long time ago,' Preston said. He wanted to go now. He wanted to forget it. It was all very well picking at the past like this if it helped to exorcise the demons, but he wasn't sure that was what William wanted. He was drawn to it in some weirdly obsessive, almost dangerous way. Preston half understood this because it was in him, too, but he rejected it, also, because it scared him too much.

They drove back in silence for a while and then, just before they reached the house where William's mother now lived, William said, 'It was the reason my mum went into business, you know.'

Preston was puzzled.

'What was?'

'What happened to Mary Moxton. She wanted to be safe, and the only way she knew how to be safe was to be rich.'

Preston shook his head, but it was true that within a few weeks of Mary Moxton's death William's mum had bought her first shop. Big Nan said she used the money the Master Sergeant had sent her 'for the boy's education'. She was running a whole chain of them by the time he went to university. She specialised in DIY and Home Brew and Clothing Kits.

William's mum was an early exponent of the self-help society.

And now she had *the* shop – Mary Ann Evans's, with its wood-panelled lifts that went up seven floors and a turnover of so many millions a year. And a home in Woolton with eight-foot walls round it and floodlights and padlocks on the gate and burglar alarms linked to the nearest police station and curtains so thick and so wide they never left any gaps even without Velcro.

They were all afraid. His own mum and his Auntie Ethel were sometimes too scared to go out of the house. Certainly there were some areas of the city they thought it was Death to enter. They kept newspaper cuttings on how dangerous the streets were, and stuck them to the door of the fridge with little magnets.

'NEWSBOY ABDUCTED ON PAPER ROUND.'

'MASKED RAPIST HUNTED.'

'HEADLESS TORSO FOUND IN WOOD.'

'STREET GANG CRIPPLE BOY VICTIM.'

'SCREWDRIVER ATTACK ON BUS DRIVER.'

They thought it was best to know what you were up against, but Preston wasn't sure it had done them a lot of good in the long run. And it hadn't helped him much either. All things considered he'd rather they'd got rich, like William's mum.

'We all need to feel safe,' he said, not really thinking about it, thinking about Emily. Thinking how quiet she'd gone when he said he was coming up for the funeral and how she'd seemed to withdraw into herself. He imagined her pacing alone in her bedroom like Mary Moxton and the light on and no curtains, and he was suddenly afraid for her.

'You know what you should do,' said William suddenly. 'You should come into this house with us.'

As if he had been considering Preston's problems and this was his solution to them. And perhaps it was. At least there'd be a garden for the twins to play in. But he rejected it almost as soon as it crossed his mind. He was feeling vulnerable, that's all. He must beware. All the wrong decisions of Preston's life had come from feeling vulnerable.

I'd have to be crazy, he thought. He wants me to be his Minder again.

But all he said was, 'I'll think about it.'

17

The Commune

The first thing they did when they moved in was get rid of the curtains.

They were net curtains, grimy and faded, and they were on every window on the ground floor.

'Pull them down,' said Kate, and down they came, great grey cobwebs thick with dust and dead flies. And Kate doing most of the pulling, thinking of Miss Haversham in her terrible room with her mice and her bits of cake. What a waste and all over a bloody man. Kate would soon have sorted her out.

'Let there be light,' said Kate, tugging away like John Mills in the David Lean version, and there *was* light.

It was their first collective decision, a rare moment of unanimity. An initial burst of optimism.

But it hadn't lasted.

'We've been here almost a month now,' said Kate, 'and we've done nothing.'

She was in the kitchen chopping carrots.

Plus ça change but it's the same old carrots.

They have a roster of House Duties pinned to the wall of the kitchen but Kate seems to do more than her fair share. Some people always have an excuse. They're working late at the office or they've got a student with a problem or there's essays to mark or they're in the middle of a sentence.

Don't interrupt me in the middle of a sentence.

Creative people, thinks Kate. Bah.

131

Give me an electrician any day, give me a carpenter, give me a dishwasher, give me someone who'll chop carrots.

'Give us a chance,' said Tess. 'I'm still exhausted after the move.'

But she doesn't look exhausted, even though she's just been for a run on the Common. She stands in the doorway leading to the dining room in a pale blue tracksuit with her hair tied up with a blue ribbon and she *glows*.

'We can't let things stagnate,' said Kate. 'We've got to make this place *work*.'

Sometimes she feels overwhelmed by it all. What is she doing here? In this monster house. This Gothic horror with its fourteen rooms, all needing decorating, and its dirty old fireplaces, all needing cleaning, and its three bathrooms, all deficient in some vital function, and its umpteen windows, all needing curtains. How can she ever have thought it might be Fun?

I am a cottage person, wails Kate silently. I want a cottage in the country with a little cottage garden and a patch for me taters.

Why do we never get what we want, why do we seem to go out of our way to pursue the opposite?

Shake yourself out of it, Kate, says Kate. It has to be made to work. Like marriage.

'We've got to think positive,' said Kate. 'We're letting it get on top of us. Some people aren't pulling their weight.'

And Tess sighs.

'I know,' she said. 'It's Louis. I knew he'd get through to you, sooner or later. He just thinks there's a good fairy around who does everything for him. Picks his dirty socks up and sprinkles elf dust over them and Hey Presto, they're back in his drawer smelling of soapflakes . . .'

'I don't just mean Louis.'

'Oh.'

'William's just as bad.'

And Tess could try harder, she thinks, but doesn't say; she needs one ally at least.

'He seems a bit distracted,' said Tess. 'Is anything the matter with him?'

'He's always distracted,' said Kate.

But he was worse than usual lately. Had been since his grandfather died. Kate wished now that she'd gone up with him for the funeral, but there'd been a crisis at the office. You couldn't just drop everything.

'It's down to you and me, Tess,' said Kate. '*They* won't do a thing. They'll just wallow in it, given half the chance. They live in a dream world, the pair of them.'

'I'll talk to him,' said Tess. 'But I don't know if it will do any good. He likes chaos. He says it helps him create.'

She put her head round the door of the Study on her way to the shower.

They called it the Study because they'd put all their desks in here and all their books. But the books were still unpacked in the cardboard boxes they'd used for the move and the desks were piled high with files and folders waiting to be organised and the only person who worked here was Louis.

His desk was in the best position in the room, just to one side of the window bay, and he was in the middle of a sentence.

Tess stood in the doorway watching him for a moment as he tapped away at his laptop. After a moment or so he looked up.

'Hi, sweetheart,' he said.

But she knew from the vague, distracted look in his eye that he was not really seeing her. He was seeing Starstruck of Stilton-Minor, or Elfinstrudle, or Moongirdle, Queen of the Outer Isles. A little thought alighted like a butterfly in the complex labyrinth of his mind and was netted before it flew away. He started typing again.

Slenderwraith descended the dark, dank steps of the dungeon carrying the sword of Gorefangle before her . . .

Louis in his dream world. Subterranean mythology, he called it. He said Jung would approve.

. . . and as she reached the bottom of the stone stairway it began to glow with an eerie intensity . . .

He was a serious student of Jung once, when she had met him. Now he wrote fantasy game books.

It's a living, Louis says, and it is, too, a good living, but that doesn't make it Real.

Some people are just playing at life, thinks Tess, who has never met William's nan and would be horrified to think they had anything in common.

. . . In the far corner of the cell, something moved. What was it, this crouching figure in the darkness? Was it Ashoran, her liege lord, Wizard Prince of Ulthuria? Or something else? Some loathsome creature of the Black Abbot's bestiary . . .?

From the doorway of the Study, Tess watches him, the dark, crouching shape bent over the green, glowing screen, her Wizard Prince. He does not see her. She watches him for a few moments as he types away and then raises her eyes beyond him to the great, black, uncurtained windows. A ghost image of the room floats in the darkness with Louis in one corner hunched over his crystal ball and herself in the middle, framed in the doorway, a slight, distant, vaguely anxious figure. Alice in the looking glass. And she feels vulnerable suddenly, as if she is on a stage and there is an unseen, hostile audience out there, looking in.

It's not going to work, she thinks, wearily.

But then, she never thought it would.

Plus ça change, but it's the same old fairy tale.

Except that she doesn't believe in fairies, any more, or handsome princes.

Read on, typed Louis, *or Turn to p.58.*

He filed it in memory.

Where to, now?

But something had disturbed his train of thought. He frowned and looked around, but the room was empty.

He glanced at his watch.

Time for a little something, he told himself in conscious parody. Pooh Bear with a rumbling tum. Mentally, he pictured the interior of the fridge, remembering it from his last visit, saw wine and cheese, a bowl of olives. Ah, a little fairy keeps filling it up as if by magic.

He was halfway across the hall when the front door opened and William came in.

'My dear fellow,' said Louis. 'What perfect timing. I was about to open a bottle of wine. What will it be? Red or white?'

William stared at him, as if he wondered who he was, as if he wondered if he'd walked into the wrong house by mistake.

In a bloody dream, thought Louis, as usual.

William took his wine up to the communal room on the first floor where the television lived.

The kids were watching a video.

'Daddy!' Edwin climbed up on the back of the couch and threw his arms round William's neck. Edwin always gave William a hug when he came in, whatever the competition, but how long would it last?

'What are you watching?' asked William, sitting down to watch with them.

'*Robin Hood*. He's a fox and Prince John's a lion and there's a snake called Sir Hiss.'

The sanitised version by Disney.

When he was a child William used to watch a different version which had seemed fairly sanitised but wasn't. It was subversive. It was a series called *Robin Hood and his Merrie Men* and it was on television every Saturday evening, and though William had not known it at the time it had been scripted by a load of American Lefties who had fled from the McCarthy witch hunt. They had subverted William and most of his generation into thinking you could rob the rich to help the poor and flout authority with impunity.

But they'd soon been put right.

He felt Kate's arms around his neck, smelling of soap.

'I didn't know you were in,' she said. 'Good day?'

'All right,' he said, squeezing her hand. 'You?'

'So–so . . .'

Louis came in and flopped into an armchair with his wine.

'What's this?' he said. 'More sex and violence?'

'Social banditry in the Middle Ages,' said William. 'It's very educative. There's a book that goes with it by Hobsbawm.'

Louis frowned at him as if he wasn't sure whether he meant it seriously or not. William grinned to reassure him.

'I usually set an essay for them afterwards,' he said. ' "The Peasant Outlaw in Feudal Society, Criminal or Freedom Fighter? Discuss." '

It was, in fact, the title of an essay he sometimes set for the first years, and there *was* a very good book on it by Hobsbawm which he recommended, but there had been a decline in interest of late. It was a bad time for social bandits and the Sheriff was winning all the battles.

Perhaps it was best left to Disney.

'I'm writing an essay for *Psychology* magazine,' declared Louis, with an air of modest achievement. 'It's called "The Collective Ideal in an Age of Predatory Individualism". What do you think?'

'Shhhhh,' hissed the kids.

'Good title,' whispered William.

Louis sipped his wine complacently.

'We've got to demonstrate that collectivism *can* work,' he said, 'provided the motivation is there.'

'We've got to have a House Meeting,' said Kate, an ominous presence in the background. 'It's time we organised a few things.'

'Shhhhhh,' hissed the kids.

'I know it's difficult for some people at the moment,' said Kate, in her best conciliatory tone, 'with work and all that . . .'

She did not look at William but the 'all that' was meant for him. Whatever it was.

'. . . but I really think we have to get some things done right away or we'll never really feel this is a proper home.'

They have convened around the dining-room table with the kids in bed and the supper plates cleared if not washed yet, only soaking in the bowl; it's Louis' turn in the kitchen and he's waiting for the fairies.

'We can't just let things drift,' said Kate.

Pity, thinks Louis, who quite likes Drift, or thinks he does. Decadence, decay, anarchy. Gormenghast in its final decline and the waters rising, Darcy Dancer's ancestral pile and the onion eaters digging at the foundations, and the cellar full of classic wines.

The house suits him like this, though the wine could be improved.

But he says nothing, for the time being.

'It's a question of where to start,' said Tess, with that slightly worried frown of hers.

'So we have to have priorities,' said Kate. 'All right, let's make a list. Now, we obviously need to get some essential building work done. We need new wiring, we need central heating, we need a lot of plumbing work and a lot of replastering. Then we need the whole place decorating.'

'Oh God,' said Tess.

'Well we knew this when we came in.'

Kate isn't going to stand for any nonsense. No defeatism. There's nothing you can't achieve given the collective will. But sometimes you need an individual to get it started.

'I've got a list of builders and decorators here. Shall we invite tenders?'

Everyone nods, easy decision that.

'But what about colours?' said Tess.

Tess is a designer. She designs exhibitions. Colours are important. They dictate atmosphere, mood. They are an indicator of personality.

Colours can be a problem.

'Well, obviously we paint our own rooms whatever colour we want . . .' said Kate.

Each couple has three private rooms which they can use as they like. They all agree that private space is important.

'But what about the other rooms?' said Tess.

She can't quite bring herself to say, the Communal Rooms, as Kate does.

'Well, I've got a load of colour charts here . . .'

Kate passes them round the table.

'This could take a long time,' said Tess.

It does. After half an hour they're still arguing and they haven't got past the entrance hall yet.

Tess wants shades of grey.

Kate wants yellow. A sunny aspect is important, she says, particularly when you come into a house.

Louis wants heavy embossed red wallpaper and red gloss banisters.

A dramatic entrance, that's what Louis wants.

William says he doesn't care, much, but then he looks at the colour charts and says he quite likes lilac.

Or green.

Or perhaps a combination of the two.

'I don't know if you've noticed,' said Kate, 'but it's already green and brown. I don't really think green and lilac would be that much of an improvement, do you?'

Finally they settle on magnolia.

Magnolia emulsion for the walls, white gloss for the paintwork and the banisters stripped bare.

'We'll end up painting the whole house bloody magnolia,' said Tess, who is not happy.

'It's called compromise, darling,' said Louis. 'Next business?'

'Curtains,' said Kate.

'Well we can't decide on curtains until we decide on what colour rooms we want,' said Tess, 'but I think we should put something up as a temporary measure. I keep on feeling people are looking in.'

'It's like being on a stage,' said Louis. 'I quite like it really.'

'Great for the burglars,' said Tess. 'And your laptop right in the window.'

She knows this will worry him and it does.

'Perhaps we were a bit hasty with the net curtains,' said William.

Kate gave him a withering look.

'It's only the Study we need to worry about,' said Louis. 'The rooms at the back aren't overlooked.'

'Except by the railway embankment,' said William.

They stared at him.

'What railway embankment?' said Kate.

'Sorry,' said William, 'I was thinking of somewhere else.'

Louis tried to catch Tess's eye but she was looking at the colour charts. Louis worries about William sometimes.

'What about the floors?' said Kate. 'I'm not talking about colours,' she added hastily, 'but are we going to get them stripped or have fitted carpets or what?'

'Carpets,' said Louis, decisively. 'I vote for carpets. Thick pile carpets in every room. Shag. Is that the word? I've always wanted a shag carpet. And I get to phone the shop. Two hundred metres of your finest shag, I'll say. Always wanted to say that. And we can fuck on the floor in front of a coal fire. Fancy that, Tess? Just like the good old days in your mum's house.'

Tess is from the class that goes in for thick pile carpets, though not, overtly, for fucking. Or so Louis maintains, who is not totally reliable on such things. Her father is a prosperous architect and her mother shops.

'Is that it?' she said. 'Have you finished?'

'Well, we must have carpets, my love. Deadens the sound, apart from anything else. Personally I don't give a shit, but you have to think of others. People are sensitive, aren't they, William?'

William is blushing, so he must be.

'Carpets and coal fires,' said Louis, 'that's what we need.'

'Let's get the essential work done first, shall we?' said Kate.

'All this is going to cost money,' said Tess.

'I know,' said Kate. 'And that's the other thing we have to talk about. We did say we'd try and get somebody else in. It's not only for the money. I think it would be good for us. We're just two families at the moment, sharing a house. Five people, I mean adults, or even six would make us a proper collective. It would bring in fresh impetus, more energy. And it would be better if we weren't so close to them. At present we're continuing with too many bad habits.'

Tess raises her cool eyes towards Louis, but he's keeping his head down, saying nothing.

'Anyone in mind?' said Tess.

She hopes Kate has a couple of hardened feminists tucked up her sleeve, battle trained at her Women's Centre and ready to be sicked on Louis every time he leaves a sock on the floor and to pin him to the kitchen sink with a half nelson.

But apparently she doesn't.

'Well, there is William's friend,' she says, with no particular enthusiasm in her voice, but a kind of resignation. 'Preston.'

They all look at William.

And William looks quite enthusiastic for a change.

'Yes,' he said, 'I think Preston would be a great idea.'

'But I thought he wasn't keen,' said Tess.

'He wasn't,' said William, 'but I think I've talked him round.'

18

The Refugee

The flood was all Preston needed.

He knew something was wrong when he opened the front door of his flat and smelt it. A kind of damp, mildewed smell, a smell of fungus ripening in a bog.

Then he opened the door of his sitting room and saw the ceiling on the floor.

'What can we say,' said the couple upstairs, 'except, of course, that we're extremely sorry.'

Preston had never liked the couple upstairs. They came back late at night in their TVR Vixen and made a vroom-vroom noise before they switched off the engine. They raced each other up the stairs. They were loud and boisterous in their love life.

At least, he assumed it was their love life.

He lay there awake sometimes listening to the noises, trying to work out what was going on. They didn't have fitted carpets to deaden the sound, that was the trouble.

The thing that really puzzled him was that when the banging and the shaking seemed to reach a climax, the man would shout, 'Jump!'

Then there'd be one final thud and it would go quiet.

He finally decided, after rejecting many alternatives, that it was a form of coitus interruptus. The man yelled 'Jump!' just when he was coming and the women hurled herself off him.

It wasn't entirely satisfactory as an explanation but he didn't suppose he'd ever get a better one and it wasn't the kind of thing you could ask.

All things considered, he wasn't surprised the ceiling fell in. The only surprise was the water.

They said they'd left the bath taps running and the bath had overflowed.

'We were soaking the bole of a tree,' said the woman, 'and we went away and forgot we'd left the taps on.'

'Ah,' said Preston, as if this made perfect sense. And perhaps it did to a woman who jumped to avoid conception.

'It's hollowed out,' said the man, 'and you put plants in it.'

'I see,' said Preston.

But they obviously thought he didn't.

'You have to completely immerse it in water,' the woman explained patiently, 'and then you fill it with soil and plants and you don't have to water them for weeks and weeks. It's wonderful if you go away a lot.'

She switched on a bright, charming smile.

'Doubtless the insurance will pay,' said the man. 'Yah?'

Preston couldn't risk having the twins for the weekend in case more bits fell down.

'I don't like issuing ultimatums, Preston,' said Polly, 'but if you don't sort yourself out soon we might have to go to Court.'

And then there was Emily and the abortion.

She'd had it while he was at the funeral.

'There was no reason for you to be there,' she told him, 'and I didn't want to wait any longer.'

He couldn't fault her reasoning and it was her decision, as he'd kept telling himself and her, but he felt dreadful about it.

He felt guilty. He felt he'd let her down. He felt he'd put his own needs before hers.

But he also felt a faint unease.

Call it what it was – what he felt was suspicion.

What if she hadn't had an abortion at all?

What if she hadn't even been pregnant, or she'd miscarried and hadn't told him?

He knew this was appalling. It made him feel even guiltier. It was an incredibly crass, mean, nasty thing to think.

But once he'd thought it, he couldn't get it out of his mind.

It didn't help that she wouldn't talk about it.

'But where did you go for it?' he said.

141

'Don't ask,' she said. 'I want to forget all about it. I want to forget it ever happened.'

And so it festered there, an ugly little pustule of doubt, growing bigger and uglier by the day.

What if she just wanted him to think she'd had an abortion to make him feel guilty? To punish him for not feeling love?

He was in a terrible state. He hated himself. What did he want her to do, bring him the aborted foetus? Would he believe her then? What right did he have to doubt her? Hadn't he done her enough mischief?

He saw her as much as she would let him. He lavished affection on her. He kept buying her flowers. He tried to give her a cheque for the abortion but she wouldn't take it.

He could not exculpate his guilt.

But there was something else, too. He was terrified she was going to move in with him. She kept saying how difficult it was at the flat, she was having a bad time with Brenda, she thought they were going to have an enormous bust-up any day now.

He could imagine the conversation where she suggested they find a place together. It makes sense, she would say. And he'd feel so guilty he wouldn't be able to say no.

He felt guilty about thinking this, too.

And then William phoned him.

'Have you thought about it?' he said. 'We need you in with us, Preston. We need you to make the chemistry work.'

So finally Preston said okay. Why not? It can't be any worse than it already is.

I need a refuge, thought Preston. I need walls up around me, I need ceilings that won't fall in.

'You need your head seeing to,' said Edward, his friend at the BBC.

Edward was a senior reporter on *Newsnight*. He and Preston had an alliance going against the rising stars of the Corporation but so far no one had noticed. They convened periodically at the BBC Club to swap calumnies and spread malicious rumours, but Edward had been off on an assignment in Prague and this was their first meeting for a while.

'A commune,' he marvelled, 'in this day and age. Have you heard what's happened to communism?'

'This isn't Eastern Europe,' said Preston, 'it's Clapham.'

'Ah,' said Edward. 'That should make all the difference.'

'Anyway, it's not a proper commune,' Preston confided, who wasn't sure yet what the rules were. 'It's just kind of sharing.'

'In my experience,' said Edward, 'the older you get the less sharing you want to do. That kind of sharing anyway. You want to have more control over your own life, not less.'

'Yes, but I don't seem to have any control,' said Preston. 'That's the point. I'm isolated. I'm vulnerable. I need a bit of collective security.'

But Edward shook his head.

'Show me any collective and I'll show you so many individuals all with their own individual hang-ups and at least one of them wanting to be Stalin,' he said. 'Call me a cynic, but don't say I didn't warn you.'

'I had to do something,' said Preston. 'It was getting desperate.'

'Talking of which,' said Edward, 'how's things in Religion now they've finally decided there isn't a God?'

'They haven't gone quite that far,' said Preston. 'They've just decided he isn't a member of the Church of England.'

But Edward had touched on another source of Preston's present misery. He wasn't sure he was doing enough to impress his head of department. There'd been one or two acid remarks, almost bordering on rebukes, about his lack of progress with the Devil documentary.

'She says I need more experts,' he complained to Edward. 'But that's not the problem. It's what they say about him.'

'Who?'

Edward's glass was nearly empty and he was trying to catch the eye of the barman.

'Satan,' said Preston. 'They all say different things. I'm just going round in circles.'

'I'm not surprised,' said Edward. 'An elusive character, Satan. Like this fucking barman. I say, Frank, when you've got a moment . . .'

143

That was the trouble, sighed Preston, no one took the Devil seriously.

'I need a Thesis,' he said. 'I need to make some kind of a Statement.'

But no one was listening.

'I'd better not have another drink,' said Preston. 'I've got to get round to the commune to talk about the conditions.'

Kate did most of the talking. Louis nodded emphatically at times, Tess looked faintly amused and William just sat and grinned whenever Preston glanced in his direction. Doubtless he meant it to be encouraging.

First she ran through the financial arrangements and the Get Out Clause.

'If anyone wants Out,' she said, 'they have to give six months' notice. In that time the rest of us can either, A: find someone to buy their share; B: buy it ourselves; or C: sell up the whole house.'

Preston nodded, but he was having trouble taking it all in. He kept on looking at the ceiling.

He'd been allocated a suite of rooms in the attic so he probably wouldn't have to worry about ceilings. Only the roof. There was a problem with a rotting floor, though, in his bathroom. Kate said they were going to do something about that, when they got the builders in.

He tried to concentrate.

'People can do what they like in their own space,' said Kate, 'within reason, but we have a Duty Roster for the communal areas for things like cleaning and tidying and washing dishes. And we take turns shopping and cooking. Is that all right?'

'Fine,' said Preston.

He kept saying that.

Or, 'That sounds reasonable.'

He wished he could think of something more intelligent to say.

'But don't you have a cleaner?'

It was the wrong thing. He knew as soon as he'd said it. He was looking at William and William's smile turned to glass. He

144

looked round the table, his own amiable beam feeling more and more like a grimace. Louis pursed his lips and looked as if he was scanning distant horizons for a sail. Kate frowned, Tess seemed to have something stuck in her throat.

'We decided not to have a cleaner,' said Kate.

Louis made a kind of Humph noise, not as good as Preston's nan's used to be, but getting there.

'It was felt,' said Kate, deliberately, 'that if we were a genuine collective we should clear up our own mess, not pay somebody to do it for us.'

'Except the dustmen, of course,' muttered Louis. 'And the carpet cleaners and the people we get in to clear the drains when they're blocked.'

'That's different,' said Kate, with an edge to her voice, 'as I said at the time.'

Oh God, thought Preston, the ceiling's about to go.

'There was a proposal to have a cleaner,' said William, nervously, 'but it was vetoed.'

'I should have explained,' said Kate, 'that if any member of the collective is violently opposed to something, say on political or moral grounds, even when everyone else wants it, they have a right of veto. We thought that was the only way it could possibly work.'

She glanced around the table as if daring anyone to contradict, but they didn't.

'What was all that about?' Preston asked William later when William took him for a tour of the garden before the light went.

'All what?' said William.

'You know, all that about the cleaner?'

'Ah, well, it was a bit of a bone of contention, that,' said William.

'So I gathered. But why?'

'Well, three of us wanted to get a cleaner in to do the areas we all share, but Kate wouldn't have it. She said it was exploitative.'

'It seems to have caused a bit of tension.'

'Well, it's Louis really. He's not very good at it. Cleaning up,

145

that is. And he's sort of making an issue of it. He skimps on his duties and kind of leaves things lying around.'

'What sort of things?'

'Well, socks and things.'

'I see.'

'It's a question of who's going to crack first. He thinks she will, and that she'll agree to get a cleaner in, but I'm not so sure about that.'

Nor was Preston.

'Wonderful,' he said.

'It's not putting you off is it?' said William, anxiously. 'It's only a small thing, it'll blow over. When you move in I'm sure it will ease things.'

'Are you?' said Preston.

But he couldn't back out now. He was committed.

Committed to an asylum for the criminally insane.

He looked up at the house. It looked a bit like an asylum with all those windows and drainpipes and a small leakage of steam from one of them. One of the windows even had bars across it, but he supposed that would be to stop the children from falling out. The twins would love it. All those rooms. All this garden.

'We've got to stick together,' said William. 'You and I.'

He moved in at the weekend. There wasn't much to move. The furniture went with the flat. He had a portable CD with a couple of speakers. He had about a hundred books he'd taken with him when Polly gave him the boot. He had some framed photographs of the twins, a trunk full of their toys, a typewriter and three suitcases full of clothes.

It all fitted into the back of a medium-sized family hatch-back.

He borrowed that from Polly.

'Is this it?' said William, when he came out to help carry it into the house.

'This is it,' said Preston.

He didn't know if he should feel depressed or liberated.

'I'll go out tomorrow,' he said, 'and buy some furniture from one of those big warehouse places that stay open on Sundays.'

'We can let you have some things,' said Kate. 'Don't rush into anything.'

She was very welcoming. They all were. Tess went out and came back with some flowers for his room and Louis and William went scavenging round the house and found him a bed and a chest of drawers, and they fixed a curtain rail across an alcove for him to hang his clothes on.

They hung a sheet across the window for a curtain.

'The sun comes pouring in on this side of the house in the mornings,' they said. They wanted him to like it.

'It's great,' said Preston.

He'd have probably said that anyway, but he meant it.

He began to relax. He hadn't come home – it wasn't quite like that, yet – but he'd found somewhere to rest for a while. That's what it felt like.

But he couldn't get rid of the feeling of being committed to some kind of institution. It was partly the Duty Roster on the notice board in the kitchen, and the way they designated the Communal Rooms as the Television Room and the Music Room and the Meeting Room and the Utility Room. But it was there also in the way they all padded around the place, he thought, as if they were always aware of intruding upon each other's personal territory. And they were so polite, almost deferential. They were always saying, 'Sorry,' or 'Excuse Me.' Or, 'Do You Mind?'

Perhaps it's just me, Preston wondered, it's because I'm new and I'm a stranger to some of them, but that was an aspect of the Institution, too. He was a New Inmate and they hadn't quite worked him out yet.

He liked them, though, and he hoped they liked him.

He'd taken a week off work to move in properly and paint his room and buy some things, and this gave him a chance to get to know them better. The Other Inmates.

Louis worked at home all the time, but Preston didn't see much of him, not to talk to. He was always in the Study, buried in his computer, and their conversations tended to be of an amiable but perfunctory nature while Louis was on his way backwards and forwards to the fridge. One evening they shared a bottle of wine before the others came home and Louis asked him a lot of questions about himself and William as children, but in a rather professional way. Preston felt as if he was being analysed. He didn't mind, in fact he rather enjoyed it, as people do, but he didn't feel he'd got to know Louis any better at the end of it.

Tess was even more difficult to pin down. Partly because she went away for a couple of days to a conference somewhere almost as soon as Preston moved in. She gave Preston the impression of being something of a supermum, efficient and organised and 'together'. She seemed kind and friendly and was given to sudden thoughtful gestures like the flowers, but he felt as if she was a bit distant, not in any cold or condescending way, but as if she was preoccupied. As if there was a part of her that was not properly engaged, but grappling with some inner problem that no one knew anything about, and she had a way of suddenly drifting out of the room, as if the solution had suddenly occurred to her and she needed to write it down while she remembered it. She had a computer in a room of her own somewhere upstairs that no one else ever went in. She said she couldn't work in the same room as Louis.

But it was difficult for him to think about Tess in any detached, objective way because of what she looked like. It wasn't a provocative sexiness, but a cool, almost careless beauty. She reminded him of a sixth-former he had known once, distantly, at a neighbouring girls' school, whom they'd all lusted over madly but didn't know how to approach. Inevitably they'd called her the Ice Maiden.

She emerged one evening from a bathroom as he came down the stairs from his attic, a long towel wrapped round her and another round her head, her shoulders bare, trailing a subtle scent of something wonderful, and smiled innocently at him. He'd felt a bit winded for a while.

But he didn't really talk to her. The person he talked to most was Kate.

There were hidden depths to Kate, he decided. She watched people a lot, and she listened. She had deep blue, almost violet eyes, and though he'd seen them glinting and striking sparks, there was a soft, easy warmth to them, too, at times. She mothered him a bit and he didn't mind it. He felt he needed a bit of mothering.

He'd always thought of her as very English, very middle class, a doctor's daughter from the Midlands, but her roots were Irish, she told him, and she seemed proud of it.

'But not Catholic,' she said, firmly. 'One Catholic in the family is quite enough.'

He assumed she meant William.

'But he's not practising, is he?' he said.

'He may not go to Mass but it's still there,' she said. 'All that superstition.'

She'd either forgotten he had the same Catholic upbringing, or didn't know, or didn't care, but he said nothing.

Her father, it turned out, had a strong prejudice against the Catholic Church, in spite of having been brought up a Catholic himself, or perhaps because of it.

She loved her father, she said, and she loved Ireland, too, for all that it was full of Catholics. She'd spent holidays as a child in the family home on Kinsale Head, a big, rugged old house on the cliffs, and he could imagine her there, with the wind blowing her hair, a wild tomboy, and was surprised he'd never seen that in her before.

She didn't talk about her mother much. 'She never really loved my father,' she said. 'She had three children by him but she never quite forgave him for not being more than he was.

'And I don't think I've ever forgiven her,' she added, thoughtfully, 'for not loving him.'

He'd thought living with Kate would be a bit of a problem, but it wasn't.

It was William who was the problem.

William, the one he knew best, the one he should have felt most at home with.

There was something going on with William. Something not quite right about him, something in his head.

It was difficult to pin down. Sometimes it was just the way he came into a room, almost shiftily, almost as if he'd been up to something and was afraid of being found out. Sometimes it was something he said, a cryptic statement, almost like a private joke which no one else could understand. At least, Preston assumed they didn't. Certainly no one ever laughed. They seemed vaguely embarrassed, and Kate irritated.

But on the whole, Preston felt he'd made the right decision. They'd moved all the kids into one bedroom to make space for him and he had the whole attic to himself. There were two fairly large rooms up there, and a bathroom which was officially designated a Communal Room, but no one else ever used it. There was little need, with two other bathrooms in the house, and there was a slight problem with the rotting floor. He did one room up as a bedroom for himself and the other for the twins when they came to stay at weekends. He bought a bunk bed for them and some children's furniture. He painted the walls blue and yellow and he hung up some of their things on the walls. Finally he splashed out on two wooden rocking horses, one for each of them. One was dapple grey with a white mane and tail made of real horse hair, the other more like one of the traditional fairground gallopers with lots of gold and red paint.

Preston liked the atmosphere in the attic. He liked the sloping garret ceilings with their odd corners and the view from the window across the other roofs to the Common. There were a lot of trees and they were just coming into leaf. Sometimes he'd go into the twins' room with a book while they were away during the week and just lie on the floor reading for an hour or so.

Kate helped him shop for the furniture and did most of the choosing. She didn't like the horses though. 'They've got glaring eyes,' she said. 'They look a bit mad.'

And she thought they were a ridiculous price.

She called them Preston's mad horses.

'You have to be careful what you put in a child's bedroom,' she said, when they left the shop. 'You can give them nightmares.'

'Do you think so?' said Preston. He was alarmed then.

'I hadn't thought of that,' he said. 'I suppose that's where the word comes from, too. Nightmares – female horses.'

But she shook her head.

'It comes from the Anglo-Saxon, *Mara*, meaning incubus,' she said, 'and that means a male demon who has sexual intercourse with women in their sleep. So you can't blame females. They're the victims, as usual.'

Preston was impressed.

'How do you know that?' he demanded.

'William told me,' she said. 'Need you ask?'

It was one of the things William *would* know.

'I worry about William, sometimes,' said Preston, not meaning to be too serious about it.

'So do I,' said Kate. And he had a feeling she was.

William knew a lot about nightmares, except the most important thing.

It was Louis who explained this to Preston, one day after he'd been to the fridge.

Preston was in the kitchen at the time doing his Duty for the Day, which was washing the dishes, and Louis took a bottle of wine out of the fridge and said, 'Fuck that. Come and have a drink.'

So they did, and Preston told him the story about the incubus. He thought he might be able to fit it into his Devil documentary and he wanted to know if Louis knew of any books he could read on the subject of the Devil and female sexual fantasies.

Louis was putting himself through analysis with the intention of becoming an analyst himself some day, so Preston thought he would be the right person to ask. But he said he didn't know anything about the Devil and though he knew quite a lot about female sexual fantasies, they had nothing to do with nightmares.

'More to do with wet dreams,' he said, and chuckled.

But then they started to discuss nightmares and he became more earnest. It was, after all, his subject.

'Stories that give you nightmares are good for you,' he argued. 'They're good for children, anyway. They're like an emetic. A natural way to expel hidden terrors. But it's very important that in the stories the goodies always win in the end.'

'Unlike real life,' said Preston.

'Ah, but they can learn this at a later age, gradually,' said Louis. 'The same way they grow into disillusionment with their parents and teachers. If it happens suddenly and too soon they become terrible pessimists, always expecting the baddies to win. That's the problem with William. William encountered a real-life nightmare when he was too young to make any sense of it. It made him

151

frightened and angry and desperately insecure. That's why he's hopeless with relationships.'

There was a lot to pick up on there, but Preston settled for, 'What nightmare?'

'Well, the sudden abandonment by his father,' said Louis, 'closely followed by the murder of his mother's best friend.'

Preston was surprised, and vaguely disconcerted, that Louis knew about all of that.

'One event would have been sufficient to throw him off balance,' Louis continued. 'The two together must have been devastating.'

'It was the same for me,' Preston confided, 'except that my father didn't run off with another woman. He died.'

'Ah,' said Louis, 'I didn't know.'

Is that why I'm hopeless with relationships, Preston wondered, a lot more hopeless than William, on the available evidence?

'You have a lot in common, you and William,' said Louis, 'don't you think?'

'We don't actually,' said Preston, resentfully. 'We just had the same nun who gave us Instruction.'

He meant it to be evasive, but Louis was interested and he found himself talking about Mother Bernard and the terrible legacy of guilt and superstition she'd left them.

'It's probably the same with all Catholics,' he said, 'but I think we had it particularly bad. And then there was William's grandad telling us we could never get away with anything, something was always going to get us in the end. No wonder we were paranoid.'

'So why didn't you like it,' said Louis, 'when I said you had a lot in common?'

Preston considered.

'Perhaps because I see certain flaws in William that I know I've got in myself,' he said. 'Certain . . . fears. Certain dark imaginings. Except that I think they're much worse in him. But then I would, wouldn't I.'

'Maybe he's your dark shadow,' said Louis.

But Preston didn't think he was being serious.

He thought he was just playing games.

19

The Adultery Department

The Demon had started as a game.

It's not *Real*, William told himself. *He's* not Real. I made him up. He doesn't really exist.

But he did, once.

Once upon a time, a long time ago, in a little village of no importance in the diocese of Winchester . . .

William's Demon was the plague priest, the randy rural cleric who had committed adultery with the wife of the steward of the manor and let the Evil out into the world and killed off half the population with bubonic plague.

Or thought he had.

And so hanged himself in his own church and descended into Hell, there to remain on the very bottom floor of Mother Bernard's department store, the pit of depravity, with all the other adulterers and their companions in crime, the murderers.

Until William conjured him up.

It had seemed more interesting to choose someone who had an identity. A history.

A good idea at the time.

But not now.

William was losing control.

It was as if the shadow game he had played as a child had gone badly wrong and the shadow had refused to diminish, to shrink back when he walked towards it, but had grown bigger and bigger and more and more threatening with every step.

And now the shadow had taken to springing out at him at times of its own choosing. It could initiate a dialogue.

'Adultery and murder,' the Demon mocked, as William swayed in the tube on his way home from work. 'Who are you trying to kid?'

William was considering a paper on the reasons why the two crimes were treated with equal severity by the medieval Church. 'The Violent Coupling', he planned to call it. It was his way of rationalising the subject, imposing some order on it – and the chaos it threatened.

'You're just trying to titillate,' said the Demon. 'Historical pornography, that's all it is. I've got the measure of you, my lad. Have done ever since I saw you on that embankment.'

'I only wanted to see her in the nude,' William protested. 'It's perfectly natural for a child of my age to want to . . .'

'I know what you wanted, you little shit,' said the Demon. 'And so did she. She knew you were out there, you know. That's why she didn't have any curtains up. She *wanted* you to watch her.'

'That's not true,' insisted William. 'And anyway, I didn't see her, did I.'

'*He* did, though, didn't he,' said the Demon, cunningly. 'He was your surrogate. He did it for you. He did what you'd have really liked to have done – with your sex and violence.'

'Oh . . . balls,' said William.

He'd taken to using crude language in these discussions, because he'd realised that there was nothing the Demon liked better than a lengthy reasoned argument. It kept the dialogue going, and he only existed when there was dialogue.

So far.

William got off the train and walked home in his usual trance, on automatic pilot, past the stand for six Hackney cabs and the row of shops and the corner pub where they'd discussed buying the house. He was level with the boarded-up laundry when a voice behind him said, 'Your turn to cook tonight.'

'Fuck off,' said William.

He thought it was the Demon, following him home, but it wasn't. It was Preston.

He looked surprised.

'God, I'm sorry,' said William. 'I didn't know it was you.'

'Who did you think it was?' asked Preston, curiously.

But William thought it prudent not to go into that. People worried about you if they knew you were talking to demons, even Preston.

'Oh, just some drunk who was pestering me,' he said. 'What did you say?'

'I said it was your turn to cook tonight. What are we having?'

William gave some thought to this as they walked up the road together.

'I suppose I could do my bean casserole,' he said, but then he frowned. 'Except that I haven't soaked any beans.'

'Thank God for that,' said Preston. 'We've had bean casserole every time it's your turn to cook. Can't you think of something else for a change?'

William was rather hurt.

'Don't you like my bean casserole?'

'I didn't mind the first time,' conceded Preston, 'once I'd stopped farting. But the novelty wears off when you've had it four weeks running.'

They turned the corner into their street.

'I suppose that's what the fleas felt about Manchurian marmot,' William brooded. But Preston wasn't listening. He had stopped dead in his tracks and was staring up the road. He looked a bit white.

'What's the matter?' said William.

Then he noticed the taxi outside the house and the woman standing on the pavement with the two suitcases.

20

Screams in the Night

'I had nowhere else to go,' said Emily. 'It's only for a few days.'

Brenda the bathroom designer had thrown her out.

'But why?' said Preston. 'What did you do?'

'What did *I* do? Why should it be *my* fault?'

'I meant what reason did she give?'

But Emily just shrugged and said it had been building up for some time.

'If you don't want me here,' she said, 'just say so and I'll go and find a hotel somewhere.'

'It's not me,' said Preston. 'I'm just a bit worried what the rest of the house will say about it.'

But to Preston's dismay, the rest of the house had very little to say about it.

'There's no rule against having people to stay,' Kate told him.

'You can do pretty much what you like in your own room,' said Louis, 'short of murder.'

'It could come to that,' said Preston darkly.

He caught them exchanging glances and was sorry he'd said it, but not as sorry as later when he and Emily were in bed and she rolled over to face the wall and muttered, 'I'm such a mess, I wish I was dead.'

'It's going to be all right,' he said, kissing the back of her head, but she didn't believe him and he certainly didn't believe himself. He imagined finding her in the morning in the bathroom, in a bath full of blood and water with both wrists slashed, or hanging from the ceiling light in the twins' bedroom. He'd made sure she was on the side of the bed nearest the wall so she'd have to climb over him to get out, and he stayed awake stroking her hair until he was sure she was asleep.

His own sleep barely sank beneath the waves of unease that slapped him half awake every half-hour or so to lie there in the dark, tense and fretful, listening for the slightest sound or movement beside him, until the sound he'd been waiting for all night finally slammed him into full alert at the darkest hour before the dawn, when he was least able to cope with it.

'Please,' he hissed urgently. 'Please, not here.'

But the low keening note rose a pitch and she began that awful rhythmic rocking motion.

'Please,' he begged. 'You'll wake the children.'

The next wail was almost a full-blooded shriek.

Preston groped for the light switch. She was lying on her back with her eyes wide and staring and her arms crossed tightly across her chest, rocking herself furiously from side to side.

'Shhh,' he crooned. 'It's all right, it's all right.'

But it wasn't. There was no expression in her eyes, not even terror, unless this was a terror so profound he did not recognise it. He didn't think she was awake, or, if she was, not in any rational sense.

He tried to hold her still, but she lashed out suddenly and caught him full on the nose with her fist.

It brought tears to his eyes, and when he put his hand up he felt blood. Large dark red blobs began to drop onto the duvet.

He jumped out of bed and ran around the room in small circles holding his nose and searching for a tissue. And then, as suddenly as it had started, the screaming and the rocking stopped. Emily turned over on her side, sighed, put her thumb in her mouth and went to sleep.

Preston didn't move for a minute, while the blood ran down his chin and neck and chest. Finally he began to back slowly away from the bed and towards the door.

He was halfway across the landing on his way to the bathroom when something made him look down the stairs.

157

The Other Inmates, all four of them, were gathered on the landing of the floor below in their dressing gowns, staring up at him.

Preston smiled through the blood and the tears.

'Gob a dose bleed,' he said. 'Sorry ib I woke oo.'

He carried on to the bathroom and closed the door behind him and sank down on to his knees and howled.

'Aaaaaaaaghhhhhhhh,' howled Preston as he pounded with his fists on the rotten floor of the attic bathroom.

And on the floor below Kate looked at Tess and Tess looked at Louis and Louis looked at William and Kate said, 'I think someone should go up and see if she's all right.'

'Well don't look at me,' said William.

But by now they all were.

'You're his friend,' said Tess.

'But she might be in the nude,' said William.

'She might be dead,' said Kate.

'She's very quiet,' said Louis.

In the end Kate and Tess went up together.

'She's asleep,' said Kate, when she came down. 'We could see her breathing.'

And they all went back to bed.

Preston detected a bit of an atmosphere at breakfast.

Kate and Tess were coolly polite, William was embarrassed. Only Louis and the kids seemed relaxed.

And Emily, of course, who looked positively glowing.

But Preston knew that even though he was the one with the swollen red nose and the dark rings under his eyes, he was forever damned as the Monster Who Made Women Scream in the Night.

He knew that somehow he had to put the record straight, but it wasn't an easy subject to raise, not over breakfast, and with Emily there, sipping placidly at her coffee and nibbling a piece of dry toast.

Everyone except him was in the usual morning frenzy, getting the kids off to playgroup or school or themselves off to work or all three. Preston had decided to work at home, typing up the

158

latest treatment for his Devil film, and by nine o'clock only he and Louis were left in the house.

He caught him in the Study before he switched on his computer.

'I expect you were a bit puzzled by all that business during the night,' he began.

'Not me,' said Louis, amiably, but not entirely convincingly. 'I assumed you were fucking. Bit difficult to sleep through, though. Is she always like that?'

'Fucking?' Preston was astonished. 'With that much noise?'

'Well, I assumed it was a multiple orgasm,' said Louis, knowledgeably, as if this was a commonplace phenomenon in his experience.

'A what?' said Preston. He was aware, once more, of the limitations of his sexual education.

'No? Oh well, none of my business, of course,' said Louis.

'Is that what you all thought?' said Preston.

'Well, Tess and Kate had other ideas. They always think the worst. But I said you'd be on the job.'

'Well, I wasn't,' said Preston, indignantly. 'I wasn't doing anything. It's some problem Emily has.'

He described the symptoms.

Louis looked thoughtful.

'Sounds like a panic attack,' he said. 'Have you tried using a paper bag?'

'What?' Preston stared at him, despairingly. 'What for?'

'To breathe in,' said Louis. 'Next time it happens try and get her to breathe deeply and regularly into a paper bag, so it expands and contracts. It invariably has a calming effect. Alternatively you could tell her to go and see her GP and get an oxygen mask, but I'd try the paper bag first.'

'You mean this is quite normal?'

'Well, I wouldn't call it normal, precisely,' said Louis, 'but then, what is? Does anything trigger it off?'

'I don't know,' said Preston, 'but it always happens in the middle of the night.'

'Often?' Louis looked mildly concerned for the first time in the conversation.

'Often enough,' said Preston. He thought they might have a House Meeting and tell him Emily would have to go. But then, his responsibility wouldn't end there. He must try and find her a flat.

But first he must find a paper bag.

This proved more difficult than he had anticipated. There were none in the house and you didn't get them in the shops any more, they were all plastic. Finally he had to buy one from a rather posh chemist's with a selection of Olde English Rose pot-pourri in it. He flushed the pot-pourri down the lavatory and practised breathing into the bag, but it didn't expand and contract the way he had imagined. Perhaps it was a bit on the large side, he thought, and the paper was a bit too stiff. But he folded it and stuck it under his pillow, thinking it was better than nothing.

He spent what was left of the day worrying about their relationship.

I don't want to get involved, he kept telling himself.

But he *was* involved. The problem was how to stop being involved.

He worried that he was using her as a sex object.

Sex with Emily *was* very good. He thought about it a lot. He'd never had such good sex.

But sex wasn't everything.

He worried about her husband. He didn't even know his name; Emily had never mentioned it. She always said 'He'. Preston thought of him simply as the Corsican.

He wondered where he was.

He drew up a balance sheet. In the plus column he wrote:

Strong Physical Attraction.
Great Sex.
I like her.

He thought about the 'I like her' for a moment. It was strange but he did, rather. He wondered why this was. Because she's warm, and kind, and generous, he thought. So he added 'Warm, Kind and Generous' to the list. Then he did the minus column:

Screaming Fits.
Highly Strung.
Neurotic.
Moody.
Suicidal Tendencies.
Background of Mental Problems.
Mad Corsican Husband.

It was no contest, really. But what could he do?

He couldn't just write her off because she had too many entries in the minus column. But why not? Other people did. They were doing it all the time.

He went into work after lunch and didn't get back until late. He found William in the kitchen washing dishes but there was no sign of anyone else.

'Seen Emily?' he enquired.

'She's in our bedroom,' said William, 'talking to Kate.'

He didn't seem too pleased about it. Nor was Preston. He didn't know why, but he felt decidedly uneasy at the thought of Emily having long private conversations with Kate.

He took himself off to the twins' bedroom with a book but found it difficult to concentrate. Finally he gave up and came downstairs again to watch television.

He didn't see Emily until he went to bed.

She was already there, sitting up, reading.

'How are you?' he said.

'Fine,' she said, brightly.

'What's the book?' he said.

It was *The Mill on the Floss* by George Eliot.

'Kate lent it to me,' she said.

'Ah.'

He sat on the bed to pull his shoes and socks off.

'Getting on all right with Kate?' he enquired, in what he hoped was the right casual tone.

'Yes,' she said. 'We had a nice long chat.'

'Ah,' he said.

He finished undressing and climbed in next to her.

'About anything in particular?'

'What?'

'Your chat with Kate.'

She looked at him. 'It wasn't about you,' she said, 'if that's what you were thinking.'

'I wasn't,' he said. 'It never crossed my mind.'

'Yes, it did,' she said, matter-of-factly. 'Men always think women are talking about them. But they're not. We were talking about books.'

He lay awake in the dark, too tense and restless and irritable to sleep, waiting for her to panic again. But she didn't. She slept soundly. Preston didn't. Every time he moved his head the paper bag rustled under the pillow.

21

The Hidden Room

'The best orgasms I ever had,' said Emily, 'were with a boy I went out with when I was in the sixth form, during my summer holidays, and we didn't even fuck.'

'They're always the best, aren't they,' said Kate, who was ten years older, and knew.

'Are they?' Emily seemed surprised.

'Oh, yes. I've always been sorry I moved on from heavy petting.' She amended this hastily. 'Apart from having Edwin, of course.'

Her eyes moved instinctively to where he was playing with the other children down the far end of the garden. There was a tree down there big enough to build a den in and a pond deep enough to drown in. The kids loved this part of the garden, which they called 'The Wildness', but Kate had less romantic feelings about it. The pond would have been filled in if she'd had her way, and the den rebuilt at ground level, but Louis had accused her at the House Meeting of 'being neurotic' and she'd given in for the time being.

It being Saturday, the twins were here and Preston in theory keeping an eye on them all, though he was actually reading a book, sitting on an old rusted garden roller by the pond. The voices of the five children drifted up to where the women sat at a table nearer the house, but the garden was big enough for them almost to feel that they were alone.

They kept their voices discreetly low, all the same.

'I rather missed out on heavy petting,' said Emily. 'Two short years and then it was all Bonk. Not that I don't like bonking,' she added, in case there was any misunderstanding about it. 'And you can have both.'

'Yes,' said Kate, but she didn't sound too sure about it. 'It's never been quite the same, though. Not for me, anyway.'

Emily studied her curiously with her cat's eyes.

'How long have you known William?' she enquired.

Kate wasn't quite sure she liked the sequence of thoughts.

'Since university,' she replied, cautiously.

'At Cambridge?'

'No. I didn't go to Cambridge. We met on the picket lines during the miners' strike. The one they won. In seventy-four.'

It seemed so long ago, and Emily would have been about seven or eight, she thought.

'It was a different world then,' she said. 'And we were different people, I think.'

She pictured herself as she'd been then, all anorak and enthusiasm, mittened hands clutching a home-made banner, crushed in among a large crowd of miners and students with the police trying to push them back off the road and a convoy of trucks coming up the hill towards them, strike-breakers hired by the Coal Board to bust the picket.

She remembered how cold it was. It never seemed to get that cold any more.

All those issues they'd had then, all those struggles they'd got involved in. Miners' pay and workers' control and US imperialism and Chile and human rights and CND and Greenham and Cruise missiles.

And now all they talked about was the weather. The Greenhouse Effect, the Ozone Layer, Global Warming.

'We were stamping our feet to keep them warm,' she told Emily, 'and he stamped on my foot by mistake and apologised. That's how we met.'

'I didn't know he was political,' said Emily.

'He wasn't. I was fooled by that. I thought he was a bit of a rebel. Then I discovered he was only rebelling against his mum.'

She remembered the trucks coming up the road and how they all surged forward, through the lines of police, and shouted, 'Out, out, out.'

And the trucks turned back and they all cheered and went to

the pub, and a few weeks later the government fell. It was like that in those days and all things seemed possible.

It was in the pub that she'd met William again. And he'd apologised again for standing on her foot. It was the beginning of a clumsy and apologetic courtship.

She did fancy him, though. He was tall and lean and darkly good-looking. There was also something about him, a kind of little-boy-lost quality. She'd always been a sucker for that. And as she'd got to know him she'd liked his sense of history, too, his knowledge, his obsession with detail. It was as if there was this great detective story about the past and the clues were all there but she'd never noticed them. He did. He showed her them, he opened them up, a distant, mysterious world. It seemed to speak to him, he was in harmony with it, he brought it alive for her, he made the shadows dance. She thought it was like magic.

Their first holiday together, they'd gone to France, camping in Provence, and they'd wandered round all those ancient cities and hill towns and he'd told her about the troubadours and the shepherd preachers who believed in powers of Darkness and of Light and the crusade against them by the Catholic Church, and the massacres and the Inquisition and the Terror.

Other men she'd known tried to be so cool, so *bored*, and they succeeded so well they *were* boring. William couldn't hide his fascination for things. His involvement. She loved it. She loved him for it.

Only later she realised he was only fascinated by *some* things, and they stopped somewhere round the year 1500. And later still she began to realise that his involvement in history was a means of escape from being involved in the present. In Real Life.

But by then, it was too late.

'The best sex I ever had with William,' she said, 'he didn't even touch me. It was in his room at college not long after we met, early summer. He'd brought these strawberries. We were having tea. You always had to have tea in his college, whatever else you had. And he very shyly asked me if I'd take all my clothes off and eat the strawberries in the nude, while he watched me.'

She lowered her voice even more, so Emily had to lean forward to hear her, mouth slightly parted, eyes bright with a child's curiosity.

'So I took all my clothes off and sat on his bed and ate the strawberries one by one from the punnet, and he just sat opposite me in this chair at his desk watching me.'

She sighed.

'And afterwards I tossed him off,' said Kate, who had always been a practical girl.

Emily laughed and leaned back and stretched in the sun.

'I love it out here,' she said after a moment. 'The garden's the best thing about this house.'

Kate looked round it, unconvinced. It was a wild, unruly 'Wildness' of bramble and unpruned fruit trees and climbing plants, and they must get round to taming it some time, imposing some kind of order. The only flowers, at least at this time of the year, were daffodils planted by some previous tenant and past their best now, dying in sombre ranks in the overgrown beds and the uncut grass.

'It certainly goes with the house,' said Kate. 'Like the Beast's garden, only no roses to pluck.'

Emily shivered and clasped her hands round her arms. She was wearing a thin cotton dress and not much under it.

'You want to go inside?' said Kate, solicitous of her welfare. She liked Emily. She knew she mothered her a bit. She was more satisfying to mother than Preston. And she needed it more.

But Emily shook her head, reluctant to disturb the mood.

'When did you meet the other two?' she asked.

'Tess and Louis?'

Emily nodded.

'Well, William and Tess met before any of us.'

'Did they?' Emily's voice rose a tone. 'Did they really?'

'Why? Does that surprise you?'

'No. No, not now I think about it. In fact . . .' But whatever it was she was going to say she thought better of it, and shook her head. 'How did they meet?'

'Well, Tess was at Cambridge. For a year after school. At some sort of crammer to do with the Cambridge entry, but in the end she didn't go there, she went to one of the London colleges. I don't know why, exactly. Anyway, that's when they met.'

'Did they go out together?'

'Not properly. I mean, I don't think they got to heavy petting.'

She looked at Emily, curiously.

'Did you think they did?'

'Well, I thought there was something . . .'

Her voice trailed off again, embarrassed.

Kate smiled.

'Well, not to my knowledge,' she said. 'And certainly not since.'

'Oh, I didn't mean . . .'

'I know. But you're right, they've always had a bit of a thing going, but William would never do anything about it. William thinks that if you commit adultery you go straight to Hell and spend the whole of eternity having little demons shove radishes up your bottom, so I should think the chances of him taking that kind of a risk are pretty minimal.'

'Radishes?'

'Apparently that was the punishment for adulterers in ancient Athens. They shoved a radish up your bum. William knows about things like that.'

'So how did you all meet? Did William and Tess keep in touch?'

'No. Not to my knowledge.' She wished she wouldn't keep saying that. 'Tess met Louis in London and they got married and came up to Cambridge when Louis came to do his PhD and she was pregnant with Alice.'

'So she met William again?'

'No. That was the odd thing about it. I met her. We met at NCT classes.'

'What?'

'NCT. National Childbirth Trust. I was pregnant with Edwin and we became friends. It was only later she discovered I was married to William and they'd known each other before.'

She still felt rather peeved about that. She'd liked Tess immediately. She was pleased with herself for finding a new friend and then it turned out she was William's friend first, and then Louis came into it, and they were Two Couples.

167

'I see,' said Emily, but she didn't seem to be interested any more.

They sat in silence for a while, gazing down the garden towards the children, and Kate noticed her shivering again and was about to insist they go in, or she at least fetch a jacket, when Tess called out to them from the kitchen and asked them if they'd like some wine.

'Great,' said Emily, and the sun came out from behind a cloud and she seemed to cheer up.

Tess brought a bottle and three glasses.

'Whose copy of Gramsci is it,' she enquired, whilst pouring, 'in the middle loo?'

Emily made a spluttering noise and Tess raised a puzzled eyebrow.

'Sorry? Did I say something funny?'

'I think Emily thinks we're a load of champagne socialists,' Kate explained. 'And that's one of the definitions.'

'Well, I just wondered,' said Tess, her voice rather brittle.

'I think it's probably Preston's,' said Emily. 'Gramsci's very in at the BBC.'

'And I noticed he's started using the middle loo lately,' said Kate, who'd had trouble getting in it. 'He's afraid of falling through the floor in his.'

Tess sighed.

'The whole place seems to be crumbling around us,' she complained.

Kate was recalled to her sense of duty.

'I'm still trying to pin down a builder,' she said. She'd been appointed I.C. Builders at the last House Meeting. 'There's this Women's Co-operative I heard about who are very good but they're booked up months in advance.'

'Well, frankly,' said Tess, 'I'd rather give feminism a miss on this one if it means waiting that long, and get a man in.'

Kate looked at her anxiously. Tess seemed to be a bit tense with her lately. She kept thinking she had to mend some bridges between them, but she didn't know how they'd come down. Perhaps they'd never built them. Builders. She seemed to think about nothing but builders these days.

168

'I'd get a man in,' she said, 'if I could find one.'

'Have you tried the Yellow Pages?'

'Yes. I've tried all the obvious places,' she said, coolly. 'It's a question of pinning them down to a time when they can come round and give us an estimate.'

'Don't you know any builders?' Emily asked Tess. 'Being a designer and all that.'

'Not those kind of builders,' said Tess, with an edge in her voice.

Kate winced.

'Anyway, let's change the subject,' she said. 'It only depresses me.'

But Tess was on her favourite hobby horse and it was raring to go.

'You'd think,' she said, 'that at least one of us would be able to do something. I mean, have you ever seen a more useless bunch? We hardly possess a single valuable human skill between us.'

'It depends what you mean by skill,' said Kate, cautiously, who knew this was aimed at Louis rather than the rest of them.

'I mean, the ordinary basic skills that enabled human beings to survive all those years,' said Tess. 'Like feeding themselves, clothing themselves and erecting a crude shelter. I mean, there's been God knows how many thousands of years of human progress, so-called, and here we are, helpless. We can't build, we can't sew, we can't grow our own food, we can't even replace a few rotten planks in a lavatory. What would happen to us if we were suddenly dumped in the desert somewhere?'

'We'd shit in the sand,' said Kate.

'We'd sit around whinging,' said Emily, cheerfully, 'until some-one turned up to rescue us. Like we do here.'

They both looked at her and then at each other. Tess raised her eyebrows fractionally.

'Is that what we seem like to you?' said Kate. 'God, how depressing. I don't want to be like that at all.'

Emily shrugged.

'You get by,' she said. 'You've got other skills.'

'But we're so useless,' said Kate. 'Tess is right. We're like that row of shops on the trendy side of the Common, with four art

169

galleries, three wine bars, two boutiques, a stripped pine warehouse and a deli. You can buy eighteen different types of salami and a designer belt, but try shopping for a can opener or a box of Tampax. We've lost touch with the basics. We can't do anything for ourselves, and we don't even know people who can.'

'That's because it's boring,' Emily said. 'And the people who can are boring.'

The two older women exchanged glances again.

'Emily,' said Kate, 'if you don't mind my saying so, that is not the attitude. That is precisely why we have lost touch with the working class.'

'Who?' said Emily.

'The builders, the plumbers, the electricians, the painters, the decorators, the man who comes to mend the fridge when it goes wrong – I hate to be sexist, but it invariably is a man. We don't know what they're *thinking* any more.'

'I'll tell you what they're thinking,' said Emily. 'They're thinking how much they can take you for.'

'God, you are so cynical,' said Kate, horrified. 'And so young.'

'She's got a point though,' said Tess, pouring more wine. 'That's why I'd rather we did it ourselves.'

'Well, that is a typical middle-class attitude,' said Kate. 'That is why we are so out of touch. That is why they all voted for Her for so long.'

'I knew we'd get on to politics,' said Tess, 'sooner or later.'

'But it's true,' said Kate. She felt as if she'd been prodded into her role as House Agitator and she rather resented it.

'We don't meet them, we don't talk to them, we don't get our message across to them . . .'

Tess smiled.

'Kate, I honestly don't think that if the man who mends the fridge spends half an hour in your company he is going to change his mind and vote for the Workers' Revolutionary Party, or whatever it is you're into at the moment. And frankly, I'd rather you didn't try to persuade him. I'd rather you just let him get on with mending the fridge.'

Kate stared at her angrily and the bile rose. She swallowed it back before she said something she'd regret.

170

'Now there is a picture of content,' said Louis, from the open door of the kitchen. 'Like one of those nineteenth-century French masterpieces. Three women at a table in a garden, a bottle of wine, the children in the background, playing up a tree. And a solitary man under it, watching over them, like a guardian angel.'

'He's reading a book, actually,' said Kate, tartly. 'If you mean Preston.'

But Louis was as immune to acerbity as he was to sarcasm, or scorn, or anything short of physical pain.

He ambled out on to the terrace with a piece of chicken he had found in the fridge and studied them appreciatively.

'I feel like a bit like a lion must,' he said, 'with the lionesses lying there in the sunshine and the cubs playing on the veldt.'

And Kate unsheathing her claws.

'Daddy,' yelled Alice, up the tree. 'Look at me, look at me. I'm higher than anyone.'

'Daddy, I want a pee,' wailed Ben, who was younger, and lower.

'Go find a flower and pee on that,' called Louis, from the kitchen.

'Your father's philosophy of life in a nutshell,' murmured Tess.

And Kate laughed and forgave her. It takes a man, she thought. She looked at Emily to share the joke, but Emily was staring up at the back of the house and frowning. Kate stopped laughing.

'What's the matter?' she demanded, anxiously following her gaze to see what latest problem she'd discovered.

'Well, I was just counting the windows,' said Emily, thoughtfully.

'Oh,' said Kate, puzzled. 'They're still all there, aren't they?'

There were rather a lot of windows at the back of the house, and they came in all shapes and sizes with no thought for symmetry or style. It all went into the front, the spirit of the age.

'Yes, but I think there's one too many.'

'What?'

'I mean, I'm sure there's one more than there is on the inside. On the first floor. Look, those two are the kids' bedroom, right? And then there's the skylight where the landing is, and then there's the bathroom and the Utility Room, but then there's that other little one at the end. See?' She pointed it out, a small, rather dingy window, slightly higher than the one next to it, rather like the window of a lavatory and almost as opaque.

'That *is* the Utility Room,' said Kate.

'But I'm sure it's only got one window,' said Emily.

'It must have two windows,' said Tess, trying to picture it from the inside.

But they were curious now. They went into the house and up the stairs and into the Utility Room. They called it that because the washing machines were up here, but they hadn't been plumbed in yet, and they just used it as a kind of store room for all the junk they couldn't fit anywhere else. They still washed their clothes down the launderette. All William's medieval prints were here, the ones Kate called his Hell and Damnation pictures from the cottage. No one would let him put them up in the Communal Areas and Kate wouldn't have them in the bedroom, they gave her the creeps.

Emily was right. There was only one window.

'Good God,' said Tess. 'There must be another room through there.'

She banged on the wall.

'Seems solid enough,' she said. 'It's not a partition.'

'Why did we never notice that window?' Kate couldn't get over it. 'And how come you did?' she said to Emily, almost accusingly.

Emily shrugged.

'But there can't be a room,' Kate objected. 'There's no door, there's no access.'

'Perhaps they had it bricked up,' said Emily.

'But why should they?'

'Perhaps they bricked someone up in there.'

She was doubtless being flippant, but Kate shivered.

'Don't,' she said.

They went out on to the landing and Tess knocked on the wall there, but that was solid too. They went into William and Kate's room.

'You know, now I come to think of it,' said Tess, 'I've always felt there was something wrong with the proportions of this house.'

'What do you mean?'

'Well, there's not as much room at the back as there is at the front. Downstairs it's the same. That dining room is really small, nothing like as wide as the living room, and they're the only two rooms on that side of the house.'

'Why did you never say anything?'

'Well, you don't think, do you. You don't come into a house and think there must be a bricked-in room somewhere.'

They all filed downstairs and into the dining room. It still had the old wallpaper – faded yellow roses on a creamy background.

Kate knocked on the wall.

'Get a shock if someone knocked back, wouldn't we,' said Tess.

'Little man been living in there for years,' said Emily. She raised her voice. 'Hello, little man.'

'Stop clowning around,' said Kate. 'This is serious.'

'What's serious?' said Preston.

He was standing in the kitchen doorway watching them.

Emily explained. While she was explaining William came in from shopping and she had to explain to him, too.

'Emily thinks there's a body in there,' said Tess, complacently.

'That's why we get those bad smells sometimes,' said Emily, who seemed to be enjoying herself.

Preston was feeling his way along the wall and knocking at regular intervals. As he reached the end the sound changed.

'Listen,' he said, 'that's not brick. That's plasterboard.'

Kate began to tear at the wallpaper, suddenly determined.

'Where's that sledgehammer?' she said.

'Shouldn't we have a House Meeting?' said Tess. She may have meant it ironically.

'We're all here,' said Kate. 'Get the sledgehammer.'

'Louis isn't,' said William.

'Oh, for God's sake,' said Kate. Sometimes she wished she wasn't a democrat.

And then a knife turned in her stomach and she remembered the kids.

'Preston,' she said. 'You've left the bloody kids.'

She ran then, panicking, seeing the body face down in the water, the broken figure at the bottom of the tree, but when she reached the garden they were all there, undrowned and in one piece and playing quite happily.

She called them in.

'Oh, Mum,' whined Edwin.

'Well, play nearer the house, then,' she said, but she felt foolish now.

When she went back inside they'd fetched Louis out from the study and he'd brought the sledgehammer.

After a few minutes there was a large hole in the wall and a lot of plaster dust. Louis stepped through.

'Christ Almighty,' he said. 'Come and look at this.'

They followed gingerly and found themselves in a passage about four feet wide. In the dim light that filtered through the dust they could see a staircase leading up.

Kate had brought a torch and she shone it up the stairs. There was a left turn at the top and a doorway.

Louis led the way, still clutching the sledgehammer.

The door was not locked and it opened into a small room, about twelve feet by six, with the tiny window Emily had noticed set high in the wall and a single black iron bedstead.

'Well,' said Louis, breaking a stunned silence, 'there's no bodies.'

He sounded slightly disappointed.

'What can it have been?'

'A bedroom? For the servants perhaps?' suggested Preston.

'Looks more like a prison,' said Emily.

'Well,' said Kate, 'you found it, Emily, you can have it.'

'Thanks a lot,' said Emily.

'Well, what *are* we going to do with it?'

'Guest room?' suggested Louis.

'For guests we don't like, you mean?'

'But why did they brick it up?' insisted William.

'Well, you're the historian, sunshine,' said Louis. 'You find out.'

But William shook his head.

'Too recent,' he said. 'Not my period.'

So in the end they decided that Preston should.

22

Couples

'I think we should brick it up again,' said William to Kate later
that night in bed, before they went to sleep.

'And pretend it isn't there?' said Kate, scathingly.

Typical, she thought.

'There's something about it,' said William. 'An atmosphere.'

'It'll be fine when it's decorated,' said Kate. 'Like the rest of
the house.'

She rolled over on to her side and switched out the light.

'Why did they brick it up?' said Louis, not for the first time.
'That's what I want to know.'

'It was probably something to do with the original builders,' said
Tess, wearily. She was tired and wanted to go to sleep. 'Someone
probably plastered over a door by mistake. Or for a joke.'

'You know your trouble?' said Louis. 'You've got no imagination.'

'You've got enough for both of us,' said Tess. 'Now close your
eyes and imagine you're asleep.'

'I don't think they love each other,' said Emily.

'Who don't?' said Preston. He lay in bed watching her at the
window. She had no clothes on and he had an erection.

'The other couples. Tess and Louis. William and Kate. I think
that's why they came here. Because they don't love each other.'

'Maybe they don't,' said Preston. It didn't bother him much at
the moment. Not like Emily did, standing naked in the window
and no curtains.

175

He was sure she'd put on weight, and it suited her.

She turned round and came over and sat on the bed and looked at him thoughtfully.

'Has William ever talked to you about Tess?' she asked.

'No,' said Preston, firmly, not wanting to talk about it. He wanted her to notice he had an erection and do something about it.

'I think he's got a thing about her,' said Emily. 'I think he's got it very bad and I think Kate knows it, and I'm pretty sure Louis knows it, too. I think probably the only one who doesn't know it is Tess.' She found his foot beneath the duvet and squeezed it. He kicked it free. He didn't want her squeezing his *foot*.

'What do *you* think?' she said.

'I think you're crazy,' said Preston. 'I think you live in a complete fantasy world.'

He grabbed her by the wrist and pulled her on top of him.

'I was right about the windows,' said Emily.

23

A Harmless Passion

It was all perfectly harmless, William told himself. A Perfectly Harmless Passion. He liked the sound of that, the juxtaposing of the two words, Harmless and Passion. To be safe but excited. To play with fire but not get burned.

It was not impossible, he told himself. You just had to stay in control.

And he was in control, totally in control. Or perhaps not totally, that's what made it exciting, like being on a horse and not knowing if it was going to run away with you, thought William, who had never been on a horse, only a donkey on Southport beach.

But nothing had happened and nothing would happen. It was a Perfectly Harmless Passion.

So why did he feel guilty?

Why did he feel he was being watched all the time?

He felt it now, sitting in the little Italian restaurant near the college which had been designated by them as the Usual Place. He was sitting alone at a table in the corner, waiting for her to join him and passing the time quite happily browsing through Morrell's *Medieval Torture and the Inquisition* when it suddenly came to him again, an awareness of being under observation.

It had happened several times in the past week and in all kinds of places; in the tube, in the pub after work, once in a supermarket. He'd be idly pursuing some train of thought, some obscure piece of history, or talking to one of his colleagues, or pushing his trolley around worrying about how much he was allowed to spend on breakfast cereal and which brand was ecologically sound and which one wasn't, when he'd have this strange conviction. It was like when you suddenly felt there was something wrong with you, but you couldn't pin it down, you just knew you felt a bit odd. He wondered if he *was* ill, but there was no specific pain, no dizzy fits, no inexplicable nausea. He even wondered if he was being followed, but that was ridiculous. And yet there *was* something. It was as if in the patchwork quilt of images and faces that crossed his vision over a period of several days there was a jarring but not instantly recognisable regularity.

When he felt it in the restaurant he began to look around for a possible cause. Not in any obvious way, he was quite careful about that. He propped Morrell's *Medieval Torture and the Inquisition* up against the large wooden pepper shaker in the centre of the table and pretended to be engrossed in making notes, but every now and again he swiftly raised his eyes and stared straight at one of the other diners hoping to catch them at it, watching him.

He thought he had once or twice. One or two people were looking decidedly shifty, he thought. He tried to recall if he'd seen them on any of his previous visits here, but he hadn't really been looking.

They had met here on four occasions since moving into the house, and the Italian waiters had started to treat them with an air of proprietorial complicity, as if they were all part of some delicate deceit.

And yet it was all so harmless. A Perfectly Harmless . . . He wished he could tell them that, except that it was quite agreeable in a way, being treated like that, quite exciting. Like it was part of the game.

'So why haven't you told Kate about it?' asked the Demon Father Robert, popping up on cue.

But he had an answer to that. He had met Tess before any of the others and therefore they had a special kind of relationship which he wished to preserve. It was important to maintain individual friendships and not have them expropriated as communal property. Of course he was attracted to her, always had been, he'd never tried to deceive himself about that, but he was in control of it, there was no problem.

He had it all worked out.

And then she appeared in the doorway of the restaurant, looking for him with that slightly apologetic air of always being late, which she was, always in a hurry to catch up on lost time. She wore a pale yellow dress, sandals, a large blue shoulder bag in some towelling material – she might have walked off the beach after a cooling swim, and William drowning, not waving.

A sudden performance of waiters descending on her like dolphins and whisking her to the table and making great play with chairs and napkins and bread baskets and swooping away again, leaving William nodding and rather breathless, as if he had just been *bounced*.

'Sorry I'm late but I've had a morning of meetings and you know what they're like . . . What on earth are you reading?'

She picked up Morrell's history.

'It's for a lecture,' he said. 'I'm just trying to find a good line . . .'

'For God's sake put it away,' she said. 'You'll put people off their lunch.'

He put it under his chair.

'Lunch is on me today,' she said. 'I've just cracked the Brighton job.'

'Really?' said William, wondering if this was something he should know about. He was never quite sure what Tess did. He knew it was something to do with Design and Exhibitions but that was about as far as his knowledge stretched. He thought it might be like shop-window dressing.

'Six weeks setting it up and it runs the whole of the summer,' she said. 'Isn't it great?'

'Great,' he said, and then the dolphins came back and there was more splashing and swooping, and when they'd gone he had a large glass of wine in front of him and a small green bottle of aqua minerale and he'd ordered a pizza that cost an extra 10p to help save Venice.

'Will you stay down there?' he asked. He began to pick at the bread nervously.

'Oh, I don't think so. It's easy enough to commute. Though I suppose I could a bit, during the school holidays, and leave the kids with my mother . . .'

'I'd have thought you'd jump at the excuse to stay away,' he said. She looked sharply at him and he added hastily, 'with the house in the state it's in . . .'

They'd finally got the builders in and the house was barely habitable. Communal meals had ended with the disappearance of most of the dining room. They ate their meals individually now, or in family units, huddled in their rooms as if in a state of siege. House Meetings resembled on-site inspections, when they'd gather around a hole in the floor, or under a pair of step ladders and a plank. No decision had yet been made about Emily's discovery. In typical house parlance it was known as the Hidden Room.

'I thought you meant because of Louis,' said Tess.

And William blushed, because he had.

'The way things are between us at the moment, I think the longer I'm away the better,' she said.

William hated it when she talked about Louis like this, but he didn't know how to stop it. It had become part of the ritual of lunch together and it was threatening to become the main topic of conversation. There was even a strong possibility, he conceded, that the sole purpose of these lunches, so far as she was concerned, was for her to whinge about Louis. Perhaps she hoped he'd intercede for her, persuade him to mend his ways.

'Perhaps it's the house,' he said. 'Perhaps you were better off when it was just the two of you and the kids.'

'Oh, come on,' she said. 'You know what we were like. We came into the house mainly because we couldn't continue living as a couple.'

William maintained what he thought of as a diplomatic silence. He was helped by the arrival of the waiters again with their food but it didn't divert the conversation.

Louis had proved impervious to what Tess had hoped would be the civilising effect of living with other people beside herself. If anything, he was worse.

'He just thinks there's more people to clean up after him,' she complained.

But Louis' slobbishness was only a small part of the problem.

'He's just a visitor,' she told William. 'He has no emotional commitment. He just drops in when he feels like it. God knows where he is the rest of the time. He could have another woman, for all I know. He could have lots of other women, he could have an entire family.'

She was watching William carefully for clues but he shook his head, because he really didn't have any. But he'd always thought of Louis as a bit of a womaniser. Wonderful word that, he thought, a womaniser. Would he like to be a womaniser?

'Try it and see,' said the Demon.

He had a sudden mental image of Louis ambling happily between women, looking at his watch and frowning when he remembered he should be with the next one, the way he did sometimes when he thought it was time for a little something from the fridge.

'I don't think I'd care,' said Tess, 'that's the thing. Mind you, I'd be pretty pissed off about the way he's treated me all these years if he did have someone else.'

William knew now that Louis was going to dominate the lunch, as he invariably did. He sighed.

'Well, I don't expect you to say anything,' said Tess. 'You're his friend, after all.'

'I honestly don't know,' protested William. 'And anyway, I'm more your friend than his.'

'Yes, but you're the same sex, you're bound to sympathise with him. I know what you're all like. You feel so trapped . . .'

She was teasing him now, because he'd said that to her the last time they had lunch together – how he felt trapped and couldn't do anything about it because of Edwin. It had been worrying him ever since, because he loved Edwin more than anything in the world and it seemed to be tempting fate. He felt it was unfair of her to tease him with it.

'I'm sorry,' she said, 'but it's true. Men have always got this, "*If it wasn't for you*" thing. It makes them feel they'd be so adventurous if they weren't tied down by responsibilities. It makes me sick. I think I will stay away,' she said. 'It'll do me good.'

Then, surprisingly, she changed the subject and they talked, more agreeably to William, about other things, and drank their way through a bottle of wine with the meal and ordered more when it was finished. But then, inevitably, the conversation drifted back to Louis.

'We always have to do things his way,' said Tess, 'have you noticed? If I want anything different he just refuses to take me seriously. He used to try to ridicule me out of it, but lately he's got more vicious – '

'Oh, hardly vicious,' William was moved to protest, but he knew that Louis' teasing banter, always an irritant with Tess, had developed a sharp, cutting edge of late. It was close to being mean, almost cruel. William wondered if it did have something to do with the house, as if the minor flaws in Louis' personality had swollen out of proportion since the move and left no room for anything else.

Tess suddenly turned and looked around the restaurant, as if she was searching for somebody.

'What's the matter?' he said, alarmed without knowing why.

'I was looking to see if I was missing something,' she said. 'You keep looking past me at the door.'

'Do I?' he said. 'I'm sorry.'

'You're not expecting anyone?'

'Of course not.'

He caught her eye for a dangerous moment and then looked away. Not at the door.

'I suppose we're both pretty selfish,' she said. 'One of us always has to give way. At first, when we met, it was always me, that's how I kept us together. But he started to take it for granted, and I don't know that I'm that bothered any more what happens to us.'

'Perhaps you should do something that will stop him taking you for granted,' said William.

He wasn't really thinking about it. He was thinking how wonderful she looked. She had a way of pushing her hair back from her forehead with one hand and holding it there while she was talking with one long strand falling down her cheek. It made her look very young and vulnerable. He suspected it was something of a pose but it was no less attractive to him for that. It was so unlike Kate, who never posed, but was always so practical, so down to earth.

'You're right,' said Tess, 'I should. I should have an affair, that would soon sort him out.'

182

William was seriously alarmed.

'Oh, I shouldn't do that,' he said, panicking.

'Oh, I shouldn't do that,' she mimicked, mischief in her eyes, and William had to look away again.

Outside, the city had seized up in a midday traffic jam and the cabbies nailed and expiring in their black coffins and only the cycle messengers moving through it all, like quick darting fish in multi-coloured wet suits.

'Looks hot out there,' said William.

'The trouble is,' said Tess, 'the only person I want to have an affair with is you.'

They emerged into bright sunshine and the city, still in a coma.

'Did I shock you?' she said, inserting her arm chummily through his.

William said no, not at all. But he was lying. He felt pole-axed.

And then he took a deep breath and stopped walking and turned to face her.

'I feel the same way,' he said.

She let go of his arm and looked up at him, frowning with her schoolgirl look, as though puzzling over her homework. She pushed her hair back again with her hand.

'But there's nothing we can do about it,' he said.

'No,' she said, thoughtfully.

Or was it 'No?'.

'We'll just have to keep it as a kind of fantasy,' he said.

'I've had enough of fantasies with Louis,' she said.

William bent forward and kissed her, not for the first time, but the first time on the lips, and he half meant it to be a brotherly kiss but it wasn't; it wasn't Passion precisely, but it wasn't Harmless either.

And he could not stop himself from looking around immediately in case someone was watching.

It was a bit of a jolt to find that someone was.

24

The Urban Survivors

And Louis sits in a corner of his dark den killing off Threats on his computer.

It is dark because Louis has found some ancient shutters in the cellar and propped them up against the window to keep the light out. On bright sunny days Louis finds it hard to read the words on the screen.

But otherwise the study is almost as it was when they first moved in, with the books and the newspapers and the files stacked in great heaps on the floor, and all the better for it, in Louis' opinion, who resists Kate's sallies with the tenacity of Byzantium defending its hegemony against the Turk. The shutters are grimy with dirt and grim with cobwebs, and beams of light pierce the gaps like the spears of an invading army.

Louis likes chaos. Chaos is good for creation.

He is working on a new game. It is called *Master of the Labyrinth*. The player has to journey through a series of subterranean caverns, each containing a complicated eco-structure of plants and creatures, some dangerous, some helpful, some harmless. Through the computer, the player has to analyse each life-form and decide whether to kill it, leave it alone, or put it in his collecting bag and take it with him in the hope that it will prove useful. The safest thing is to kill everything that seems vaguely alarming, but if you do that, you risk destroying the whole delicate balance of the environment. Also, something you kill instead of collecting might otherwise have enabled you to kill something that would otherwise kill *you*.

The subtlety of the game is that it is not just about winning.

When the game is over, assuming you have survived, the computer gives you an Ecological Grading. The top grade is Master of the Labyrinth. That goes to the player who has made all the right judgements and overcome all the Threats *and* succeeded in improving the environment. The player who has killed everything and avoided being killed himself but left an ecological wasteland is designated a Dangerous Primitive. The player who just about survives without doing any damage is designated Harmless.

Louis thinks it is just right for the current political climate. He intends to market it as 'An Ecological Adventure'.

This is the first test run and Louis isn't doing too badly. A couple of cave bears have been annihilated without noticeable detriment to the balance of nature and now he is confronted with a faintly glowing fungus clinging to the walls of the tunnel.

He taps out the code for Analyse and peers at the information as it appears on the screen, and decides, on balance, and after due consideration, to leave it alone.

The street was empty. Empty, at least, of any apparent threat. But how could you be sure?

William watched his unknown neighbours dribbling home from work, torpid in the unaccustomed heat of the early evening, and exposed each of them to a rigorous observation, and did not perceive in them any degree of menace.

But nor could he categorise them with any confidence as entirely harmless.

William was deeply troubled.

The trouble is, the only person I want to have an affair with is you.

Those words assailed his mind like a battering ram, pounding away at the few pathetic defences he had. He could think of little else, except one thing, and that was disturbingly related: the thought of the man who had been watching them when they came out of the restaurant.

He was a tall, well-built man probably in his late fifties and their eyes had met for an instant only, but in that instant William had seen recognition. Or something. Something more than neutral curiosity, anyway, at the sight of a couple kissing in the street. And then he'd turned quickly away and started walking in the opposite direction.

William kept reminding himself of the incident because he wanted to keep it sharp in his mind and it kept fading. He was beginning to doubt if the figure was real. Or perhaps he had imagined the expression on the man's face. Perhaps it was all some deep projection of his guilt?

When he reached the house he pretended to inspect the privet, as if for leaf rot, but really he was inspecting the street for hidden watchers. But there were none. None he could see, anyway. He went in.

Kate was in the kitchen staring into the sink. She was wearing a bra and a pair of thin pants.

There was something William had meant to ask her but he was temporarily distracted.

'Look at that,' she said.

William peered over her shoulder.

The sink contained a plastic washing-up bowl filled with dirty dishes and soupy water with a scum of grease and food floating on the surface.

'Excuse me?' said William.

'Well, look at it.'

William gathered that Kate was not pleased.

'Whose turn is it to wash up?' enquired William, hoping it wasn't his.

'That's not the point,' said Kate. 'For God's sake, what good is it leaving the damn things in the water?'

'That's Louis,' explained William, with relief. 'He always does it. He says it takes the grease off.'

'Oh yes?' said Kate, who must know it was Louis. 'And what else does he think happens to them in there? I mean, by what chemical or mystical process does he think they are washed and dried and put back in the cupboard?'

'I expect he thinks that's done by the person whose turn it is to wash the dishes,' said William helpfully.

'But it's foul. Look at it. Why doesn't he just stack them neatly on the draining board?'

'I don't know, Kate,' said William, trying to edge past her into the garden.

'Men,' said Kate, unfairly, in William's opinion, Louis being in a quite different category. Now if she had said, 'Trolls.'

'And another thing,' said Kate, pulling him up short a step or two from the open door and the sunlight. 'Why is it that none of you can ever finish anything?'

'Excuse me?'

'Why is it that you always leave one dish dirty, or you never Hoover under one chair? I mean, is it some kind of statement? Are you trying to say, Look how good I've been, I nearly did it right this time, or what?'

William pretended to think about this, frowning, because he didn't know what to say, except, 'Excuse me?' again, and he knew this irritated her.

'Or is it some kind of protest? Are you trying to say you shouldn't be doing this, really, it's not macho enough for you?'

'I'm sorry, Kate,' said William, but he was beginning to get annoyed now. 'Is something upsetting you?'

If Kate didn't say Humph, her look did, and far more eloquently. She began to wash the dishes.

'Why aren't you wearing any clothes?' William enquired.

'Because it's hot,' she said.

'Not bothered about the builders, then?'

'The builders are not here,' she said, through a suggestion of clenched teeth. 'Apparently they have not been here all day.'

'Oh. Why not?'

It was obvious, even to William, that they hadn't finished.

'I don't know,' said Kate. 'Perhaps you'd care to phone them and find out. Or do I have to do everything in this house?'

William wandered out into the garden thinking about bottoms.

Some bottoms were peaches and some were apples and some were pears. Tess was in the apple category. Kate somewhere between a peach and a pear.

'Daddy, Daddy.' Edwin came running up the lawn for a hug.

He was in his swimming trunks and wet from the plastic paddling pool where he'd been playing with Ben and Alice.

Here is Daddy, home from work, William thought, and his wife near naked in the kitchen and his son jumping up into his arms smelling wonderfully of sunshine and warm earth.

And the worm Adultery writhing restless in William's breast.

Then he noticed, with a jolt, another bottom. He thought it was Tess's for a moment, but it wasn't. It was Emily's, but it was definitely an apple, and in even thinner knickers than Kate's.

She was lying face down on a rug on the lawn reading a book, but she twisted round at his approach and said, 'Hello.'

She wasn't wearing anything on top.

'Hello,' said William, not quite knowing where to look. He settled for shading his eyes and looking at the sky.

'Fabulous day,' he said.

He'd seen enough, though, and very nice too. His eyes hurt after a while, looking at the sky, and he settled for the end of the garden where the children were playing. He couldn't help but be aware of Emily, though, nearer to hand. She'd seemed such a slip of a girl, too, he thought, with clothes on.

He must stop this, he really must. There'd been quite enough of this for one day.

'Preston home?' he said.

'Not yet,' she said. 'I knocked off early.'

'Ah, yes, very wise,' he said. He sounded like her bloody uncle. Or her grandad.

'Fancy a beer?' he said, briskly, as if she was one of the chaps.

But Oh God, that meant he'd have to hand it to her.

'Thank you,' she said. 'That'd be great.'

Kate was still in the kitchen, still washing dishes.

William remembered what it was he'd meant to ask her.

'Kate,' he began, cautiously. 'You know I told you about my grandad being worried about a man who'd been to prison?'

She turned to look at him.

'Yes?'

It wasn't an encouraging response, but he persevered.

'Well, you couldn't find out what happened to him for me, could you? I mean, through the probation service or something?'

'What do you mean?'

'Well, whether he's still in prison or, if they let him out, what happened to him, where he is, what he's doing, that sort of thing.'

'Why do you want to know?'

She wore an expression he had come to recognise if not precisely define. Sort of cautious professional concern. The way he imagined doctors in mental hospitals looked at patients who might turn out to be seriously disturbed.

'Is it worrying you?'

'No, no, not me. Not *worrying* me. I was just curious, that's all.'

She shook her head.

'Well, I'm afraid I can't help you. I'd need a good reason to get that kind of information, and I haven't got one, and I'm not sure who'd tell me even if I did.'

'Oh well, it isn't important.'

He got the beer out of the fridge.

Emily stretched out on the rug and felt the sun on her back and lost herself in George Eliot.

Our life is determined for us – and it makes the mind very free when we give up wishing and only think of bearing what is laid upon us and doing what is given us to do.

Emily felt a strong sense of identification with Maggie Tulliver, but she was beginning to feel irritated with her. She hated this acceptance thing. She could see it all ending in tears and most of them would be Maggie's, she suspected, and though she knew it wasn't Maggie's fault, she wished she wouldn't be so co-operative. Fight it, she thought, fight *them*. Don't just let it *happen* to you.

Something was happening to Emily. She didn't know quite what it was yet, but it felt quite positive. She felt as if one phase of her life was over and another was about to begin, and this was the period in between when she was lying low, in the chrysalis, and it felt good. She was in no hurry to move on.

She'd felt good most of the time since moving into the house. She liked having the other people around, it felt comforting, even if they were a bit mad, some of them. She liked Kate very much. Unlike the others, Kate seemed entirely sane. She'd had lots of good talks with Kate. She'd told her about the abortions and the

189

crazy marriage and the breakdowns, and even about the terrible times in the middle of the night when the screaming came on her. Kate told her it wasn't all that unusual. She called them anxiety attacks. She said the cause probably went back to something in her infancy, something far too deep to remember. All she could do was try to fight them when she felt them coming on. Breathe deeply and regularly, try to think of something relaxing or funny, or anything, until it passed. Try not to be frightened of them. Kate made her feel that some of the things that had happened to her hadn't been entirely her fault. She'd been a little too eager for experience, that was all, and she hadn't had the resources to cope with all of it. But it wasn't just because she was a stupid idiot, like she thought she was sometimes. Some things just happened, like they did to Maggie Tulliver, like they had to George Eliot, but it didn't mean you had to lie down and accept it, it didn't mean you shouldn't fight back.

Emily was learning to fight back.

In the meantime she felt an almost catlike content with being here. She felt she had come into the cave and, like the cat in the *Just So Stories*, she loved the warmth, she loved the company, but she walked alone. There was something deeply satisfying in that.

She even had an appetite. She was eating more than she'd ever eaten in her life before, and getting fatter and sleeker and stronger. This was partly because she felt more secure, having other people in the cave with her, but it was also because she looked at the people and didn't feel weaker than them. They had partners and children and good jobs and money and *resources*, but they were vulnerable, too, and in ways she didn't think she was. She knew, deep down, that she was a survivor, and she wasn't sure they were.

The only nagging problem was how long she'd be able to stay. She knew Preston wouldn't actually throw her out on the streets, but she knew, too, that he didn't want her here.

Oh, he wanted her physically, sure, he wanted her body, but he didn't want anything else particularly. That had made her unhappy once, but it didn't any more. She was broadening her base. There has to be more to life than a man, Kate said.

She wondered what was going on inside Preston sometimes. She'd thought *she* was neurotic, but my God, *him* . . . He was so neurotic it was weird. He worried about the most peculiar things. Things she'd never dream of worrying about. Like this thing about being torn to pieces by Rottweilers. Well, all right, it was a risk, like flying, or travelling on the underground, but you didn't spend your whole life worrying about things like that, the way Preston did.

He thought you were crazy if you didn't.

He was always doing really weird things, and when he explained about them, when he told her the 'thought-process' that lay behind them, she thought he was weirder than ever. Like when they were going for a walk in the Common with the twins and he took this steel comb out of the drawer and pushed it under the lining in his shoe.

'Excuse me,' she said. 'What's with the comb?'

'It's in case we get attacked,' he said.

He had the grace to seem a bit embarrassed about it.

'Attacked by what?' she said.

'A dog,' he said. 'A Rottweiler, or a pit bull. Or even a cocker spaniel. Apparently they're the worst. They get things called Avalanches of Rage.'

'So when this pit bull terrier or cocker spaniel or whatever attacks us, you're going to jump on its back and comb its hair?' she said. 'Does this have a calming effect or something?'

'No,' he said, 'it's for cutting their throats.'

'I see,' she said.

She seriously wondered about Preston sometimes.

'I've filed the teeth down so they're razor sharp,' he explained.

'Wouldn't a knife be more convenient?' she asked him.

'Probably,' he said, 'but they're illegal.'

'But why in the shoe?' she said. 'Why not the pocket?'

He looked at her in surprise.

'Because it rips the lining,' he said.

'Ah, of course. Silly me. What does it do to your foot?'

'Well, it's not so bad in your shoe because it lies flat. It just makes you limp a bit.'

Mad, absolutely barking.

And then there was this paper bag she'd found under his pillow. She hadn't asked him about that yet.

She'd thought at first it might have been because he was feeling sick one night and put it there for emergencies, though why he didn't use a bucket like anyone else . . .

But they changed the bed linen and she checked the next night and it was still there.

Perhaps it was some kind of comfort, she thought. Perhaps he couldn't sleep without it.

She didn't like to ask him about it in case he told her something that made her realise he really *was* crazy.

'There you go.'

She looked round and there was William with her beer.

'Thank you,' she said. She smiled at him and sat up, tucking her legs under her.

He was trying not to look at her tits.

'How's rats, lice and history?' she said.

There was a sudden cry from inside the house.

William spilt his beer. Emily jumped up and would have run inside, but then it came again, and it was not so much a scream as a roar of rage, and a moment later Louis appeared in the french windows that opened out from the kids' playroom.

His fists were clenched and his face wild.

'Harmless,' he shouted at them in a voice high with incredulity. 'Me? Harmless?'

Kate came out of the kitchen door and glared at him, and Louis glared back at her as if it was all her fault.

They looked, Emily thought, like those figures in the weather house who tell you if it's going to rain or shine, appearing together for once and not knowing quite what to make of each other.

'Harmless.' It was more of a growl now. 'I'll show them who's Harmless.'

He turned his back on them and retired once more into the darkness of his cave.

Mad as a rat, thought Emily, stark, staring, the lot of them.

She raised her eyebrows at William.

'What was that about?' she said.

'I don't know,' he said. He looked a bit shaken.

'You've gone all white,' she said.

'I thought someone was hurt,' he said. He sat down at the table with his beer.

Emily shrugged.

'Who's turn is it to cook supper tonight?' asked Emily.

25

The Last Supper

Here is Louis in the kitchen cutting up cucumbers.

There are radishes, too, but Louis does not cut them. Louis likes his radishes whole. When Louis is chef of the day a number of sub-chefs are required to do the menial tasks, like the washing and the peeling and the setting of the table. Louis is a good cook, an artist. The kitchen is his palette and it is inevitably going to get messy and somebody else will naturally clean it up. An artist can only do so much.

Preston has been given the job of slicing up onions and chopping up carrots and crushing up garlic. He weeps over the chopping board in a corner of the kitchen. William is setting the table, outside on the terrace because the evening is warm and, the theory goes, they will be able to eat without getting dust in their mouths. It is their first communal meal together for a fortnight.

Louis, the Cook, drains the fat from the red snapper that is frying in the frying pan and pours a cocktail of white wine and vinegar and cayenne over the top of it. He snaps his fingers for Preston's vegetables and adds them to the pan with a sprinkling of allspice and leaves it to simmer. This is for starters.

Pudding is in the fridge. Homemade vanilla ice-cream with a sauce of mangos and bananas mashed with pineapple juice, which Louis says is a Nigerian dish and no one is arguing. Louis spent much of his childhood in Nigeria. The recipe, he says, was written out for him on a piece of paper, by the family cook.

The main dish is in the oven. An English dish from the West Country, Roast Saddle of Lamb with Plum Sauce. No one wrote this recipe for Louis, he had to find it in a cookery book, of which he has an impressive collection. The lamb is in a moderate oven with rosemary and black pepper and the plums in a pan with wine vinegar and brown sugar. Louis glances to his right. Preston is now chopping mint, fresh from the garden, found, spreading rampant, in one of the unkempt beds.

'Hurry with the mint,' commands Louis.

Timing is everything.

'And is everybody ready? No one in the bath?'

'No one in the bath,' says William. 'Everyone ready and waiting.'

If they are not, there will be trouble. A serious tantrum has been slowly simmering and is ready to boil over.

'Right,' says Louis.

He takes out the lamb from the oven. Oohs and aahs and Louis demonic in a blast of heat and rising steam and the sacrificial lamb roasting in its own juices.

'A glass of red wine.'

William pours and offers up the glass, and Louis tastes, mingles the wine with the juices from the meat and holds his greasy hands clear for Preston to turn the pages of the cookery book. Thus had Father Michael conducted Mass and changed the bread and the wine into the Body and the Blood while Preston and William officiated as altar boys or sat in the front row of the pews making sure he did it right, according to the pictures in their missals. But the picture in the cookery book shows mummers parading through a Devonshire market town with an effigy of the Devil . . . 'which later they did burn, and afterwards, sheep-roasting on the village green', and Louis, more shaman than priest, stirs the juices in the big pan and dispenses herbs with a lavish, careless hand so that they flare and sparkle in the flames.

'Get the white wine out of the fridge.'

William rushes to obey.

'And open another red to let it breathe.'

He pours the flavoured blood back over the roasted beast and shoves it back in the oven to keep warm with parsnip and taters.

And now the fish is ready.

'Summon the women,' he commands.

Dinner is served.

'Three murders in a decade and all in the same few streets,' said Preston, reporting back on his research amid the remains of the murdered meal.

'But none in this house?'

'None that I can find. Yet.'

In the darkening sky above them the feast has just begun and the bats and the birds swoop through herds of unseen insects, slaughtering on the wing. The garden is overhung with trees and they could be in the country, but those who listen, like Emily, can hear the heartbeat of the city and are comforted.

'Only three?' Louis reflected. 'There must be more than that every few weeks these days, judging from the headlines on the Give-aways we get through the door.'

'Not famous murders.' Preston will not have his discovery trivialised. 'These were Famous Victorian Murders and all within a few streets of here.'

'So go on,' said Kate. 'What were they?'

'Charles Bravo was one. Poisoned by his wife's lover. With arsenic. Died in agony in a house round the corner.'

'Good solid Victorian poison, arsenic,' said Louis, approvingly. 'What is it today? Some synthetic rubbish, no doubt.'

'Pesticides, nuclear waste, carbon monoxide, the air we breathe.'

'Thank you, Kate,' said Louis, 'I knew you'd know.'

'And the lover was the family doctor,' Preston persisted.

'Hurrying through the gaslight with his black bag,' said William. 'Yes, I remember.'

'You *remember*?'

'I read the book. *The Night Charles Bravo Died.*'

'Gaslight,' said Louis. 'Ah, gaslight, that is why Victorian murders were famous. Not the same without gaslight. And fog, of course.'

The conversation lapping and surging around the table, wash and backwash, current and undercurrent, some waves bigger than others and they are usually the ones Louis makes, beaming with

196

the success of his meal and the best part of the two bottles that are inside him, one white, one red. Beaming but dangerous.

'And what were the others?'

'A man murdered his wife with an axe and pretended it was burglars. She was a bit of a holy terror with a terrible tongue on her and he wanted her money so he could marry the maid, who was kind to him.'

'I expect it was the uniform, too,' said William.

They all looked at him.

'Pardon?' said Kate. 'Did you say something?'

William blushed.

'The uniform,' he repeated. 'On the maid. Black frock. I expect it turned him on.'

Kate sighed.

'Go on, Preston,' she said.

'And the other was a woman who murdered her lodger,' continued Preston. 'She went into a hardware store and asked for a knife that would cut through bone . . .'

'They sold them in those days,' said Kate, nodding approvingly. 'You wouldn't be able to find one today, not round here.'

'You'd have to use the stuff they strip pine furniture with,' said Tess. 'In the bath.'

'Disguised with bubbles,' said Kate. 'Yes, I like the sound of that.'

'Shut up,' said Louis. 'Why the lodger? Rent problem?'

'In love with him,' explained Preston, 'and he was two-timing her with a neighbour, so she went up to him in the street while he was getting out of a hansom cab outside the other woman's house and plunged it through his breastbone and into his heart.'

'Isn't that typical of a bloody woman?' said Louis. 'Why didn't she kill the neighbour?'

'Do you think if she'd asked for a knife that went through *breast*bone the shopkeeper would have realised?' asked Tess.

'I don't know,' said Preston doubtfully.

'No imagination, shopkeepers,' said Kate. 'That's why the country's in the state it's in.'

'But there must have been more murders since then,' objected Emily.

197

'Not in the local history section of our library,' Preston assured her.

'Is that all the research you've done?' demanded Kate, not very impressed. 'Spent an hour or so in the library?'

'No, I've traced the previous owner,' said Preston, with a modest air of achievement.

'You mean the landlord – when they were flats?'

'Yes.'

'And?'

'Well, he didn't know anything about the room.'

His balloon blown, and burst.

'If he had,' said Louis, 'he'd have rented it out to a family of four.'

'But he did give me the address of the person who sold it to him,' said Preston. 'The trouble is, she lives near Brighton.'

'She?'

'Mrs McNab.'

'Mrs Mc*Nab*?'

'He's making it up.'

'I promise you . . .'

'Tess is working in Brighton,' said Louis. He gave her his teasing grin. 'You could drop in on her, darling. One of those evenings you stay down there.'

And the danger in the eyes, not the smile.

'I certainly could not,' said Tess.

'Why not?'

'Why not? Because I'm not the least bit interested, I'm far too busy, and also . . .' She hesitated.

'We might not like the answer,' said William.

They all looked at him again, but he just shrugged.

'And also,' continued Tess, 'I wouldn't know what to say to them. Well, can you imagine, just turning up on someone's doorstep and asking them do they know anything about a bricked-up room in a house they used to own . . . how many years ago?'

'Twenty-four,' said Preston. 'That's when she sold it. Anyway, I've written to her, explaining what it's about. I said someone might come and see her.'

But Tess shook her head.

'Well, it won't be me.'

'You'll have to go, Preston,' said Kate. 'We'll pay your expenses.'

'A weekend? With the twins?'

'One cheap-day return from Victoria.'

'And what if William's right,' said Emily, 'and you don't like the answer?'

She looks at Preston coldly. She has noted her exclusion from the weekend in Brighton and will be revenged.

Some day.

'What if something awful did happen there,' she said. 'And that's why they bricked it up?'

'Well, I think I'd prefer to know,' said Kate. 'Whatever it was.'

'Would you?'

'Yes. I'd always rather know the truth – even if I don't like it.'

'I think something Evil happened there,' said William. 'I can feel it, like a kind of force . . .'

There was a small silence.

Louis broke it.

'Bollocks,' he said.

'Don't you believe in Evil?' said William.

There was a challenge in his voice, and Louis was not one to ignore a challenge, especially not from William.

'No I don't, as a matter of fact,' he said. 'Not in the way you do, at any rate.'

'How do I believe in it?'

'You believe there's some kind of Devil and a host of lesser devils who stir it up in a big pot and dispense it to suitable clients. You believe people can't do the bloody awful things they do unless they're possessed by some demonic force – '

'Don't you think there are forces, then, that push people in certain directions?'

'What forces?'

'Well, I think it's been established that there are certain inexplicable universal forces – '

William looked like he might be planning a fairly lengthy lecture on the subject but Louis strangled it at birth.

'Universal bull*shit*,' he sneered. 'Universal forces don't make people commit murders. Something inside them does. Read Conrad. The universe is like a huge knitting machine, totally mechanical, amoral, all it can do is knit.'

Preston looked up in surprise.

'Did Conrad say that? I thought it was William's grandad.'

'Well, you know my view,' said Kate. 'I think it's just a convenient excuse for people. I was possessed, your honour . . .'

'I'm not saying people aren't responsible for their own actions,' William argued. 'All I am saying is that there may be some kind of force that influences us, and if it gets out of control, or too strong, it inclines us to chaos and destruction – '

'So don't blame me,' said Kate. 'Blame the force.'

'It's known as Splitting,' said Louis. 'Everyone has a dark side but some people don't like to admit it, so they try to put it on some imaginary character they've invented, their *alter ego*. Sometimes they give him a name, sometimes it's just the Devil. But it's all my arse.'

It was becoming a three-way contest between William on the one hand and Kate and Louis on the other, and Preston didn't think it was fair. Nor did he think it was altogether about theology. He decided to weigh in on William's side.

'But it is possible to think of the Devil as a metaphor,' he said, cleverly, because he knew this would fox Louis. Louis was into metaphors.

'A metaphor for what?' said Louis, turning on him.

'For some failing within us, some obstacle, which cuts us off from the love of God, or, if you prefer the humanist line, whatever is best in us. So why not call it by its metaphorical name – the Devil?'

'Because it's misleading,' said Louis. 'And also because it enables people to deceive themselves and others as to the true nature of their psychosis.'

'Exactly,' said Kate.

'Nice to know you two can agree sometimes,' said Tess, sweetly.

'But if Evil does exist,' said Emily, 'where *does* it come from? Where did it come from originally?'

'It comes from deep within the individual psyche,' said Louis. 'Triggered by some severe emotional upset. It comes from our ancestors, who were part reptile and park killer ape . . .'

'It comes from the hole in the wall,' said William.

And they laughed, with relief, or derision, and because they'd had enough of the conversation and they thought he was joking.

And the stars were out, and the bats and the swallows still killing.

'I wanted to ask you a favour,' said William to Preston later, while they were washing up.

'Go on,' said Preston, cheerfully. He was slightly drunk.

'Do you remember my telling you about Grandad being worried about something before he died?'

'You mean about Barry Moxton?' More warily now.

'Yes, that's right. Well, now my nan is.'

'Your nan?'

'Yes. She must have picked it up from him. Mum was telling me. She's quite bothered about it.'

'I'm sure there's no need to be,' said Preston. He passed him another plate to dry. There were a lot of them. Kate wouldn't let them buy a dishwasher on the grounds of energy conservation.

'No, of course not,' said William, 'but I rather stupidly said I'd find out what happened to him. And I don't know how to go about it. I wondered if you could help.'

'Me?' Preston stopped scrubbing dishes and looked at him. 'How?'

'Well, you're used to making enquiries about people, aren't you? For your work?'

'It could take a lot of work. My God, I've got enough on my plate trying to make a documentary about the Devil. You've got me running around like a loony with this bloody room and now you want me to find out what happened to Barry Moxton.'

'Well, I was thinking, I could take over about the room, if you could just make a couple of enquiries about him for me, for my nan.'

Preston frowned at him. A distant alarm bell rang but his head was befuddled by drink. He couldn't think straight.

'If you gave me the address of this woman,' said William, 'I could go and see her for you . . .'

201

26

Demons

Preston awoke, on cue, at about three in the morning, and could not get back to sleep. Emily breathed placidly and regularly beside him and made happy little gurgling noises from time to time, but Preston lay in torment, his mind projecting a dismal repeat of past sins and failures and an even more dismal trailer of those yet to come; the usual darkest-hour-before-the-dawn stuff, more terrible and depressing than any television horror. Finally he crawled out from under his duvet and fled out on to the landing.

The house was in darkness but the moon shone through the uncurtained windows and he could see clearly down four flights of stairs to the hall, where a pair of Louis' socks lay like two inky blobs on a sheet of blotting paper.

He descended quietly, listening to the strange night sounds of the house. He felt, on these nocturnal ramblings of his, as if he could hear its heartbeat, he could hear its breathing, as if in sleep, recuperating from the hammering it took during the day. Or perhaps it was dying, damaged in some fundamental way in its innards. It *looked* damaged. The wallpaper hung in shreds from the walls and the old wiring had been ripped out of the plaster and whole sections of floorboard removed to replace the old lead piping. He felt, absurdly, as if it was nursing its hurt and brooding on revenge.

He was planning to sit in the Study where the desk lamps were still functioning and he could read, but he was halfway down the hall when he saw a glimmer of light coming through the half-open door of the dining room. He could feel his own heartbeat then, though there was no reason to be bothered, it could easily be one of the others. The kitchen was through there and someone else might have found it difficult to sleep and be raiding the fridge. Except that there was no sound. He stood there, straining his ears, but there was only that strange, breathing silence of the house. The light appeared to be coming from a torch, though that was not in itself cause for alarm with all the rewiring that was going on. Even so, he crept cautiously towards the doorway and inched his head slowly round the edge of the frame until he could see with one eye into the room beyond.

At first all he could see was the beam of light. It did not waver, or search. It cut directly across the room, starting from the corner opposite the door and ending at the hole in the wall that led up to the Hidden Room. Then he saw what he took to be a crouching figure against the window and he cried out, 'Who's that?' in unthinking alarm, and the beam swung swiftly towards him, blinding him.

And a voice said, 'I'm sorry, it's me, William, is that Preston?'

Preston opened the door and stepped into the room, shielding his eyes from the glare.

'What the hell are you doing?' he said.

The light fell, making a pool on the floor, but the area around it, and William himself, were now in deep shadow.

'I'm sorry,' said William, again. 'I was just sitting here.'

Preston's brain adjusted to this information rather more slowly than his eyes to the light. He could see now that William was sitting on a chair directly opposite the hole in the wall.

But why?

He was pointing the torch down so its light bounced back off the floorboards, almost but not quite reaching his face. Preston felt his way across the room and bumped into a chair, nearly knocking it over. He sat down on it and peered at William, trying without success to read his expression.

'Do you often do this?' he said.

'I was thinking about the room,' said William.

He raised the torch again and Preston followed the beam across to the wall and the jagged hole Louis had made in it with the sledgehammer.

'What about it?' said Preston.

'Have you ever been up there?' William asked him. 'On your own?'

'No,' said Preston, tartly. 'Can't say I've wanted to particularly.'

'Do you want to try?'

'What? Now?'

He almost giggled with the absurdity of it all, except that he felt strangely nervous too. He wished he could see William's face.

'Yes, now,' said William. 'I've just tried, you see. But I can't.'

'What do you mean, you *can't*?'

'I went through the hole,' said William, 'but I couldn't go up the stairs. I was too scared.'

Preston took the torch off him and walked over to the hole in the wall.

He didn't like the look of it. It worried him, for some reason. It was like his fear of the viaduct as a child. But he was grown up now.

He ducked through the hole and shone the torch up the narrow staircase. It ended in a blank wall, the faded paper of which resembled a landscape of stark, wintry trees. The door to the Hidden Room was immediately to the left.

Preston began to walk up the staircase, slowly, his courage draining with every step. It was something about that wallpaper . . . No . . . It was something about having to turn at the top of the stairs and confront that empty room.

Because although he knew it *was* empty, he had a terrible, totally irrational feeling that there was someone, or something, in there, something that was so completely outside his experience and comprehension it would freak him out. It would disturb his sense of order in some irrevocable way.

He got halfway up the stairs and then turned and went down again. He went down quicker than he'd gone up and when he stepped back through the hole he shuddered with relief.

William was still sitting there, watching him.

'I didn't fancy it,' said Preston.

'No,' said William. 'I know.'

'It can't be anything,' said Preston. 'It's just us.'

He handed him the torch.

Bloody William, he thought. He felt like when they were kids and William had talked him into some stunt or other he immediately regretted. He felt aggressive.

'I'm going back to bed,' he said. 'Are you going to stay here staring at it or what?'

But William stood up.

'I want to show you some things,' he said.

Preston wondered what he meant.

'What things?' he said.

But William just led the way into the Study and Preston followed, reluctantly.

He thought William meant to show him something to do with the house, some other curious feature of its architecture, but he switched on one of the desk lights and slid open a drawer and took out a pile of newspaper cuttings.

'I've been keeping them,' he said.

Preston took them from him, mystified.

'What are they about?' he said.

'Evil,' said William.

Preston could see his expression now. It looked tense, but otherwise normal. Not staring mad, anyway.

'I thought they might help you,' he said.

'Help me?'

What was going on here?

'I mean with your programme. About the Devil.'

Preston studied them in the light of the desk lamp. The top one was about the Hungerford killings, when sixteen people had been shot dead one summer afternoon in a small English market town by a crazed gunman. Someone, presumably William, had ringed one of the paragraphs in red ink. It was the testimony of one of the witnesses, who described coming out from her house to see what the noise was and finding the killer standing there with the rifle in his hands. She had looked straight into his face. It was sweaty and blotchy, she said, and he was smiling, but there was nothing in his eyes. She said it was as if he was 'brain dead'.

Preston frowned at William, puzzled, but William only nodded, as if to reassure him, and he skimmed through the cuttings, picking up a sentence here and there, a headline, a photograph.

They were all about murders or violent crimes and the bits he read were enough. There was one story about a woman who had murdered her two young children by suffocating them in their sleep because she was afraid they were going to be sexually abused by her neighbours. She loved her children to distraction, said a neighbour. There was another about a man who had just been gaoled for life for kicking and beating his pregnant girlfriend until her unborn child was destroyed in her womb. There was a photograph of him being driven away from the court in a police van after sentence. He was smiling through the bars of the rear door and giving the photographer a V-sign. The story described how he had stood with his hands on his hips as the judge told him, 'You treated this lady with a savagery and sadistic brutality which is unsurpassed in my experience, culminating in the most terrible experience which can befall a woman, having her baby kicked to death in her womb while she is lying naked in the snow.'

Preston did not want to read any more. He handed them back to William and shook his head, not knowing what to say.

'Do you ever feel people might be possessed?' William asked him.

'I don't know,' said Preston. He didn't want to talk about it, not to William, not now.

'You've never felt anything sort of inside you, that wasn't a part of you, but kind of urged you to do things you didn't really want to do?'

'If you mean like that,' said Preston, 'no, I have not. Why? Have you?'

'No, no,' said William. 'Not like that. It's just that, when I read about people doing things like that, that are so terrible, so *inhuman*, I just worry about it.'

Preston knew he should be sympathetic but he just felt irritated.

'It's three o'clock in the morning,' he said. 'It's the wrong time to think about things like that.'

He left him and went back to bed. But sleep was quite impossible now and he lay there in the dark, staring at the ceiling with tears in his eyes and a heavy pressure on his chest as if the incubus of the nightmare was riding him, and he could almost have screamed with the pain and fear of it, like Emily used to.

And William sat alone in the study with the cuttings until it was almost daylight, and then he went upstairs to the room where the children slept and he knelt down by the side of the bed where his own child lay and looked into his face and listened to him breathing, and then he pulled the bedclothes up from where the child had kicked them away and tenderly tucked him in again. And over and over again, like the replay of a terrible video, he saw the smiling face of the man on the front page of the newspaper and the naked woman lying in the snow.

27

Friends

'So I feel,' said Preston to his friend Edward in the BBC Club, 'as if I ran into this cave for protection and found it was full of cave bears. Also vampire bats and dark, slimy creeping things clinging to the walls . . .'

'Not to speak of rising damp,' said Edward.

They were discussing the house.

'I don't think we've got any of that, yet,' said Preston, doubtfully. 'I think I could cope with a bit of that if we got rid of the other problems . . . It would seem almost consoling.'

'So, just let me recap,' said Edward. 'I think I've got it right. You went in with this lot because you felt you needed a bit of security and a home for your kids where the ceiling didn't keep falling in – '

'There were a few other things, but more or less,' said Preston.

'And you now find yourself living in a Gothic horror whose occupants appear to be in various stages of mental disintegration and which is, in itself, in an advanced stage of structural collapse?'

'Well, I wouldn't put it quite like that – '

'But from what you tell me it doesn't sound the sort of place to put your feet up while life slips heedlessly by . . . I mean, I might have the wrong impression . . .'

'No, no,' said Preston, 'that would seem to sum it up.'

'Not *quite* the kind of secure refuge that would reassure your wife that her little chicks were in safe hands for the weekend?'

Edward had, as usual, put his finger on the pulse of the problem.

'Or are they impervious to the various goings-on you have described to me?'

'Not exactly,' admitted Preston. 'They seem a bit tense sometimes. Particularly going to the lavatory.'

'Going to the lavatory?'

'In case they fall through the floor.'

'I see. Yes, it would make you tense, that. Bit constipated, too, I should imagine. And now this Emily has moved in with you, yes?'

'Yes. Temporarily.'

'And she keeps waking up in the middle of the night and screaming?'

'Well, she did at first. She's got better lately.'

'I'm glad to hear it. Mind you, I think I might wake up screaming in that place. I'm surprised you don't. How are you getting on with the haunted room?'

'I've passed that on to William.'

'He's the one who thinks he's possessed, yes?'

'Well, not exactly. He's just a bit worried that he might be – one day. And sometimes I've seen him sort of muttering to himself . . .'

'Muttering to himself?'

'Yes, like just sitting there with his lips moving as if he's talking to someone and a sort of distant look in his eye.'

'I see.'

'I mean, he's always been a bit strange, but, well, I'm a bit worried he's going totally round the twist.'

'I'd be a bit worried if he wasn't,' said Edward.

'Sorry?'

'Well, the alternative is somewhat more alarming. But if you really want my opinion, I think *you*'d be totally round the twist to stay there another day, not to speak of night. I think you should come and stay with me immediately.'

But Preston shook his head.

'I couldn't do that to you,' he said. 'If it was just me I might, but there's Emily and the twins . . . and William.'

'Well, I could cope with the twins – I'm not there at the weekends, anyway – and I might even manage to hack Emily

209

for a while provided she's stopped screaming, but I'm not sure about William,' said Edward. 'Why would you have to bring him along?'

'I didn't mean I'd have to bring him. What I meant was I don't think I can leave him in this state. I'd be a bit worried about what might happen.'

Edward sighed.

'It sounds hard,' he said, 'but you're not his keeper.'

'Well, I am, sort of,' said Preston. He shrugged. He didn't know how to explain. 'It goes back a long time,' he said.

But he thought about it while Edward got another round in. It wasn't just that business of being William's Minder at school. He needed William, too, perhaps more than William needed him sometimes. He could go years of hardly seeing him, of hardly thinking about him consciously, just exchanging Christmas cards, but the continued existence of William as His Friend, even as a friend he didn't know if he really liked or not, was important to him. In a sense, it was like touching base. It reminded him of who he was and where he came from.

'It's funny with friends,' he said to Edward when he had the next pint in front of him. 'I mean, with a lot of my friends I'm not Me at all, I'm whoever I think they want me to be. I was like that with Polly. I've been like that with most women I've been out with. I don't know if it's because I lack confidence or I just find it easier that way. I usually get it wrong anyway or they don't know what they want, or they change their mind about what they want just when I'm getting into it. But with William, there's none of that. It would be a waste of time. He knew me when I was the kid next door. When I'm with him I know who I really am. At least, I think I do.'

'I know a few couples who married for that reason,' remarked Edward, critically. 'Met each other at school and stuck together ever since. It seems to work, as marriages go, but they don't really know who they are, not as individuals, quite the opposite, in fact. I think they stay together mainly because they're terrified of finding out who they bloody are.'

Edward had been married three times and was, presently, single. He claimed it was the best state to be in. Edward was happy with himself as an individual. He didn't need anybody else. Or at least, he said he didn't. But Preston sometimes wondered why he kept getting married.

'We all go through an identity crisis from time to time,' Edward told him. 'It's no big deal. It's probably a bloody good thing. We handle it in whatever way we can. But, frankly, I don't think this William bloke is going to help you, not in the state he's in, and I don't think living in this collective is, either. What you need to do is stop being so bloody introspective, chum. Lose yourself in a few good fucks, that's what you ought to do.'

'I tried that with Emily,' said Preston. 'It doesn't work with me. And besides, I keep worrying about the Corsican.'

'The who?'

Preston realised he hadn't told Edward about the Corsican. He did. Edward listened with growing concern.

'Whenever I'm with Emily,' Preston told him, 'I'm worried sick that he's watching us, or else he'll suddenly come barging in through the door. But I don't know his name, I don't even know what he looks like . . .'

'I imagine you'll know him when you meet him,' said Edward. 'He'll be the one that left the stiletto in the back of your neck.'

'Thank you,' said Preston. 'That's really helpful.'

Later that night Preston returned, unsoberly, to the house. It was in darkness and looked empty, but when he went in there was a chink of light coming from a room at the back, and this time it wasn't William with a torch. It was Kate with a candle.

She was washing something in the sink.

'Hi,' said Preston.

'Hi,' she said. But she didn't sound delighted. There had been a recent cooling in their relationship. Preston didn't know whether to blame Emily for this or William. Or perhaps it was him.

'Like some coffee?' he said. 'Or herb tea?'

'I wouldn't mind some herb tea,' she said. 'If you're making some.'

While the rewiring was being done they were boiling up the water on the gas stove. Preston took the kettle over to the sink.

It was full of socks.

He wondered for a moment if they belonged to Louis, but this was because he was not sober.

Kate was unlikely to wash Louis' socks for him.

Whenever Kate saw a pair of Louis' socks lying around she picked one of them up – just one – and put it in her handbag and dropped it into a litter bin on her way to work. She had told Emily this, who had been amused and told Preston.

But Preston didn't think it was at all funny. It seemed to him yet another indication of collective madness.

Kate pulled one out of the water. It looked like one of the children's.

'William in?' he enquired, for no particular reason.

'No,' said Kate. 'He's away for the night.'

She seemed a bit tight-lipped about this, and in fact it was unusual. William didn't do the kind of work that took him away at nights.

'Apparently, he's gone to see this woman of yours,' said Kate.

Preston, startled, wondered who she meant.

'The one in Brighton,' said Kate. 'About the room.'

28

Mrs McNab

William rang the front doorbell of the bungalow and it tinkled a suburban tune.

He saw the woman approaching through the frosted glass of the door, but she didn't open it. She just shouted through it.

'Yes? Who is it?'

'Mr Moody,' William shouted back. He felt the whole street could hear and would know it was a lie. 'I wrote you a letter.'

Silence. But he could hear it breathing.

'About the house you used to live in.'

Silence. But he could hear it thinking.

Then the sound of bolts being drawn back, chains being rattled.

The door opened a fraction, to the end of its leash but no further. He saw an eye pressed to the crack and smiled, encouragingly.

The door closed.

William stayed smiling but a small perplexed frown appeared in the centre of his forehead, where it belonged.

But she was only taking the chain off and the door opened properly to reveal a very small, very square old lady dressed in check.

She looked like a rug with eyes. Large eyes, magnified through large spectacles, and a very large, very peculiar jaw that operated a very straight, very thin mouth.

The mouth spoke.

'I never got round to writing back.'

She was probably a couple of inches under five feet tall and almost as wide about the hips, though the check two-piece might have exaggerated that impression, along with the hairy shawl in a

213

clashing pattern around her shoulders. She had very bright dyed red hair, cut short in a fringe above horn-rimmed spectacles.

But the most remarkable thing about this lady, despite the spectacles, despite the check, despite the eyes, was the jaw.

It was the Habsburg jaw. No doubt about it. She looked as William imagined the Empress Maria Theresa must have looked in her declining years. Like a large piranha fish disguised as a rug snapping up generals for breakfast. The kind of jaw that would make them stand up to Frederick the Great and all his cannon and all his horse and all his strapping grenadiers rather than go back to face that jaw in defeat.

'I'm sorry,' said William, as *they* must have said once, or a few times, given the number of battles they lost, 'I hope it's not inconvenient.'

Inconvenient? Snap. Silesia gone. Half of fucking Bohemia. Two entire armies lost in the mud and that bloody Prussian fag with his boot poised over Vienna. Inconvenient!

'It was a long time ago,' she said.

'I know,' said William.

They stood looking at one another for a moment. She had a stick and her hands grasped it tightly in front of her, trembling slightly.

'The first house we ever owned.'

'Ah.'

'Well, I suppose you'd better come in, then.'

The inside of the bungalow was dark and dingy and smelt of cat food, and she limped ahead of him down the hall, stocky in seamed stockings, leaning on her stick. And something about it, perhaps the faded flower-pattern wallpaper, perhaps the dull varnished paintwork, perhaps the woman herself, reminded him of the passage they had found and the staircase that led to the hidden room.

The cats were waiting for him in the parlour, a furry, purring conspiracy of cats, prowling through the brown and orange foliage of the carpet or draped like unwashed grey antimacassars over the backs of the chintzy three-piece suite.

And every one of them watching, like courtiers with eyes full of secrets and a nose for mischief, and their axe-jawed empress poised over another apologetic general, about to be minced into cat food.

'Made me feel quite peculiar,' said Mrs McNab, 'getting your letter. It was all so long ago. I expect it's the room, is it?'

William was taken aback. Preston had decided not to mention the Hidden Room in his letter in case it alarmed her. All he'd said was that he was interested in the past history of the place and would like to call on her to discuss it.

'Well, isn't it?' she said.

'Well, we did find a room,' William confessed. 'On the first floor. We did wonder . . .'

And the cats watching, with their secret eyes.

'I thought it was,' she said, with satisfaction. 'It was still bricked up then?'

William looked at her, warily, as if this presaged some appalling confession.

'So you did know about it?' he said.

'I ought to. It was Father bricked it up.'

'I see.'

Not seeing at all, not having cat's eyes.

'Erm, why exactly . . .?'

'Because of the noises,' she said, surprised, as if it was a silly question.

'The noises?'

'Like someone crying.'

He felt as if a spider had crawled up the back of his neck, and was crouching there, wondering whether to bite.

'Haven't you heard them, then?'

'No, we've heard nothing. We just wondered why it had been bricked up.'

'I thought she was still at it. This long after.'

'Excuse me?'

'The crying and the sobbing. Father said it was cats when we told him, but we knew it wasn't cats. Cats don't sound like that.'

Her voice was as peculiar as her jaw, drawn deep from the well of the throat but with a distinct nasal intonation as if it had tried that route first before finding its way through the thin crack between the thin lips.

'Can you tell me about it?' said William.

She looked at him for a moment as if she was weighing up the consequences. Then she began.

'Well, it must have been, what, seventy years ago we moved in. Early nineteen-twenties anyhow. I was the eldest. Eight years old, or ten, perhaps. Can't remember now. I can still remember that noise, though, I'll remember it to my grave.

'I had the room above, with my sisters, in the attic. I used to lie awake at night, listening to it, half petrified.'

William tried to imagine her as a little girl, like the illustration from a childhood book, like Alice, or Wendy Darling, with her long nightdress and her long hair spread on the pillow, whatever colour it was then, and her eyes wide with fear, and no spectacles. But it wasn't easy, looking at her now, squat and solid on the edge of the sofa and her thick little legs planted wide to show the tops of her stockings.

'Cats, he said. But you couldn't argue with your father, not then, not like they do now. But Mother must have said something to him because he started to take more notice. Then we found out about the maid.'

'The maid?'

'That belonged to the people who had it before us. This doctor fella and his family. They said it was him that did it, and him a doctor, too, and with three children.'

William was lost.

'Did what?'

'Got her into trouble. Catholic girl, too, from Ireland. Not that that makes any difference, in my opinion, but people seem to think it does – '

'You mean she had a baby?'

'She would have, if she hadn't took something. I don't know what, no one ever found out, I only got the details myself years later, but it was some kind of poison. They got her to hospital but it was too late. Seems an odd way to do it, poison, but I suppose if she was in a state. There was some doubt about it, though, with her being a Catholic. Some said it was him give it her, to get rid of the baby, or the both of them, but there was never any charge.'

216

'Him?'

'The fella. The doctor. Him we bought the house off. Father said he'd never have bought it if he'd known, even at the price it was, when he thought of all the misery in that little room. That's why he bricked it up. It didn't stop it right away. Still went on for a bit. Then there was just the knocking. Then that stopped, too. And after a while we almost forgot it was there.'

When William came out of the house it was raining, a fine spray whipping in from the sea. He lifted his face up to it as if he could shower himself clean. Clean of cat fur, free of the claustrophobia induced by the house, the woman, her terrible story. It only partly worked.

He had been walking aimlessly but in the general direction of the sea. Now he set off back towards the town.

It wasn't too late. Just past five o'clock. He could be back home by seven or eight. He might even be in time to see Edwin before he went to sleep, and read him a story.

But he knew it wasn't going to happen.

He felt as if his route had been decided a long time ago and there was nothing he could do about it.

He phoned the conference centre, half hoping she'd already left, or they wouldn't be able to find her. But she hadn't, and they did.

'William,' said Tess. She sounded pleased. 'Where are you?'

He told her. And why.

'You came down from London for that? What did she say?'

'She wasn't in,' William said. 'I'll have to try again later . . . or tomorrow.'

He wasn't sure why he lied. He told himself, later, that it was because he didn't want to alarm her.

'Come over,' she said. 'Ask for me in reception. I'm in Room 208.'

Room 208 was an expansive office equipped for a number of people, but by the time he arrived only Tess was working there, at a desk in the window with a view of the sea. The white horses were racing in from a long way out and great spumes of spray breaking over the end of the pier.

217

'Something's cropped up,' she said. 'I'll have to work on for a bit. But if you're not in a rush we could meet up later and have a meal or something.'

'That'd be great,' said William. It was odd seeing her at work. He'd never seen her in her working environment before. She wore a grey pin-striped suit and her hair was pulled back from her forehead and tied in a ribbon. He thought she looked wonderful.

She suggested he wait for her at a pub behind the conference centre where she said she sometimes had lunch. It was almost empty but quite cosy, with a fire that could almost be real. He ordered a glass of wine and took it to a table in the corner and sat there with a book, trying not to think about what Mrs McNab had told him, trying not to think about what he was doing here, trying not to think about anything much.

He'd drunk three glasses of wine by the time she arrived, looking flushed and windblown, and frowning at him as if she didn't know quite what to do with him.

'Look, if you want to stay the night,' she said, 'I could probably book a room for you at my hotel.'

It was as if she had to get that over with, quickly.

'That'd be fine,' he said.

'I think you must be mad,' she said, 'taking all this trouble just to find out about a stupid room.'

He shrugged and smiled, but awkwardly.

'It's because I'm a historian,' he said.

'It's because you're obsessive,' she corrected him. 'Or neurotic, or both.'

They ate at a French restaurant in a small Regency square, and all the time they ate and drank and talked William knew that she hadn't phoned the hotel, but he did not remind her.

'Well,' she said, finally, when they were deciding to give pudding a miss and have another small carafe of wine, as usual, 'I think you've left it a bit late for the train . . .'

It was as if they hadn't had that earlier conversation.

'I'd better phone the hotel,' she said.

'Yes,' he said, nodding. 'If you don't mind.'

'Or there's a spare bed in my room,' she said, looking for the waiter to order the extra carafe. 'You could sleep there, if you like. It might be easier.'

'Fine,' he said, 'fine.'

Still nodding.

'Do you feel guilty?' she asked him, later, sleepily, with her head tucked into his shoulder and her hair untied and spread out on his chest, in the single bed next to the one that was still spare.

'A bit,' he said.

What he felt was Doomed and he did not care. Not yet.

'About Kate?'

'No. Not really. More about Louis.'

'Why not Kate?'

'I don't know,' he said, 'I just don't.' He thought about it. 'Perhaps because I don't think she'd mind very much.'

'Wouldn't she?'

She sounded surprised. Perhaps it was a surprising thing to say. He wondered if it was true, or whether he was just trying to protect her again. But he just didn't know. He felt numb in his feelings about Kate, numb in his awareness of hers.

'Do you feel guilty about Louis?' he asked her.

'No.'

She seemed quite positive about that. Perhaps a bit too positive.

'Why not?'

'I don't know,' she said, 'but I don't.'

'And Kate?'

'I don't want to think about Kate,' she said.

'I love you,' he told her.

And she kissed him, but said nothing.

William did feel guilty about Louis. He felt guilty about Kate, too, eventually, though he did not tell Tess this. He felt guilty about everything, but he was in love.

He knew this was no excuse.

He'd spent the final part of spring and the early part of summer torn between his guilt and his love. It was a time of the year when the balance naturally inclined to the latter.

219

He knew what it meant now to be in love with being in love.

It made everything so different. It was as if some kind of filter, or flaw, had been removed from his vision so that everything became so much more intense. He couldn't believe it was the same world. He felt, for the first time in his life, as if he was a part of everything that was happening around him and in harmony with it. He felt as if he had been fine-tuned.

Once, in spring, when Edwin was about six or seven months old, William had taken him to Kew Gardens in his push-chair when the cherry trees were in blossom. He had tilted the push-chair back so that all the child could see was the brilliant blue of the sky and then pushed it under a great canopy of pink blossom and watched as the child's eyes, so sleepily neutral, suddenly widened in astonished wonder.

William felt a bit like that. The odd thing was, he did not feel it so much when he was with Tess, but during the times when he anticipated being with her.

Travelling down in the train to see her, he would watch a flock of birds settle on a field and soar and go about their inexplicable business, and it was as if he had discovered some great joy in the pointlessness of it all. He became a great listener to pointless conversations. He smiled at total strangers.

He loved to sit alone at a table outside some pub somewhere, waiting for her to join him. Endlessly he anticipated the moment when he would look up and see her there.

But he always knew it was wrong and it did not stop him from feeling guilty. And sometimes, when he knew how wrong it was, the spider would tense its claws in the back of his neck and remind him it was still there, waiting to bite.

He told no one about his affair with Tess and he told no one about the story of the hidden room. He thought it would only make people worry. When Preston asked him about Mrs McNab he said she had moved house and no one had a forwarding address.

29

Something in the Post

Preston knew that William was hiding something from him and he suspected the worst.

'I was right, wasn't I,' said Emily, 'about William and Tess?'

But she didn't sound smug about it; she sounded worried.

Preston was worried, too, but he didn't know what to do about it. He thought William was going crazy.

He found him one evening in the bathroom in the attic. He was kneeling down with his ear pressed to the floorboards as if he was listening for something.

He did not seem to be at all embarrassed when Preston came in and asked him what he was doing.

'I was just wondering,' he said, 'if you ever heard any strange noises?'

'What kind of noises?'

William seemed a bit evasive about that.

'Just like crying noises,' he said. 'Or knocking.'

'Like mice?' said Preston.

But William shook his head.

'This bathroom's directly above the hidden room,' he said. 'Did you know that?'

'No,' said Preston. 'I can't say I've really thought about it.'

'That could be why the floor's rotten, of course,' said William.

Preston stared at him.

'Whatever's in there,' said William, 'it could be coming up through the ceiling. I'd keep the door shut if I were you.'

'They'll lock you up one day,' Preston told him, 'and throw away the key.'

But all William said was, 'Have you found anything about Barry Moxton, yet?'

'I'm working on it,' Preston told him, irritably. 'I'm expecting something in the post.'

He was on his way out the next morning, late and in a hurry, when the mail arrived, and he picked it up from the front-door mat and sifted through it quickly. There was the usual pile for Louis, a couple for Tess who was still away, one for William and one for him.

He knew from the writing that it was from his Auntie Ethel, and he knew from the size of the envelope what it was likely to contain, and he thrust it into his briefcase and wished he could do what Kate did with Louis' socks and drop it in the first litter bin on the way to work, unopened.

But of course, he didn't. His sense of obligation was, as usual, too strong. He opened it in the tube and tipped the contents on to his knee.

They were photocopies of newspaper cuttings from the *Liverpool Echo* and the *Liverpool Daily Post* and the *Liverpool Weekly News* of twenty-six years ago. He'd asked his Auntie Ethel to pick them up for him because they didn't keep local newspaper cuttings at the BBC and they didn't file obscure murders from a quarter of a century ago, anyway, even murders like this.

His mouth felt dry and he felt the hairs rise on the back of his neck and knew it was a warning like the danger sign on the railway embankment and the one in the hospital grounds that said Do Not Trespass, and there was a terse letter from his Auntie Ethel saying she didn't know why he was always wanting to poke around in things Best Left Forgotten.

But for a cautious man Preston was very bad at heeding warnings, and there was a morbid fascination in reading, at long last, what had really happened to Mary Moxton.

William sat in his study, staring out of the window at rooftops and a grey sky. A grey day in London town and William wanting, as usual, to be somewhere else. He was meant to be listening to an essay read aloud to him by one of his students and he

222

did catch the occasional sentence, but it did nothing to cheer him up.

'The immense power of the medieval church may be compared to a modern police state interfering in every aspect of human life from the cradle to the grave . . .

'It possessed in the Inquisition an instrument of repression to rival any modern state security police . . .'

There was little there of originality or style, or even truth – the Inquisition had no police force of its own and its filing system was bloody awful – and William had already marked the essay down for a B minus.

'. . . from crusading Popes, zealous in their pursuit of orthodoxy, to the meanest rural priest, denouncing the village lechers and fornicators and drunkards and adulterers . . .'

William endured it to the end and then sent its author packing with a B plus, out of guilt because he hadn't been listening properly, and perhaps for other reasons.

As soon as he was alone he phoned Tess.

'Hi, hope I'm not interrupting anything,' he said.

'Well, it's a bit difficult at the moment,' she said.

She sounded a bit cool. William's antennae waved frantically.

'Oh, sorry, well, I just phoned to say is it okay for tomorrow night?'

And I love you, I miss you. And a lot of other things that would have to keep.

A long pause and a gust of wind rattling the old window frame, and then she said, 'Didn't you get my letter?'

And William knew then what he should have known at least a week ago, when last he saw her, or maybe before that, maybe from the start.

But he clung to the last shred of ambiguity.

'No,' he said. 'What letter?'

'I posted it yesterday. I wanted . . . It was just that I found it easier to write.'

'You wrote me a letter?'

'I meant you to get it this morning. Look, William, I can't talk to you now. Please read the letter. I'm sorry, I have to go.'

He sat by the phone for a long while after she'd hung up. It

223

must be the guilt, he thought. It's too much for her. I should have known.

But he knew that it wasn't guilt about Louis. It wasn't even guilt about Kate, though that was there. It was guilt about him, because she didn't love him.

'It had to happen,' she'd said to him, when they first made love. 'We had to do it at least once. We should have done it years ago, and got it out of our systems.'

She'd been getting him out of her system and now she had and he was gone. Flush. Down the drain.

Though to be fair to her, she'd probably thought he would flush her out of his system too.

Only it hadn't worked for him and he didn't think it ever would.

He sat there well into the afternoon, turning things over and over in his mind. Then he thought about the letter. He'd left before the morning mail. Perhaps it was there now, waiting for him. He suddenly felt anxious about it, lying there on the hall stand, with Louis working at home all day. He had no more lectures that day, no more tutorials . . . He looked at his watch.

And then he remembered.

My God, Edwin.

He said it aloud, it was such a shock to have forgotten.

He'd said he'd pick Edwin up from school.

Their childminder was at the dentist. She wouldn't be there to collect him and it was twenty to three and he came out at a quarter past.

If he'd stopped for a moment to think about it he'd have phoned the school, but he didn't, he just started running.

Louis sat alone in the wreck of the house.

The builders had left on one of their sudden forays to the builders' yard or the betting shop or the next job or wherever it was they went in their big red van, leaving the house stunned and bleeding, like the victim of a mugging, still in shock and waiting for the pain to begin, and Louis sat at his desk, knowing how it felt.

The desk was one of six occupying the room, each a substantial guide to the character of its owner, an altar to individuality, and Louis had frequently considered that a few minutes in the company of the desk would probably tell you as much as you'd ever learn from a few years with the person who worked at it. Especially if that person was Tess. Or William.

Which was why he was staring so thoughtfully at William's desk.

He was looking for clues.

He did not know what clues he was looking for, or whether he would recognise them if he saw them, or what he was going to do about it when he did, but he felt obliged at least to look.

The deity worshipped at this particular shrine appeared to be the Beast of the Apocalypse.

There were a number of books, some open, some shut, devoted to his previous visitations. Froissart's *Chronicles of the Hundred Years War*, volume two of Runciman's *History of the Crusades*, a couple of French titles: *La peste en Normandie* by Porquet and Prat's *Albi et la peste noire*, an English volume more starkly entitled *The Black Death*, Hecker's *The Epidemics of the Middle Ages*, a couple of books on the suppression and massacre of the Albigensians, and some more general works – *Man and Aggression* and *The Anatomy of Human Destructiveness*, which William presumably read when he wanted to unwind.

Moving on, Louis' bemused gaze took in a pile of essays, which he assumed were by William's students. He read the title: *'Religion, Sex and Punishment in the Middle Ages: the role of the ecclesiastical courts in regulating public morals and disciplining their transgressors'.*

Intrigued, he sat down in William's chair and began to read, but, disappointingly after such a title, it proved to be dry old stuff and he was about to give up when, three essays down, his attention was caught by a margin note in red ink in William's handwriting.

The student had begun his essay with the sentence: 'The concept of punishment for sexual transgression is a peculiarly medieval one resulting from the dominant role played by the Church and its courts and has gradually been eradicated by the growth of the modern, secular state.'

Beside this, William had written, 'Is it? Has it?'

225

Louis considered those terse scribbles for considerably more time than it took to read them and his expression grew, if anything, more thoughtful. He read on for a while, but soon lost interest and turned instead, and more guiltily, to a wire basket full of mail on the left-hand side of the desk.

This appeared to be devoted to the current activities of William's grim horsemen – and a few allies they'd picked up on the way.

William did not belong to any political party but he was a member of Greenpeace, Friends of the Earth, War on Want and Survivors International, and their leaflets and circulars chronicled the present miseries of humankind. William's in-tray painted a bleak picture of doomed and threatened species, dead and dying seas, polluted rivers and poisoned skies. The general tone was captured in one slim brochure from Greenpeace.

Planet Earth is 4,600 million years old, *read Louis*. If we condense this inconceivable time-span into an understandable concept, we can liken Earth to a person of 46 years of age . . .

Dinosaurs and the great reptiles did not appear until one year ago, when the planet was 45. Mammals arrived only eight months ago; in the middle of last week man-like apes evolved into ape-like men, and at the weekend the last ice age enveloped the Earth.

Modern Man has been around for four hours. During the last hour, Man discovered agriculture. The industrial revolution began a minute ago.

During those sixty seconds of biological time, Modern Man has made a rubbish tip of Paradise.

He has multiplied his numbers to plague proportions, caused the extinction of 500 species of animals, ransacked the planet for fuels and now stands like a brutish infant, gloating over this meteoric rise to ascendancy, on the brink of a war to end all wars and of effectively destroying this oasis of life in the solar system.

Under these warnings, at the bottom of the pile, was a brightly coloured envelope containing photographs.

Feeling more guilty, but also elated, as if he had found his clue,

226

and also frightened, in case he had, Louis tipped the photographs on to the desk.

But they were all of William and Kate and Edwin, taken during a recent weekend they had spent in the fens. They were happy family snaps. It was difficult, looking at them, to believe that William was anything other than a happy family man.

Louis put the photographs back in the envelope and the envelope back at the bottom of the pile. There was no clue here, not the one he was looking for. He knew where the clue was but he'd been trying not to think about it. It was out on the hall stand.

He went out there again and looked at it: the letter for William.

The name and address were typed but he knew who it had to be from, he could tell from the postmark.

But why would she be writing to William?

It was a new experience for Louis, this suspicion. It had never happened to him before and he could scarcely believe it was happening to him now. It was something that happened to other people, weak, vulnerable people, victims. Not him. He felt demeaned by it but as often as he shrugged it off, ridiculed it and banished it to a corner of his mind, it would come worming insidiously back, tormenting and mocking and devouring. And even as he analysed his reasons for it, the intercepted glances, the body language, the evenings they had simultaneously stayed away from home, he felt cheapened and belittled, as he had when he sat at William's desk, sifting through his papers.

It had started shortly after they moved to the house, not in any dramatic way, or with some particular incident, but almost as if he had woken up one morning and found it was there, so alien to his nature and yet so much a part of him now, like some dreadful metamorphosis, shameful and ugly and repulsive.

Sometimes he blamed the house, as if there was some poison in the atmosphere that had corrupted him. Then he'd wonder if it had been happening before – months, even years ago – and only their proximity together in the house had made him aware of it.

And yet there was so little evidence, and so much of it could be coincidence, or his own foul imaginings, the product of this dreadful sense of insecurity and inadequacy that had overwhelmed him of late, as strange and new and destructive as his suspicions.

He returned to his own desk by the window and sat down, staring bleakly at the words he had written hours before on the computer.

Elwin has three choices:
He can turn back and try a different route.
He can go forward in the darkness and risk falling into a trap.
He can use his last flare to light the way and risk drawing attention to himself.

Elwin, his current hero. He was always having trouble coming up with new names for his heroes and he frequently borrowed or adapted them from people he knew. This one must have come from Edwin, William and Kate's son, but he'd only just realised it.

He was fond of Edwin. He was a nice kid and Louis liked kids. He was just a big kid himself, people said. If anything ever happened to William and Kate he'd want to bring Edwin up with his own. He was almost like a brother to Ben and Alice anyway.

He missed Ben and Alice. They'd be coming out of school now, except that they weren't at school, they were with Tess's mother. He'd complained that he was having to do more than his fair share of looking after them so Tess had packed them off there two weeks before the summer holidays. That was typical of Tess. She had her ruthless side.

Typical of him, too, he thought. He'd only been trying to get back at her for staying away so much and he'd ended up hurting himself more. As usual. Fuck her, he thought.

And fuck this. He smashed his fist down on the keyboard and the computer let out a shriek of anguished beeps and the screen filled with gibberish.

He left it and paced about the room.

What the hell was Tess up to? How could she do this to him? And with William of all people?

It could not possibly be true. They would not do this to him.

And now he was back on the same old track, following the same hopeless trail. It was like a nagging tooth that he could not leave alone, but must be always exploring with his tongue, feeling for the extent of the damage, trying to reassure himself there was nothing wrong, it was all in the mind, and all the time feeling that great bleeding cavity, and the pain.

He went out into the hall again and picked up the letter. He was tempted to steam it open, but he had never steamed open a letter in his life, he didn't know if it left marks. Besides, some remaining sense of schoolboy honour, or basic decency, restrained him. He held it up to the light from the window. He could just make out her writing, but not what it said. He took it into the study where the light was better and held it up again. The double thickness of the folded letter confused him, but just at the bottom, where it was thinner, he could make out the words 'without you . . .'

That was all. Right at the bottom of the letter: '*without you*' – and three dots. He held it up again, trying to see how she had signed herself, and whether there were any kisses, but those were the only words he could see: '*without you . . .*'

What could possibly precede it?

Can't live without you?

Stay here without you?

And suddenly his misery was swamped in a cold, almost vicious anger. With sudden conviction, no longer confused, he strode briskly from the room, tossed the letter contemptuously on the pile on the hall stand, and ran up to his room to pack. He did not know what he was packing for, or where he was going to go, or even *whether* he was going to go, but he wanted to be prepared. It seemed like a decisive step, and he wanted to be decisive. He would no longer be a victim, crawling in the dark, while they walked all over him.

He packed one suitcase and then started on another, breaking off to put on a tape of a rock concert they had gone to when they had first met, and played over and over when they were first making love. To its insistent beat Louis packed his bags, pulling the straps tight, snapping the locks. He pulled out a trunk from under the bed and began to throw books into it, selecting only those that were his from the shelves, leaving hers. It seemed like a very definite act of separation, this dissection of their books, and there was a certain satisfaction in it, and in seeing the gaps that appeared on the shelves. He started on the tapes, taking those that he had bought for himself and leaving the others. His gestures were brisk, definite, final. He felt as if he were physically hacking the individual out from the unit, and the more of it he hacked out the stronger he felt. It was as if he was emerging from some unnatural coupling in which he had felt diminished and belittled and betrayed.

The trunk was full and there were still some of his own things left to pack and he did not want to leave them. He did not want to leave anything of his in the room. He went downstairs for a black polythene dustbin liner, thinking he could use that for some books and bits and pieces from the shelves. On the way he noticed, with new eyes, just how ravaged the house looked, and how ugly. He was surprised he'd not noticed before.

On his way to the kitchen the phone rang and he went into the study to answer it.

It was Tess.

'Hello,' she said. 'What are you up to?'

Sounding so bright and cheerful, so innocent.

He thought about it for a moment, but only for a moment, then he told her he had been packing.

A slight hesitation down the line, or did he imagine it?

'Packing? Packing what?'

He said nothing.

'Louis? Is something the matter?'

'You know what's the matter.'

A definite hesitation.

'What do you mean?'

'Look, I don't want to play any more games with you, Tess. You just get on with your life and I'll get on with mine.'

Silence. As if they were both waiting. He looked around the room. He felt strangely detached from all of this. And quite unemotional. He was impatient to carry on with his packing. When she spoke again it was in a different tone.

'Will you wait for me to come home?' she said.

'I'm not sure I want to spend any more time here, actually.'

His own voice was cold, giving nothing.

'I was going to come back tonight. That's why I was phoning you. I thought we could go out for a late supper.'

'And I certainly don't want to run into William.'

A long silence.

'Louis . . .'

He waited.

'Look, don't go until I come back. We have to talk about this.'

She sounded close to tears now but it made him harder. And now, too, the last doubts had disappeared.

'You can't just walk away from this, Louis. You have to give me a chance to see you.'

The anger exploded then.

'I don't have to give you anything,' he said. 'I don't owe you a thing.'

He slammed the phone down and went upstairs and finished packing. The tape had finished and he could hear the phone again but he let it ring and after a while it stopped.

It didn't take him long to load the car. Before he left he picked up the letter from his wife and placed it on top of the wire tray on William's desk.

30

Late for School

It was eight stops on the underground, and one change.

Say a minute and a half between stops, that was twelve minutes, and he'd better allow five for the change.

William looked at his watch.

He should just make it. At worst he'd be a few minutes late. If only Ben wasn't away, he'd have had someone to wait with. It wouldn't be so bad if there were two of them. But they must have some system if a child wasn't picked up on time.

He changed lines and stood fretting on the platform waiting for the next train. The digital sign that was supposed to give you the times kept flashing CORRECTION, but it didn't tell you what it was. The bloody Northern line. Oh God. It was five past three.

There was a platform announcement, but as usual it was distorted and he couldn't make any sense of it. He wondered if he should give up and try for a taxi, but there were never any black cabs south of the river, not going south, anyway.

The sign finally stopped flashing and came up with a time. Four minutes.

But it was more like six before the train arrived.

There were two hold-ups between stops. One lasted nearly ten minutes. It was, for William, like one long, silent scream.

In the summer the kids waited outside the classroom in the playground until they were picked up.

Don't let him leave the playground, William prayed.

By the time he arrived at his station it was gone half past three.

He ran all the way to the school.

There were five or six older boys playing football in a distant corner of the playground, but no sign of Edwin. He tried the classroom. The desks seemed very small and very empty. He tried the staffroom next, but that was empty, too.

Perhaps he had gone home on his own. Or perhaps one of the other parents had taken him.

It took William just over three minutes to reach the house, running most of the way. Louis was coming out of the front door.

'Is Edwin home?' William asked him. He felt as if he could hardly breathe.

Louis looked at him and William knew at once that he knew about him and Tess. But he felt he could cope with that, if only Edwin was home.

But he wasn't.

'Isn't he with his childminder?' said Louis.

'She's at the dentist,' William explained. 'I was supposed to pick him up but I was late and he's not there. Has no one rung?'

'No.'

They stood looking at each other across the open doorway and a million miles.

'Oh Christ, Louis,' said William, 'where can he be?'

'Have you tried his classroom? The staffroom? The caretaker? Perhaps one of the other parents saw him waiting and took him home . . .'

The caretaker.

There was a caretaker who lived on the premises, in a kind of lodge.

'Were you going out?' said William.

'Yes,' said Louis. He sounded very positive about that, as if it was important. 'I was.'

'Could you just hang on a few minutes?' William begged him. 'In case someone rings.'

He left Louis at the front door and ran back the four or five blocks to the school. The streets seemed oddly empty for the time of day and there was a hint of rain in the air, and as he ran he looked down every side road and even into the gardens and the windows of the houses, but he did not see Edwin in any of them.

The caretaker was round the back of the kitchens, emptying something into the big rubbish bins, like grey steel drums, or vats.

'I've lost my little boy,' William told him. His voice sounded hoarse and he knew he was close to tears.

The caretaker was a small, peppery man called Mr Allcock and some of the older boys called him No Balls. Edwin, mishearing, and not understanding, called him Snowball. He thought that was the joke.

'There was some kids playing football in the playground,' said Snowball. 'Are you sure he's not with them?'

William shook his head, not trusting himself to speak, and they walked back together to the front of the building and met the football players just as they were packing up and going home. It was raining quite heavily now.

'We saw some little kid standing around by himself,' said one of them. 'He was crying. I spoke to him but he said he was waiting for his dad.'

'Why didn't you bring him to me,' said the caretaker, 'if you saw he was upset?'

William still couldn't speak.

'Oh, but this bloke came for him,' said one of the other boys. 'I saw them go off together.'

William found his voice at last but it seemed to come from a great distance.

'How long ago?' he said.

But he knew it was too long ago. Much too long ago, even as he started to run once more into the wet and empty streets.

31

The File on Barry Moxton

The trouble with being an acutely sensitive and creative person, as Preston sometimes explained to people, was that you never really knew if the pain in your chest was real or imagined. And it was the same with premonition. Preston was so used to expecting the worst to happen that he never knew if this was because there was an especially good reason why it should, like a small red dwarf approaching with a meat cleaver in his hand and a nasty gleam in his eye, or because he'd woken up in the morning with a hangover and a particularly jaundiced view of the world.

This time he put it down to the effect of reading the cuttings on the Moxton murder trial. They were enough to give most people a sense of doom and despondency and Preston had a flying start on most people in this area. But no attempt at rational explanation could relieve his deep sense of anxiety.

He even phoned Polly at work to make sure the twins were all right.

'Well, they were when I took them to school this morning,' she said.

He considered phoning the school but decided that was silly.

He did phone the Home Office, though, to ask them if there was any chance of tracing a convicted murderer through their files, even if he'd been released. He had to tell a lot of lies about a programme he said he was making.

'Not if he's left prison,' the press officer said. 'Certainly not.'

'Well, could you check if he's still in prison?' Preston asked. 'Or mental hospital?'

But he'd have to put in a written request, the man said, so they could consider it. Preston gave up.

But he couldn't stop worrying about it.

Finally, early in the afternoon, he phoned Kate at her office to see if she might be able to trace him through the social services, or the probation department.

But they said she was out on a call.

It was one of Kate's days for home visits and she did not return to her office until well into the afternoon, bringing a tuna salad sandwich with her and a carton of apple juice because she had missed lunch.

The file on Barry Moxton was waiting for her on her desk.

She sat there looking at it for a moment, wondering if she'd done the right thing. It was almost a condition of Kate's survival that she didn't take William's paranoias and obsessions and complexes very seriously. She would have become a slave to them otherwise. It would have been her life's work trying to sort them out. But she was worried about William and she was worried about their marriage. She conceded that it might be too late for that, and she didn't even know if she'd mind terribly if it was. She didn't know what she felt about William, any more. But she didn't like losing; she didn't like giving up. She felt she owed it to them both, and to Edwin, to make one last effort.

Chasing up the file on Barry Moxton was part of that. William had never been easy to communicate with, but he'd been particularly withdrawn since his grandfather's funeral and Kate thought it might have triggered off some distant memory, something to do with the murder.

But she hadn't told him about her enquiries. She needed to know where she stood first. She needed to know what had happened and how it might have affected him. She was looking for clues.

So she opened up the file and began to read.

'I never meant to hurt her when I went there,' Barry Moxton had said in his statement to the police. 'I just wanted to talk to her but she kept trying to push me out the door and beating at me with her fists and scratching with her nails so I hit her just once just to calm her down and then she rushes into the kitchen and comes back at me with this knife. She was calling me queer, mummy's boy, all kinds of names. I got it off of her but she cut me on the arm and I didn't know what I was doing, I just started stabbing at her.'

The defence went for manslaughter. After all, members of the jury, it was the woman who first went for the knife. One might almost say, its primary purpose was self-defence.

Except that he had kept on stabbing. Except that he had pursued her from room to room still stabbing. Except that when she had stopped running and screaming and started dying, lying in a pool of her own blood on the floor of the last room she had run to, he had stabbed the knife over and over again into her womb.

That was what had done for him really, and his lawyers and their plea of self-defence.

It was odd, after reading his statement, to then read the medical reports, the psychiatric reports, the prison reports, the reports from the succession of doctors and psychiatrists and probation officers into whose professional care Barry Moxton had passed, odd to see how he took over the case, moving his victim further and further out of the picture until in the end she did not feature in it at all.

It was almost as if a small industry had sprung up devoted to the care and protection and study of Barry Moxton until the reason why it had started in the first place was no longer deemed relevant, and perhaps it wasn't.

It was the rain on the window that brought her to life again and jolted her out of these reflections. It was nearly four o'clock now and the weather had changed for the worse and the tuna salad sandwich lay untouched on her desk and she didn't think she wanted it now.

She had a strange sense of foreboding. It was out of character and it irritated her, but she couldn't shake it off. She skimmed back through the file, looking for something specific, something she might have missed. She found it in one of the prison psychiatric reports, one of the early ones.

'She changed,' Barry Moxton had told his assessor. 'I couldn't get through to her any more. There was this friend of hers, I think if it hadn't been for her we'd have been all right, but she'd left her own husband and come back with this kid. My mum knew the family. Mary was always round there. I reckon that's why she changed. They turned her against me.'

For a moment Kate felt as if she'd been touched with the cold dagger of William's own insecurity. This 'kid' Moxton had referred to was him.

On impulse she rang the social services in Liverpool and asked to speak to the woman who had sent her the file. Inevitably, it was her day off. They wanted to know if anyone else could help.

Kate hesitated. She had established her own bogus connection with the Barry Moxton industry by explaining that there was an old woman on her caseload who had been a witness at his trial and who was terrified that he was going to come after her when he got out of prison. It had looked all right on paper but she hesitated to explain it to someone else on the phone, so she said it could wait until tomorrow.

When she put the phone down one of her colleagues called across to her.

'There was a call for you. Will you ring your son's school?'

Kate glanced at her watch. It was gone four o'clock. William must have forgotten to pick him up. Bloody typical, she thought. She might have known she couldn't trust him, and the poor little boy waiting all this time. She hoped they'd kept him in the classroom and not let him out in the rain.

She found the number of the school in her contact book and began to dial.

And on the far side of the city Preston felt the dagger twist so violently in his stomach he gave up trying to think it through, gave up looking for reasons and explanations, and left the office without a word to anyone and ran through the rain to the nearest subway. He was luckier than William had been and didn't have to wait more than two minutes for a train.

But then, he started later than William and he'd got further to go.

32

Fear

The rain beat across the Common, heavy as hailstones, churning the football pitch into a lake of mud and the lake into a moonscape of tiny craters. William had finished running. He stood alone among the climbing frames where the children usually played, with nowhere else to run to, soaked to the skin and shuddering, without hope, and turned his face up to the sky and howled.

It had been hope that brought him here, a thin, desperate hope, that whoever had taken his son might seek some corner of the Common to do whatever he meant to do, away from people, and free from interruption. But he had been to them all, every one he could think of: the public lavatory, the hut by the bowling green, the shed near the tennis courts where they kept the gardening tools, the wild overgrown part where Edwin played jungle games with his friends, even the old Victorian bandstand, and he did not know where else to look and it was terribly late.

He knew he should go back to the house but he was afraid that if he did and Edwin was not there and no one had phoned to say he was with them, then the last tiny shred of hope would have gone and then he would know for certain, and it was better to stay here, howling in the rain, than to know that.

He could not endure the thought of the waiting, of knowing and waiting. Sitting by the telephone in that fearful house with the clock ticking away, knowing everything except the details and his imagination filling them in step by step, minute by minute, and every minute, every hour, taking his child further and further away from him and out of reach, further and further into the darkness.

He could not bear the thought of his being frightened and crying out for help, and not being there to help him.

But he had to go back, if only to phone the police.

And Kate.

He would have to tell Kate. Perhaps she'd phoned already to check Edwin was home all right and spoken to Louis.

The thought of Louis brought the guilt flooding back, and with the guilt came an even greater fear.

He slowed down at the end of the street and began to walk more slowly towards the house. His mind seemed to be shivering in rhythm with his body, shivering and out of control. He did not know what made him look in the back of Louis' car. He certainly did not know what he expected to find. But what he saw was a black polythene bag, a dustbin liner, the kind of thing the government told you would be handy in the event of nuclear war for the disposal of bodies.

He wiped at the rain on the window but all he could be sure of was that it contained something solid and lumpy and about the size of a child.

He tried the door handle but it was locked. He hesitated, but only briefly, not long enough to think more rationally about what he was doing, and then he picked up the brick from the garden and smashed the window, and opened the car door and dragged the bag out on to the pavement.

The bag split while he was trying to open it and the contents fell out on to the kerb.

It was full of books. Books and some tapes and a silver-framed photograph of Tess with Ben and Alice.

William knelt to pick it up and tried to wipe the rain off it, and then Louis was there, staring down at him.

'William? What the hell are you doing?'

'I'm sorry,' he said, and then he looked up and saw Edwin.

He was standing in the doorway of the house, looking mildly surprised, with some people behind him.

William ran up the path and knelt down and held him, closing his eyes, feeling the warmth and the solidness of him, and the life.

'Daddy, you're all wet.'

'We tried to get hold of you, we knew you'd be worried.'

240

It was one of the teachers. William didn't know her name.

'I'm sorry I was late,' he said to Edwin. He was still shivering. Like the plague. He could hear his teeth chattering.

'That's all right,' said Edwin. 'My grandad came for me.'

'You see, his grandad came by,' said the teacher, 'and found him crying and brought him across to the staff room. We didn't know whether anyone was coming to pick him up or what, so in the end I ran them back here. We must have missed you on the way.'

William let go of Edwin and stood up.

'What do you mean his grandad?'

She turned, and for the first time William noticed the man standing in the doorway behind her. A tall, thin man in a grey plastic mac. He wore round-rimmed spectacles and his eyes stared brightly through them at William.

'That's not his grandad,' said William. 'I've never seen this man before in my life. What the hell is going on here?'

The man put his hand out in a gesture that might have been intended as a handshake. Or just vaguely imploring. They were all staring at him now. William, the teacher, Edwin.

'He said he was my grandad,' said Edwin.

'I am, son,' he said. 'I am.'

He used the hand to ruffle the boy's hair but he was still looking at William.

'And you have seen me before, Billy,' he said. 'A long time ago. I'm your father, Billy. I'm sorry.'

And then William felt Louis' hand on his shoulder, pulling him back and turning him round.

'What did you think was in the bag?' said Louis, and his fists were clenched, too, and his face tight with anger and hurt. 'What did you think was in the fucking bag?'

33

The Master Sergeant

'You seem to have picked rather an awkward time,' said Preston, when he'd swept up the glass from the pavement and returned to the kitchen where he'd left William's dad.

The former Master Sergeant had taken off his grey plastic mac to reveal a lightweight suit, also grey, in some kind of crushed fibre, or perhaps he'd just slept in it. He wore spectacles and a look of anxious, slightly apologetic enquiry.

'Do you think he'll be back?' he asked.

Preston assumed he meant William.

'I don't know,' said Preston. 'It's a bit of a mess, I'm afraid. Can I make you some coffee?'

Preston had arrived with Kate just as Louis was leaving. William had left a little later, carrying a small suitcase, after a private talk with Kate up in their bedroom. He hadn't said a word to his father. He didn't even acknowledge his presence.

And now he seemed to be Preston's problem.

Preston studied him while he made the coffee. He was incredibly thin. He looked a bit like a stick insect, only grey.

'Mr Quirk . . .' he began.

'Max – please.'

'Max, what exactly were you doing in the school playground?'

Max spread his arms in a helpless gesture. He seemed close to tears.

'I just wanted to see my grandson,' he said. 'I had no intention of approaching him. But then when I saw him sitting there, crying . . . well, what could I do?'

'I can understand that,' said Preston. 'But how did you know it was Edwin? I mean, how did you know you had a grandson, how did you find the school?'

'Oh, I got all that from the detective agency,' said Max.

'I'm sorry?'

'The agency I hired to find Billy. They've been keeping me informed about the family circumstances, that kind of thing. They even took photographs.' He fumbled inside his suit and produced a wallet.

'I'm sorry, let me get this straight,' said Preston. 'You hired a private detective?'

'That's right. Well, I had no other way of tracing him.'

He pulled out a selection of photographs. There was one of the three of them, William, Kate and Edwin. One of William alone. And one of William with Tess coming out of a restaurant together.

'My God,' said Preston. 'You were having him watched?'

'Watched? No, not *watched*. Well, just kept sight of.'

There was a small, delicate silence.

Max spread his arms in that helpless gesture again. It reminded Preston of William a bit.

'The fact is, I needed to know how things stood,' he said. 'Whether there was family, that kind of thing. It sounds crazy now, in view of what transpired, but I wanted to make the right kind of entrance.'

'My God,' said Preston again.

But he felt sorry for him. He tried to explain.

'William's going through a bit of a rough patch at the moment,' he said. 'He's having a bit of an emotional crisis.'

Well, it was a start, anyway.

'I had an idea about that,' said Max. 'There's a woman involved?'

Preston nodded.

'Like father like son,' said Max.

Preston continued nodding but decided this wasn't quite the correct response, not polite, not quite what his Auntie Ethel would have advised in the circumstances. If she could ever have imagined circumstances like this.

He poured more coffee.

'How long have you been in England?' he enquired.

'Two days,' said Max. He smiled a very tired smile. 'Been plucking up my courage, timing my entrance . . .'

Preston wondered what he was going to do with him. And where had William gone? Perhaps he should have tried to stop him, or talk to him, but what could he have said? He didn't know what had been said between him and Kate up in their bedroom before William had come down with his suitcase and headed off into the sunset.

He looked up and saw her standing in the kitchen doorway looking at William's father. She seemed a bit tense, but otherwise not unduly distressed.

'Coffee?' said Preston.

'Something stronger,' she said. 'Is there any wine in the fridge?'

Max stood up and put his hand out.

'You must be Kate,' he said.

Kate sat down at the table opposite William's father.

He looked at her with an expression of polite enquiry.

'Erm . . .' said Kate. How could she begin? She felt the way she did sometimes when she was trying to sort out a domestic quarrel involving one of her clients, or arbitrate between the various parties to a marital breakdown. She felt as if she'd left one party in one room and now she was going to have to sort out the other. It was an effort to comprehend that she wasn't an outsider looking in. She was right in the middle of this one. This was happening to *her*.

Preston handed her a glass of wine.

'How do you feel?' he asked.

'Okay,' she said. 'Thanks.'

'I guess you must be feeling pretty shell-shocked,' said William's father. 'Coming home to all of this.'

Kate wondered if she was. But she didn't feel much different from the way she normally felt at the end of an averagely trying day. Perhaps she had lost the capacity to be shocked. Or even surprised.

Perhaps it was no surprise.

'A glass of wine?' Preston was asking William's father.

'No, thank you,' he said. 'I'll just stick to coffee.'

244

'Where's Edwin?' Preston asked her.

'He's watching a video,' she said. She smiled. 'I wonder what they did with the kids during a family crisis before they invented videos?'

'They sent them to play on the railway line,' said Preston. It sounded like the sort of thing William came out with.

Why didn't she *feel* anything?

'He's a lovely kid,' said William's father.

She heard him coming down the stairs, shouting for an apple juice.

'Don't yell,' she yelled back, automatically.

He came into the kitchen, grinning, but with that cautious look he had sometimes when he knew something was going on and didn't quite know how it was going to affect him.

'Now I've got two grandads,' he said to Preston.

'Aren't you the lucky boy,' said Preston.

'Go and get your apple juice,' said Kate. 'And then it's off to bed.'

'Can he come up and read me a story?'

William's father looked at her hopefully and she didn't have the heart to say no.

He looked tragic. He looked as if he might burst into tears at any moment. Kate was a sympathetic person but she hoped he wouldn't.

'Go and clean your teeth and get into your pyjamas,' she said. 'We'll give the bath a miss tonight.'

'I sure hope his daddy comes back,' said his new grandad when he'd left the room. 'For his sake, if not for yours.'

'I don't suppose we've seen the last of him,' said Kate.

That sounded awful. She tried to soften it.

'He said he'd phone. I'm sure he'll want to see you, it's just that, at the moment . . .'

'I understand,' he said. 'Who can blame him?'

Well, me for one, thought Kate, but didn't say.

'Do you know where he's gone?' Preston asked her.

But Kate shook her head. 'He said something about a flat he might be able to use. Someone at the university.'

She looked at William's father again.

'Mr Quirk . . .'

'Max,' he corrected her, but she didn't quite get it at first.

'Max,' said Preston. 'That's his name. Max.'

She glared at him as if it was all his fault. He shrugged apologetically, as if he thought it was, too.

'Max,' she said, 'were you planning to stay long? In England, I mean?' In case he thought she meant in the house, in their kitchen.

'No. Not long. I have business to get back to in North Carolina.'

'I see.' Nodding away as if it was all perfectly clear.

What made you come now, she wanted to say, why now? After thirty years?

'The fact is,' he said. 'I had a bit of a medical problem recently.'

Of course. She should have known. She *would* have known if she hadn't had so much else to think about. You only had to look at him.

'It was operable but . . . that kind of thing never really clears. So, I figured it was time to kind of put my affairs in order. If not exactly make amends, at least try to explain a few things.'

'I honestly don't think that William has ever blamed you for anything,' said Kate.

But how would she know?

How did she know what William felt? Ever?

'The fact is that when I left them, him and his mother, I fully intended to send for them.' He was speaking carefully, not looking at either of them. You don't have to explain anything, Kate wanted to urge him, not to me. But she knew he didn't want her to say that. He wanted to explain. She was a surrogate for William, for William's mother. It was a not entirely unfamiliar position.

'It was just that . . . circumstances kind of got in the way. First it was money and no decent kind of place for them to call a home, and then, well, I did meet someone else, but if . . .'

He looked up then, turning his hands, palm uppermost, on the table, and she could hardly bear it. He looked like something out of one of William's Hell and Damnation paintings. The eternal supplicant carrying his impossible load of guilt and begging for release.

246

'I know,' she said. 'It's all right.'

'You see, we had a child.'

She nodded again, as if that had been obvious, too.

'And in the final analysis it seemed less harm done all round if they just . . . stayed where they were. At least, that's how I explained it to myself at the time. But I missed them. I missed him. He was my little boy. And now it seems to me, I look at your boy there, and, you know, I don't know how I could ever bring myself to do a thing like that.'

Kate poured herself another glass of wine, not looking at him, not wanting to see the pain, not knowing what to say. The emotional link between her and Edwin was so strong she could never imagine voluntarily breaking it. She could understand why some parents left their children, or sent them away, but she could never begin to understand *how* they did it.

'I guess when you're younger you have so many things you want to do,' said Max. 'So many other needs all crowding in on you. It's only later, they kind of recede in importance and you realise there were other things that were maybe more important in the long term . . .'

He was silent for a moment. Kate could hear Edwin shouting from upstairs.

'In a minute,' she shouted back.

'What kind of business is it that you have to get back to?' she asked him, just for something to say.

'Aircraft maintenance,' he said. 'I've got a contract with the coastguard down Cape Hatteras . . . You ever been to that part of the world?'

She shook her head.

'Great place to bring up a boy,' he said. 'I used to imagine William being there . . .'

He fell silent again. Kate looked helplessly at Preston. But he was no help.

'Maybe you could bring Ed out there some time,' said Max.

'Yes,' she said. She smiled, but she knew it wasn't very convincing.

'Where are you staying in London?' said Preston, about half a minute too late.

247

'Hotel near the Victoria Station. The Kennet. You know it?'

Preston shook his head.

'No, I guess you wouldn't,' he said. 'It's not exactly the Dorchester.'

It occurred to Kate that Max was probably not well off. Aircraft maintenance. A contract with the coastguard. He was probably a mechanic. Pity none of it had filtered through to William, she thought. She wondered what sort of family life he had back in America, if any.

'Look,' she said. 'Why don't you come and stay with us until you go back? I'm sure no one would mind . . .'

She looked at Preston, and he didn't seem to, and there weren't many others left to consult.

'And it would be nice for Edwin, to see something of you.'

'Are you sure you mean that?'

'Of course I mean it.'

'It wouldn't be too much trouble?'

'No trouble at all,' said Kate.

It's a victim syndrome, she thought. They find me out. They even cross oceans for me.

So Max was upstairs reading to his grandson and Kate was in the kitchen, peeling taters for the supper, when Tess arrived.

'Hi,' said Tess. 'Is Louis home?'

34

Decisions

Preston lurked in the study out of the way until he saw Emily coming up the front path.

He intercepted her in the hallway.

'Upstairs,' he whispered urgently, grabbing her arm.

'Mmmm,' she said, 'I'm a bit sweaty, though, from the tube. Can we do it in the shower?'

'Not for that,' he said sternly. 'I want to talk to you.'

She shrugged. 'Okay, but could I have a drink first?'

'No,' he said. 'You can't go in the kitchen.'

'Why not?'

They were both whispering now.

'Because Tess and Kate are in there,' he said.

'So?'

But then she understood and her mouth formed a silent Oh as big as her eyes.

They went upstairs.

Max emerged from the kids' bedroom on the first floor.

'Is it all right to come down now?' he asked.

'No,' Preston told him. 'I don't think so.'

Max sighed.

'I'll go and read him another story then,' he said. 'Only he's a bit sleepy.'

Max looked a bit sleepy, too.

'Give it another ten minutes or so,' said Preston.

Max went back into the room.

'Who's he?' whispered Emily.

'That's Max,' Preston told her, 'the former Master Sergeant.'

'What?'

'Sorry?'

'What's a Master Sergeant, for Christ's sake?'

'Oh. It's a rank in the US Air Force. At least, he was. Now it's just the coastguard. He mends their planes when they break down.'

Emily felt a panic attack coming on.

'But what's he doing here?' she hissed.

'He's William's dad,' said Preston. 'It's a bit complicated.'

He shut the door of their bedroom and did his best to explain.

'Do we still have to whisper?' Emily asked after a while.

Preston hadn't realised he was. He carried on in his normal voice.

'So what's going to happen now?' Emily said, when he'd finished.

'I don't know,' said Preston. It was one of the questions that had been bothering him.

'I didn't really think about what would happen,' said Tess. 'We weren't going anywhere, we were just going round in circles, but in a way there was something nice about that. At least for me, at least at first.'

'I think William thought he was going somewhere,' said Kate.

'I know,' said Tess. 'I realised that. That was the trouble. That's why I had to end it.'

They'd opened another bottle of wine and were halfway through it. Tess shook her head.

'I don't know how I let it happen, Kate. I'm very fond of William. I've known him a long time, longer than any of you. I trusted him, I could talk to him. He was there when I needed someone. I suppose, in a way, I just sort of borrowed him from you.'

'So you don't intend to keep him?'

'No.' She looked up, startled, as though alarmed at the possibility.

'Poor William,' said Kate, flatly.

'God, I'm sorry, Kate. I've behaved so badly.'

'You have a bit,' said Kate.

'I wish you'd be angry with me or something.'

Kate said nothing.

'I never really thought how you'd feel about it,' said Tess. 'I think I shut that out. It was something between me and William, as if it was some kind of unfinished business we had that we had to attend to, that came before all of you. I didn't mean it to be against you. It was almost as if you weren't involved at all . . .'

And the small alien bubble of grievance that Kate had discovered in some distant, seldom-used, hidden room of her brain swelled into a bright red balloon of rage that took over the whole house.

'Actually you probably forgot I was here, didn't you,' she said. She was surprised her voice still sounded so calm. 'Kate? Oh yes, Kate. She's the one in the kitchen peeling the taters, chopping the carrots. Isn't she the one who puts the kids in the bath? I'll tell you something, Tess, I don't mind you fucking William, I don't mind you *borrowing* him without asking, he's not mine to lend you, actually. I don't *possess* him. To be perfectly honest with you, I don't *want* to possess him. But what really pisses me off, if you really want to know, is that you didn't even *think* about me at all.'

The colour had drained out of Tess's face. After the first few sentences she rested her elbow on the table and her head in her hand and closed her eyes. Kate kept going. She felt as if she'd only just started. She just felt a bit breathless, that was all.

'When we came into this place I thought we had some kind of respect for each other, all of us, I thought that was why we did it. I thought we felt we could trust each other. It was the outside world that was the problem – not us. *We* weren't going to hurt each other. My God, and you, you didn't even think about how you might have fucked me up. The fact that you didn't – as far as I know, at least – is entirely fucking accidental.'

Tess was crying now and Kate was close to it herself, but she kept on, she hadn't finished yet.

'I really liked you, you know, when I first met you. I was really pleased with myself for meeting someone I liked. You were like a breath of fresh air. I *valued* you. I always resented it when William took you over, *claimed* you as if you were *his* friend. God, I knew there was something between you, but I never thought you'd treat me like that, I never thought you'd just walk around me like that, as if I was a piece of shit you didn't want to see . . .'

251

The anger went then, as suddenly as it had come. The bubble burst. Or else it shrank, and went back to its hidden room. She couldn't finish. She just sat there, silently, playing with the stem of her wine glass. She couldn't cry either.

After a while Tess wiped her eyes with her hand and took a deep shuddering breath and stood up.

'I'd better go,' she said.

'Go where?' said Kate sullenly.

'Anywhere,' said Tess. 'My mother's I suppose.'

'It's raining,' said Kate.

They could hear it on the windows.

Tess made a sound between a laugh and a sob.

'Sit down,' said Kate. 'I don't want you to go.'

'Why not? I don't know how you can stand the sight of me.'

'Don't be stupid.' Kate looked at her. 'If I couldn't stand the sight of you I wouldn't be so hurt.'

Tess sat down.

'It wasn't like that, Kate,' she said. 'I've always liked you, I've always respected you. I just . . . William just got in the way so I couldn't really see you properly for a while, do you understand?'

'Not really,' said Kate. 'Not at the moment. I expect I will some day. That's the trouble. I always have to understand. I have to *be* understanding. That's the trouble with being a social worker. Everyone thinks I'm so sensible, so organised, so controlled. You know why I'm like that, because I've seen what it's like when you're not, I've seen the abyss. I know if I put a foot wrong I'll be in there, too.'

She felt the tears coming then.

'People who build up that kind of, of, of . . . we need control, we need order because . . . because we've seen the chaos. But it doesn't mean, just because I'm practical, that's not all I am . . . You can be practical and sens – Oh damn.'

'I'm sorry,' said Tess.

She came round the table and put her arms round Kate and now they were both crying.

'Excuse me,' said Preston.

He was peering round the door.

'Is there any wine left?' he said.

'Bloody men,' said Kate, through her tears. She picked the glass up off the table and threw it. She didn't mean to hit him but it was a close thing. The glass bounced off the door and shattered on the floor.

The head withdrew.

'Bloody hell,' said Preston's voice from the other side. 'It was bloody Emily who wanted some actually.'

'It's all right,' said Tess, standing up. 'You can come in. I was just going.'

But Kate grabbed her hand.

'No,' she said. 'Stay.'

She was suddenly very determined.

'I'm damned if I'm going to be defeated by this,' she said. 'We can make this place work if we try.'

'Can we?'

'We have to try, Tess. It'll be awful if we just give up.'

'There's not many of us left . . .'

'There's still Preston and Emily.'

They heard Preston's voice again through the door.

'I don't think you should count Emily in,' he said. 'She's not staying very long.'

This time Tess threw the glass.

'I'd quite like to stay,' said Emily when they asked her. 'I really like it here.'

'What about Preston?' said Kate.

Preston had been sent to the off licence for more wine, so they could talk about him.

Emily shrugged.

'You'd have to ask him what he thinks,' she said. 'I don't suppose he'd tell me. Not honestly.'

'Well, you could always have a separate room,' said Tess. 'If it comes to that.'

'I think she should, anyway,' said Kate. 'Sod this couples business. We're all individuals.'

'Right,' said Tess.

'Well, what do you think?' said Kate. She was looking at Tess. 'Shall we have a bash at it?'

'I think we should get different builders in,' said Tess. 'That's all.'

They had the plans spread over the kitchen table when Preston came back with the wine.

'What's all this?' he said.

'Tess has had some ideas about the house,' said Kate.

Preston sat down thoughtfully.

'So it's carrying on?' he said.

'It is,' said Kate, firmly. 'What about you?'

Preston tried to be witty about it.

'I have to mind William,' he said. 'I promised my Auntie Ethel.'

The trouble was, he wasn't sure if he was joking.

35

The Guardian Angel

'Barry Moxton is dead,' said Preston. 'He died six months ago. Of cancer.'

William looked up from his book.

'How do you know?' he said.

'Kate found out,' said Preston.

He walked over to the window and looked out at the canal. It was an old acquaintance, this canal. He had lived beside it once before, before he was married, but in a far livelier part of the city, and he'd seen it many times since, from Camden Lock, Regent's Park, Little Venice, but never like this. Here it was altogether different. Here it was The Cut, cutting through the seedy, run-down remnants of its own past, worming through its roots. A dirty, dark, oily slick of water between boarded-up tenements and warehouses and old Victorian sweatshops with the last drop of sweat wrung out of them a long time ago.

More recently, the developers had moved in and converted a couple of warehouses into 'Luxury Flats', but the bottom had fallen out of the market and they'd abandoned the area until the prices picked up again, if they ever did.

William was living in one of these conversions. It had been lent him by a colleague at the university, who called it his 'Studio', and there were a few canvases and paints lying around for show, but William said he used it as a bolt-hole, really, for when he wanted to get away from his wife.

William had been alone there for three days before Preston found him. He'd raised no objection to Preston moving in, but he hadn't seemed too pleased about it either. He didn't seem to be able to react to anything. Most of the time he just sat in his room, reading. He didn't seem to have washed or shaved since he'd left home, and from the look of his eyes he hadn't slept much either.

'You can get a disease from swimming in canals,' Preston told him. 'It's called Weil's Disease after the man who discovered it. It's caused by rat's urine and it makes you go blind.'

He turned away from the window, but William just sat there, not reacting.

'I don't suppose you were thinking of going swimming in it though,' said Preston. 'Were you?'

William spoke.

'Devils don't like water,' he said.

Preston had wanted to draw him out but he wasn't sure if this was a step in the right direction.

'Sorry?' he said.

'That's what it says in the books,' said William. 'But I think they're wrong.'

'What books?'

'He was right about the holes, though.'

'What holes?'

William looked up at him, then, faintly surprised.

'The holes in the universe,' he said.

'Ah,' said Preston. 'St Augustine. Right.'

Sometimes he thought he was the only person who could ever understand William. Mother Bernard had taught them the same language. He hoped he didn't think like him, that was all.

'But he didn't mean up in the sky or anything,' William assured him earnestly. 'It was a metaphor, like you said. He meant bad places.'

'I'm sure he did,' said Preston, soothingly.

He didn't know how long he could keep this up. It was depressing him. He'd thought he could help William by staying here, help bring him out of himself, but he was worried about the effect William was having on *him*. They had too much past in common, too many shared experiences, too many shared influences.

Too much Mother Bernard.

Whatever it was William was going through it might be catching, and Preston had to be more susceptible than most.

'That's what the room is,' said William.

'What?'

'One of the holes. I've been thinking about it. It has a kind of energy that keeps on getting renewed. That's what we do, we keep renewing it.'

'I'm sorry,' said Preston, 'you've lost me.'

But William was looking quite animated for once, as if he'd made some great discovery.

'How many months ago, did you say?'

'Did I say what?'

'When Barry Moxton died?'

'Oh. I think it was about six, Kate said.'

'That's when we moved into the house. My God, don't you see?'

'No. See what?'

'Look, when somebody dies who's really Evil they've got all this energy left.' He was leaning forward across the table in his eagerness to explain, to make Preston understand. 'You see, it should be a balance. Good and Evil. Like all things in nature, like positive and negative ions. But sometimes it gets all distorted, like the way you get too many positive ions because of central heating, or man-made fibres and things, it's the same with Good and Evil. If there's this energy and we keep adding to it because of the things we do, it gets all unbalanced . . . The Evil starts to get really powerful.'

He stood up.

'They're in terrible danger,' he said.

'Who are?'

'The women and children.'

Preston stared at him.

'It's all coming from the room, you see,' said William. 'Do you understand?'

Preston shook his head.

'I think we need a drink,' he said.

There was a bottle of red wine but he couldn't find a corkscrew. He wandered into the front room to see if it had been left there.

257

While he was looking he noticed a book lying open on one of the armchairs. He picked it up and looked at the title. *Satan: A Portrait*. It was one of the books he'd borrowed from the London Library for his documentary. William must have brought it from the house.

He heard a door slam.

'William?' he called. There was no answer.

He went into the kitchen but it was empty. Another book lay discarded on the table. Preston read the cover.

Augustine on Evil.

He walked back into the front room and looked out of the window just in time to see William disappear round the corner of the street.

Preston grabbed his coat and ran down the stairs and hurried along the empty street after him and hoped he hadn't left it too late.

36

The Roman Matrons

Tess sacked the old builders and Kate found the new ones. They were called Bill and Sam, Bill for Wilma and Sam for Samantha, and they were members of the Battersea Women's Construction Collective.

'We've changed the plans a bit since the last lot started,' Tess told them when they came to give an estimate. 'We thought we'd have a kind of Atrium.'

Bill and Sam exchanged glances.

'What's a Atrium when it's at home?' asked Bill.

'It's a sort of inner sanctuary,' said Kate. 'We thought we'd be able to sit around in it with the kids at the end of the day, like Roman matrons.'

Bill and Sam looked at each other again.

'Are you separatists, then?' asked Sam.

'Not for any ideological reason,' Kate told them. 'It just seems to have worked out that way.'

'That's what happened to us,' said Sam, while they were doing a tour of the house. 'We had the odd bloke at first but they were fucking useless, so now it's all women. People think we're lesbians, but we're not, not all of us, anyway. I live with a bloke who works for the council teaching the correct use of weight-training facilities, but I wouldn't trust him to put a shelf up.'

'Where did you want this Atrium?' asked Bill.

'We wondered about joining the kitchen and the dining room together,' said Tess. 'And also there's this partition that could come down.'

She showed them the false wall with the hole in it and they went up the stairs and into the hidden room.

'Fuck me,' said Bill. 'Is this for prisoners?'

'We don't know why it's like this,' said Tess, 'but we'd like it to come down. We thought you could knock down this wall and join it to the next room the same as downstairs . . .'

But Sam was looking thoughtful.

'The attic's been converted since they put this wall up,' she said, 'and it's carrying a lot of weight now. There's a bathroom on top of this, isn't there?'

'We could always RSJ it,' said Bill.

This time Tess and Kate looked at each other, because the other builders used to talk like this and it usually ended up costing a lot of money.

'And how *are* we going to pay for it?' Kate asked, when they'd gone.

'We've got the improvements loan,' said Tess. 'And if we need any more, my father said he'll help.'

'You're going to need your father's money to buy off Louis,' Kate reminded her. 'That's if we don't want to sell the place. And I'll have to come to some kind of arrangement with William, when I can get to talk to him.'

'Are you sure they're not going to be back?' said Emily.

'I'm pretty sure about Louis,' said Tess. 'I think we both know it's over.'

'And I certainly don't want William back,' said Kate. 'Not all the time, anyway. I might be able to manage him for the odd weekend.'

They both looked at Emily.

'So what about you and Preston?' said Kate.

'I don't think me and Preston ever had much of a thing going,' said Emily. She shrugged. 'If he wants to come back, it's up to him. But I can live without him.'

'God knows I don't want to put any pressure on you,' said Kate, 'but it's going to be difficult if we have to buy out all three of them. I don't think we could raise that big a mortgage.'

'I could put some money in,' said Emily.

260

'Don't worry,' said Tess. 'We'll take in lodgers.'

'No, I'm serious. I've got some coming to me when I'm twenty-five and it's only a couple of months away. My gran left it me in a trust.'

'You'd be better leaving it there,' said Kate. 'How much is it?'

'I think it's about two hundred thousand,' said Emily. 'Least, it was when she died, but it's probably a bit more now.'

They were finishing off the champagne when William's dad came back with the kids. He'd been to the adventure playground with them.

'Hi Max,' said Emily. 'Have some champagne.'

'What are you celebrating?' He smiled, awkwardly, never very comfortable alone with the three women.

'Emily,' said Kate. 'We're celebrating Emily.'

Tess handed him a glass with the last of the bottle. He gazed into it a bit dubiously. He looked exhausted.

'Why don't you take it into the front room and have a little lie down,' said Kate. 'I'll call you when supper's ready.'

'I think I'll do that,' said Max, relieved.

'Poor Max,' said Emily when he'd gone.

'He's got to go back tomorrow,' said Kate.

'William still won't see him?'

Kate shook her head.

'I asked Preston to speak to him,' she said, 'but I don't think it'll make any difference.'

'Funny he still feels that way after so many years,' said Tess. 'It makes you wonder if you're doing the right thing, doesn't it?'

'It won't be like that with us,' said Kate, irritably. 'The kids will still see their fathers.' She lowered her voice in case Max could hear her. Or the kids. 'He broke with William entirely. He never saw him again, never had any contact with him. William felt utterly abandoned, he felt rejected. It shattered his self-esteem.'

'Is that why he's punishing him now?'

'I'm not sure if he is punishing him,' said Kate. 'I'm not sure he's even thinking about him.'

'Do you?'

261

'Do I what?'

'Blame him? For William?'

'Fuck, no,' said Kate. 'Why should I? I don't even blame my parents for *me*. Not since I was an adolescent. It's no longer the accepted wisdom.'

'Isn't it?' said Emily. 'Well I'm fucked if I'm going to stop blaming mine.'

Their language had taken a turn for the worse since the men had left, Kate reflected. They picked it up from Sam and Bill. But they were always very polite when Max was in the room.

'Does Grandad have to go tomorrow?' Edwin asked Kate, when she was getting him ready for bed.

'I'm afraid he does,' she said.

She smoothed his hair back from his forehead.

'Is he going to die soon?'

She was startled.

'What makes you think that?'

'Nothing.' He climbed into bed and lay on his back staring up at the ceiling. 'Will we see him again?'

'I expect so. He wants us to go and see him in America. For a holiday.'

'Can we?'

'We'll try.'

She tucked him in and kissed him goodnight. On her way downstairs she passed Tess coming to do the same with Ben and Alice.

Emily was in the kitchen scraping the taters. Kate began to tidy up. It was part of the evening ritual, a necessary part of the winding-down process. Afterwards she would put a record on and pour herself a glass of wine and pick up a novel.

'They left their pickaxe behind,' she said to Emily.

'What? Who did?'

'The builders. The first lot.'

She'd only just noticed it, leaning near the hole in the wall. She almost picked it up to tidy away, but she didn't know where to put it. Maybe they'd come back for it. She hoped they wouldn't. She didn't want to see them again. It was typical of men, she

262

thought, leaving something like that lying around when they left. Like peeing to mark territory.

She loitered in the open door of the kitchen, idly surveying the garden. That needed tidying, too; the kids' toys marked their route from house to tree-hut and back again like the abandoned equipment of a retreating army. But they could stay there, it didn't look as though it was going to rain.

She closed her eyes. The sun was balanced delicately on the roof of the house opposite, and her vision filled with a blood-red wash. She could hear the subdued sounds of the summer's evening. Birdsong, the snick-snack of a pair of shears, a hose spraying a neighbour's garden, the scrape, scrape of Emily's knife on the taters.

A jarring note intruded. The front-door bell.

'I'll go,' she told Emily, up to her elbows in the sink. Tess was still upstairs with Ben and Alice.

It was William.

Kate tried to look pleased, or at least not displeased, but she knew they had a problem as soon as she saw his face.

He looked brain-dead.

'Come in,' she heard herself say. 'Pooh's in bed, but he's probably still awake if you want to see him.'

She hadn't called Edwin that for ages, she thought. It was what they both used to call him when he was younger.

'And your father's here,' she said, 'if you want to see him. I think you should, you know.'

He still didn't speak, but he walked in past her and she followed him down the hall, mystified, and slightly alarmed.

It was ridiculous, but she suddenly remembered the file on Barry Moxton and how Mary had gone into the kitchen for a knife.

I must be crazy, thought Kate, this is William.

But she wasn't crazy. It was William who was crazy. Only he didn't go for the knife. He went for the pickaxe.

Kate opened her mouth when he picked it up but no sound came. She couldn't move.

Emily appeared in the kitchen door looking faintly surprised, with a potato in one hand and the knife in the other and both arms wet to the elbows.

I've seen it before, thought Kate, just like this, I've seen it all before. And she still couldn't scream.

And William gazed at Emily for a moment, and then at Kate as if he was making his mind up about something, and then frowned and turned and ducked through the hole in the wall.

37

The Exorcist

He wasn't entirely crazy. He knew they'd try to stop him. He knew that much.

The first thing he did when he got inside the room was push the bedstead against the door. It was cast iron and very heavy and he dragged it across the floor and wedged the head rail under the door knob.

Then he looked around the room.

The Demon was sitting in a chair against the far wall, watching him and smiling, but his clothes were soaked in blood and he had the face of Barry Moxton.

William threw the pickaxe at him.

It went right through Barry Moxton's head and bounced off the wall and brought a huge chunk of plaster down. Barry Moxton disappeared but the Demon came back as a rat. It sat in the far corner tidying its whiskers and watching him carefully.

William ignored it and retrieved the pickaxe and started on the wall.

He wasn't at all crazy. He knew he had to let the light in. It was only a partition wall, one layer of bricks thick, and the Utility Room was on the other side, and that always had a lot of light.

After the first few blows a section of brick fell out.

But something was clawing at his throat, pulling him back, choking him.

William let go of the pickaxe with one hand and tried to prise the fingers away from his windpipe. They felt reptilian, like claws.

'In the name of Jesus Christ I command you,' he said.

It was the adjuration to the demons from the Roman Catholic exorcism. Mother Bernard had made him learn it just in case.

But the claws were still tight around his throat and he couldn't breathe.

He gave up trying to prise them away and took the pickaxe in both hands again and swung it again and again at the wall. He lost his balance twice with the weight pulling him back, but each time he dragged himself back to the wall and swung the pickaxe.

Another section of wall came down, then another, and another.

The front door was open when Preston arrived and he could hear the noise as he came up the path. It took him a little while, though, to realise where it was coming from. Then he ducked through the hole in the wall and peered up the stairs.

Kate and Tess and Emily were all on the small landing at the top banging on the door to the Hidden Room and shouting. There was a loud and regular thudding coming from inside.

Preston ran up the stairs and added his weight to the door. Between them they managed to open it a few inches or so, but then whatever was jammed against it caught on something and it stuck solid.

Preston put his arm through the gap and felt around until he located the brass rail of the bed. He tried to wrench it out from under the door knob, but it was the wrist he had sprained in his fight with the Big Chicken and he felt it go again. The pain shot right up his arm.

He eased it out, his face twisted in agony.

'Perhaps I could squeeze through the gap,' said Emily, who was the thinnest.

From inside the room they heard an enormous crash and the rumble of falling bricks.

William's father had been dreaming he was on a beach he knew on the Barrier Islands. The light was fading and he was watching the waves breaking. There were several fins in amongst them and at first he thought they were sharks and was surprised they were that close inshore, but when he got down there he saw that they were dolphins.

266

Then the noise woke him.

He found Preston and the three women on the small landing outside the room they all thought was haunted. One of the women was trying to force her way in but the door seemed to be jammed and she was a bit too big in the chest area.

'It's William,' said Kate. 'He's gone mad. He's trying to knock the walls down.'

'Let me try,' said Max. 'I'm pretty thin.'

The woman came out and Max inserted his wiry body in the gap. He could see William now. He had his back to the door and he was smashing away at the opposite wall with a pickaxe. Max called to him but he took no notice.

He forced his body the rest of the way through and crept up behind him, watching the swing of the pick. William was in such a frenzy there was hardly a second between blows. But then he got it stuck in a crack in the brickwork, and while he was wrenching at it the former Master Sergeant flung himself on his son's back.

And just then, William managed to pull the pickaxe out of the wall and most of the wall came with it.

And most of the ceiling.

And the room on the floor above.

38

The Hospital

'DIY enthusiast was he?' the porter asked them while they waited at the hospital.

'Not so you'd notice,' said Preston.

'We get them in all the time,' said the porter. 'Some days it's worse than road accidents. I reckon they ought to make them take a test before they let them loose on some of them tools. Do-it-yourself? Do-*in*-yourself more like.'

Shortly before midnight one of the doctors came out.

'How is he?' Kate asked him.

'Severe concussion, two bones broken in his right foot and a mass of cuts and contusions,' he said. 'But we think he'll live.'

'Is he conscious?'

'Just about. You can go in and see him if you like, but he's not making much sense, I'm afraid.'

He was lying in bed in a small room off the main ward with a bandage round his head.

'Hello William,' said Kate gently.

William opened one eye.

'Hello,' he said. 'How am I?'

'Fine,' said Kate. 'Just fine.'

'I can only see out of one eye,' he said.

'The other one's got a bandage over it,' Preston told him.

'Ah,' said William. The eye he could see out of looked anxious.

'It's just bruised,' Kate said quickly. 'And a burst blood vessel. The doctor says it'll be fine in a day or two.'

'I feel very tired,' he said.

'They've given you a sleeping pill. We'll go in a minute. You'll have a lot of aches and pains when you wake up, the doctor said.'

'Don't go. Not until I'm asleep.'

'I won't,' said Kate.

'What happened exactly?'

'You knocked the wall down,' said Kate.

'I remember that.'

'Only the ceiling fell in, too,' said Kate. 'And the floor above and . . . quite a lot of other things.'

'Oh,' said William. 'So no more Hidden Room?'

'No more Hidden Room.'

The eye closed and they thought he was asleep but then it opened again and he sounded quite alert.

'Has my father gone back yet?' he said.

'Back where?' said Kate, after a moment.

'To America?'

'No . . .' said Kate, doubtfully. 'Not yet.'

'I'd like to see him,' said William.

Kate said nothing. She looked at Preston. Preston was chewing his bottom lip.

'Don't you remember?' said Kate.

'Remember what?'

'William, your father dragged you away from the wall.'

William shook his head.

'That was the Demon,' he said.

Kate put her hand up to her eyes.

'Don't worry,' said William, 'I'm all right now. It's gone. I'd like to see him, if I can.'

'He saved your life,' said Preston. 'He pulled you away just as the roof fell in. They found him on top of you in the rubble.'

The eye watched him carefully.

'Was he hurt, then?' said William.

'I'll go and ask the doctor,' said Preston.

He didn't dare look at Kate.

'He's asking about his father,' Preston told the doctor. 'What should we say?'

269

'Ah,' said the doctor. 'Were they very close?'

'No. Not close at all. They hadn't met for thirty years until just before this.'

'Ah. Well, you'd better tell him then. Or do you want me to?'

'No, I'll manage it,' said Preston. 'We're old friends.'

He returned to the ward.

'Is he asleep?' he whispered to Kate, hopefully.

'No,' said William, opening his eye. 'How is he?'

'I'm afraid he's dead,' said Preston. 'Lavatory fell on his head.'

'Well done, Preston,' Kate murmured, quietly. 'You should be in bereavement counselling.'

'Well, what else could I say?' said Preston.

'He'd been very ill, William,' said Kate, in her best bedside manner. 'I don't think he felt he had long to live. And he wanted to make amends. He'd probably consider that this was the best way that he possibly could.'

William nodded and closed his eye again.

'Funny about the lavatory, though,' he said, sleepily. 'Grandad must have had a hand in that.'

Kate looked bewildered, but Preston thought he understood.

'Your father was a good man, I think,' said Kate. 'I think he'll be at peace now.'

'He'll be in the Adultery Department,' said William.

'We'd like to keep him in for a day or two for tests,' said the doctor when they saw him on their way out. 'But I think we can take it there's no brain damage.'

Preston laughed, drily, and the doctor raised a faint eyebrow.

'There's just one thing that puzzles us,' he said, 'and that's the scratches round his neck.'

'The scratches?'

'Yes, quite deep ones, as if someone had been clawing at him. Perhaps when you tried to dig him out of the rubble . . .'

39

Light and Shadow

From where Kate stood in the dining room she could look up through two floors to the roof of the attic. Sunlight poured down through the hole in the ceiling and a galaxy of dust orbited silently.

'I think I rather prefer it like this,' she said, holding her face up to the sun and closing her eyes. 'It's like living in a conservatory. All that light.'

'Well, you got your Atrium,' said Sam, accepting a glass of wine from Tess. 'I'm not sure I'd have gone about it in the same way, but there you go, I'm not a man.'

'Do you think we could leave it like this?' Emily asked.

'Well, we could open it to the first floor,' Tess said. 'I don't think we'd want the Hidden Room back.'

'God, no,' said Kate. 'Not unless we want William round here again, with a bulldozer this time.'

'It could look fantastic,' said Tess. 'With a wrought-iron staircase up to the landing and a few plants trailing down. Like hanging gardens.'

'You could put a window right across where the two rooms used to be,' said Sam. 'You'd have tons more light then, even in winter.'

'Why not?' said Kate. 'It's not as if we need the rooms.'

'You're not thinking of having the men back, then?' said Sam. She was intrigued about 'their arrangement', as she called it.

'Not that I'm a separatist,' she told them, 'as you know. Only I've always wondered what it's like for women without men.'

271

'Safer,' said Emily. 'You're not forever worrying the roof's going to fall in.'

'Emotionally speaking,' said Tess, 'they were never here very much, anyway.'

'They can always visit,' said Kate. 'That's what men prefer, really, visiting.'

'And how is the demolition expert?'

'Learning his lines for the inquest, I hope,' said Kate, 'like the rest of us.'

William sat on a chair on the towpath with his bad leg stuck out to one side and his tubes of paint in a box on the floor and a big canvas propped up on an easel in front of him with a picture on it of a battleship in a stormy sea.

Preston had looked up the canal and there was no apparent sign of any battleship and the water was quite calm, but William seemed content and that was the main thing, as his Auntie Ethel would have said.

William had a patch over one eye and his foot was set in plaster, and Preston sat on a low wall next to him with his right arm in a sling and his wrist bandaged.

'We look like the fox and the cat in *Pinocchio*,' he grumbled.

Preston was coaching him in his story for the coroner's court but it was hard going.

'We don't want a verdict of manslaughter, do we?' he said.

'It's no more than I deserve,' said William. 'I killed him, didn't I?'

'They'd put you away somewhere,' said Preston. 'That's not what your father died for. We have to convince them it was an accident while we were doing some work on the house. Do you understand that?'

William squeezed a blob of black paint out of the tube and mixed it with white on the palette. He'd started the painting when he came out of hospital but it was some time before Preston had realised what it was about. He had no obvious talents as an artist.

'We could tell them the truth,' said William.

Preston sighed.

'All right, William,' he said, 'what's the truth?'

William said nothing for a moment. He concentrated on mixing the right shade of battleship grey.

'We exorcised a lot of demons that day,' he said at last. 'Me and my dad.'

'No demons,' said Preston firmly. 'Not in court, please.'

He was sounding more like his Auntie Ethel every day, he thought.

'I was speaking metaphorically,' said William with a crafty grin.

Preston watched him warily. He was only staying with William during the week – at the weekend he went back to the house with the twins – but it was a tiring business being William's Minder, even part of the time.

'So what have you exorcised so far?' he enquired. 'Metaphorically speaking?'

'Hatred of my father,' said William. 'A sense of rejection, a fair bit of self-loathing, though not all . . . Lust . . .'

'You got rid of Lust? That must have been a struggle.'

'It was,' said William. 'I'm not sure I'm entirely free of it yet.'

'I'll keep my fingers crossed for you,' said Preston. 'Must take it out of you, exorcising demons,' he said. 'Even metaphorical ones.'

'Not so much as getting rid of the holes in the universe,' William confided.

Preston shook his head. Sarcasm was lost on William, always had been, even when they were kids.

'What with Mother Bernard and your grandad,' he said, 'we had an awful lot of Negative Influence at a vulnerable age.'

'There was nothing wrong with my grandad,' said William. 'Apart from the grudge he had about that lavatory.'

William was convinced his grandad had hurled a lavatory like a thunderbolt from on high and brained his father, out of revenge for what the US Air Force did to his kneecap during the war.

'Remember how he used to paint the devil in the corner of the picture,' Preston said. 'Whenever you were cycling downhill,

273

he'd tell us, with the wind behind you and the sun on your face . . .'

'. . . some little bugger would nip out with an iron bar and stick it in your spokes,' William finished for him. He nodded. 'He was right.'

'No, he wasn't,' said Preston. 'That was a Very Negative Attitude. You can't spend your life worrying about things going wrong all the time . . .'

'You do,' said William. 'You're worse than I am.'

'Ah, but not any more,' Preston retorted confidently. 'I've stopped all that.'

He'd learned a few things from William lately. The most important was not to be like him.

'I know you're never safe,' said Preston. 'You're not safe from the moment you're born to the moment you die, but you can't spend your life in between worrying about not being. That's why I got married, that's why I came into that bloody commune of yours, and look what happened. So now I've stopped worrying about things. Emily's right. You've got to dive in and take risks.'

There was a splash, and he started, more alarmed by the coincidence than by the noise.

'Only another rat,' said William, 'diving in the water. He's probably pissing in it.'

Preston stood up.

'I'm going back,' he said. 'Don't stay out long, it's getting chilly.'

'Fear of emotional commitment,' said William, irrelevantly. 'That's the next demon we have to exorcise.'

Preston looked at him.

'Is it?' he said. 'Is it really? Well, you might be right about that, but don't go at it with a pickaxe this time.'

He set off up the towpath towards the studio.

'How do you explain the scratches on my neck?' William called after him. 'Were they metaphors, too?'

'You did them yourself, you mad fucker,' Preston shouted back, and his voice boomed off the empty buildings.

And William winked at the rat in the water and stayed painting on the towpath while the sun dropped down below the tops of the buildings and the shadows deepened around him and the air turned chill, and when he'd finished he painted the devil in his usual place, smirking at the bottom corner of the picture.

A NOTE ON THE AUTHOR

Paul Bryers began his career as a journalist and television presenter. He now works full-time as a drama director and writer. He was born in Liverpool and now lives in London.